Praise for the Ivy Meadows Mystery Series

"This gut-splitting mystery is a hilarious riff on an avant-garde production of 'the Scottish play'...Combining humor and pathos can be risky in a whodunit, but gifted author Brown makes it work."

— *Mystery Scene Magazine*

"Vivid characters, a wacky circus production of *Macbeth*, and a plot full of surprises make this a perfect read f⌐   ng. Pour a glass of wine, put your feet   funny."

tlewood,

Award-Winning Author   lysteries

"This gripping mystery is   ⌐gly clever and rich with unerring comedic timing. Without a doubt, *Macdeath* is one of the most entertaining debuts I've read in a very long time."

— Bill Cameron,
Spotted Owl Award-Winning Author of *County Line*

"Funny and unexpectedly poignant, *Macdeath* is that rarest of creatures: a mystery that will make you laugh out loud. I loved it!"

— April Henry,
New York Times Bestselling Author

"Brown mixes laugh out loud observations about the acting life with a witty and intriguing mystery. Consider yourself warned. *Oliver Twisted* is a fast-paced addictive read impossible to put down until Ivy has caught the killer."

— D.E. Ireland,
Agatha Award-Nominated Author of *Move Your Blooming Corpse*

"A definite delight...sit back, wait for the curtain to rise on this one, and then have a whole lot of fun figuring out whodunit."

— *Suspense Magazine*

IVY GET YOUR GUN

IVY GET YOUR GUN

AN IVY MEADOWS MYSTERY

Cindy Brown

HENERY PRESS

IVY GET YOUR GUN
An Ivy Meadows Mystery
Part of the Henery Press Mystery Collection

First Edition | May 2017

Henery Press
www.henerypress.com

This is a work of fiction. Any references to historical events, real people, or real locales are used fictitiously. Other names, characters, places, and incidents are the product of the author's imagination, and any resemblance to actual events or locales or persons, living or dead, is entirely coincidental.

Trade Paperback ISBN-13: 978-1-63511-207-8
Digital epub ISBN-13: 978-1-63511-208-5
Kindle ISBN-13: 978-1-63511-209-2
Hardcover ISBN-13: 978-1-63511-210-8

Printed in the United States of America

For Holly Franko

"It is not often that someone comes along
who is a true friend and a good writer."
– E.B. White, *Charlotte's Web*

ACKNOWLEDGMENTS

Gold Bug Gulch does not exist, but happily, Goldfield Ghost Town does, and is a much nicer place to visit (no murders). My fictional town is not based on Goldfield (which is located in Apache Junction, AZ), but much of my research took place there, and I'm very grateful to "Mayor" Bob Schoose for his incredible generosity, and to Mongo (Jud) Ware for the loan of his name.

Arnon Kartmazov of Bridgetown Forge (Portland, OR) was also very generous with his time, showing me how blacksmiths work with coal-fired forges. He's a wonderful teacher for anyone interested in smithing.

Once again, John Hopper of JB National Investigations proved invaluable to me, helping me figure out some of the ins and outs of PI work and legal issues.

Thanks to the folks who helped me get the details right: Bonnie Gestring of Earthworks (mining info): the Crime Scene Listserv (forensics); Anthony Petchel (non-profits and money); Dave Furman and Judy Hricko (rifles), and Steve Etling (septic tank...stuff).

As always, the team at Henery Press has been an invaluable help and a joy to work with. Thanks to Erin George, Kendel Lynn, Rachel Jackson, Stephanie Chontos, and Art Molinares.

I am lucky to have a fabulous group of reading and writing friends who make my books so much better: Lisa Alber, Delia Booth, Holly

Franko, Judy Hricko, Doug Levin, Evan Lewis, Ann Littlewood, Janice Maxson, Marilyn McFarlane, Lindsay Nyre, Shauna Petchel, and Angela M. Sanders.

I wish I could name all the people who have supported me and my writing, but this book would be several pages longer (really!). So in brief, I'd like to thank Gretchen Archer, Shannon Baker, Bruce Cantwell, Kate Dyer-Seeley, April Henry, Kelly Garrett, John Kohlepp, Erin Pawlus, the folks at Oregon Writers Colony, and the wonderfully supportive Hens of Henery Press.

And last but never least, all my love and thanks to Hal, my editor, partner, and true love.

CHAPTER 1

"Ivy, come quick! Lassie's in trouble!"

The caller hung up, but I knew it was Marge and I knew it was serious. Marge never hung up without saying goodbye.

"Gotta go," I said to my friends and flew down the stairs and out the door.

Lassie. What could have happened? I beat down my rising panic and redialed Marge as I ran across the theater parking lot.

"You okay?" I said when she picked up. "Maybe you need to call the vet?"

"No, but I called 911. They said it wasn't an emergency."

Phew, things must not be too bad.

"They, they, they..." Marge started to cry.

Dang, things *were* bad. Not only did Marge never hang up without saying goodbye, she never cried. "I'll be there as soon as I can." I jumped into my latest used car, a 2005 Nissan pickup, and squealed out of the lot. I'd met Marge last spring when we both did a show at Desert Magic Dinner Theater. I loved my friend and her dog. My throat swelled at the thought of either of them in pain.

It was Saturday, so I made pretty good time from downtown Phoenix to Marge's retirement community, west of town. I turned into an entrance flanked by rock walls and two signs, one that said "Sunnydale!" and the other "America's Favorite 55+ Community!" I zoomed past palm trees, a golf course, and a bunch of golf carts toodling down the road and pulled into Marge's driveway.

I didn't even ring the bell. I just shouted as I walked in the door. "Marge?"

Heels clicked on the tile floor as Marge rounded a corner into the foyer. "What happened?" I began, then stopped.

Marge was pale. Marge, who suntanned for all of her sixty-plus years and had skin the color of calf leather, looked positively white. She teetered on her heels. "Lassie..."

I put an arm around her and steered her back into the living room, where we sat together on a pastel sofa. The surroundings were familiar: I had stayed here last spring, taking care of the house and Lassie while Marge was ill. But though I knew the dent in the sofa like it was my own, I didn't recognize this version of my friend. Marge was "Arizona's Ethel Merman," a bold, brassy former Broadway star. But today she crumpled onto the sofa like a used Kleenex, clutching a cellphone in her hand.

I scanned the room for Lassie, afraid he was lying on the floor somewhere. Yeah, Lassie was a boy, just like all the Lassies in the movies, but that's where the resemblance ended. Lassie was a pug. And he wasn't in the room.

"Tell me," I said gently.

"You're a detective, so you'll find him, right? Right?"

Though I worked part-time at my Uncle Bob's PI firm, I didn't have my license yet, so I wasn't really a detective. I also wasn't about to correct Marge in her present state. "Tell me what happened," I said again.

"Lassie wanted a walk, but I was on the phone, so I let him out in the front yard." There was a small courtyard in front of Marge's house, ringed by a decorative iron fence. "He was taking his time, sniffing everything five times before peeing on it, so I went inside, keeping the door open so he could come in when he was done. Then I heard them."

"Them?" I couldn't imagine what she meant—no gangs in Sunnydale, no motorcades, or groups of juvenile delinquents or anything else that could qualify as "them."

"I don't know how they got in—maybe Arnie left the gate open when he got the mail—but they were yipping and..."

My stomach dropped. Coyotes. I'd seen them around, skulking around the oleanders, looking mangy and underfed. But wait. They were usually out at night. "Marge, what time—"

Her cell rang. A flicker of hope crossed her face, then died as she saw who was calling. "Arnie," she said to her husband as she picked up. "Ivy's here, but Lassie's still..." She couldn't go on.

"It'll be all right, babe." Arnie talked so loudly I could hear him, even though Marge wasn't using speakerphone. "He'll be all right." His voice broke too. My eyes filled up just listening to them. I adored these guys, and Lassie. Oh no. Tears were beginning to leak out of my eyes now. I wiped them hurriedly so Marge wouldn't see. "Let me talk to Ivy," Arnie said. Marge handed the phone over to me. "Thanks for coming over, kid," he said. "You know that little dog means the world to us. Do you think you can find him?"

"I...sure. Of course, but..." I tried not to think about what I might find, what a pack of coyotes might do to a little black pug.

"The last thing I heard, the pack was skirting the golf courses. Food and water, you know."

"Of course. There are the water hazards, and the bunnies."

"Bunnies?"

"Yeah." Oh boy. Didn't want to transfer the bloody image in my mind to Arnie's head so I simply said, "Food."

"Food, huh? Seems like they'd go more for pretzels and protein bars and stuff. I hear people throw their snacks at them to keep them away. Bunnies seem a little big, even for a pack of Chihuahuas."

"A pack could easily take down—did you say Chihuahuas?"

"Yeah. Didn't Marge tell you? It's that pack—you've seen 'em on the news."

Sunnydale had recently made the national news, courtesy of a pack of, yes, feral Chihuahuas that were terrorizing the neighborhood. "The Chihuahuas carried off Lassie?"

"He *joined* them. Little hoodlum." The affection in Arnie's voice turned to concern. "But it's not safe. They could get hit by a car. A few people even said they'd take pot shots at them if them saw 'em. And then there are the coyotes..." He didn't have to say more. We both knew what could happen to the snack pack of tasty little dogs. If I could just find Lassie before...

What was that noise? "Arnie, was that a gunshot?" I whispered, sliding a look at Marge. Either she didn't hear me or the news didn't bother her.

"Yeah." He chuckled as several more shots rang out over the line, followed by...applause? "But don't worry, it's just—oh my God!"

The line went dead.

CHAPTER 2

Marge heard that. She grabbed the phone out of my hands. "Arnie? Arnie?" Wild-eyed, she thrust the phone at me. I put it to my ear—definitely dead. I put the cell on speakerphone and redialed. The phone rang. And rang. And rang. Then it picked up. "You've reached Arnie. Leave me a message and—"

"Marge, were those gunshots?"

"Try him again." Marge leapt up from the sofa and began pacing.

I stood up too, the muscles in my legs jumping from tension. I redialed. Same message. Marge grabbed the phone from me and tried dialing herself. "You've reached Arnie. Leave me—"

"First Lassie, then Arnie. No. No, no, no."

"Come on." I grabbed my keys from the coffee table where I'd dropped them. "We'll go see what's going on."

I bundled Marge into the cab of my truck, hoping Arnie would be okay to drive home. No way the three of us would fit in my pickup, unless one of us rode in the back. It was amazing, the strangely normal worries that came into your mind in times of crisis. But maybe there wasn't a crisis. "Maybe Arnie forgot to charge his cell phone," I said as we pulled out of Marge's driveway.

She shook her head. "Saw it on the charger last night."

"Okay." My stomach dropped, but I put on a calm demeanor. "Where to?"

"Head west on Grand."

I didn't ask where we were going, and she didn't tell me. I just kept driving west, and she just kept dialing Arnie's number. "First Lassie, now this..." she mumbled to herself.

City turned to desert. "Keep going?" I said.

"Yeah."

The desert northwest of Phoenix was scrubby, devoid of any interesting features except the craggy bare mountains that ringed the valley. Still, Marge stared out of the window as if mesmerized.

After ten minutes I said, "You doing okay?"

Marge looked at me as if seeing me properly for the first time. "You come from the theater?"

"Yeah."

She eyed my green-paint-spattered jeans, t-shirt, and ball cap, which kept my bi-colored hair (brown roots, blonde hair) from being tri-colored. "You working backstage?"

"I was painting some flats for New Vintage Theater."

She nodded. "Good outfit. You doing a show for them? I thought you were auditioning for *Annie Get Your Gun*."

"I was just helping some friends. And yeah, I did audition. You won't believe it, but..."

"You got a callback?"

"Crazy, huh?" Arizona Center Stage was a regional theater company. A callback for them was a big deal, a definite step up career-wise. "How did you know?"

"I got big ears. And I know the assistant director."

"Did you...?"

"Nah. You got it on your own, kiddo. I knew you could."

I waited, but that seemed to be the end of our conversation. I rolled down my window to let the cool November air stream in (and to save gas by shutting off the AC). After another ten minutes of no sound but wheels on asphalt, I asked, "We going to Wickenburg?" It was the only place I could think of out this direction, a small desert town that still felt like the Old West, maybe owing to its history of cowboys, mining, and massacres.

"No. That new Western theme park, Gold Bug Gulch. It's just this side of Wickenburg."

"I didn't know it was open yet."

"It's half-open, what they call a soft opening. Just weekends for now. The saloon and restaurant, reptile house, and blacksmith shop are open, plus they have horse rides and roping and..."

"Gunfights. That's what we heard on the phone." Phew. "Maybe

Arnie yelled because it surprised him." I didn't say anything about him not picking up the phone. I was sure Marge hadn't forgotten about that.

"He knows about the gunfight. He's been out there almost every day the past two weeks. He's an investor."

This was not good news. Arnie fancied himself an impresario, but he'd left a string of bad business decisions in his wake. He finally had a winner with Desert Magic Dinner Theater, where I'd met him and Marge. The theater's success was really due to Marge, who headlined about half of the shows. People whispered that it was Marge's money that kept the theater afloat, since Arnie didn't have much of his own.

Oh no.

"*You're* the investor," I said. "But why? Doesn't seem like your kind of entertainment."

"You're right there, kiddo. My idea of the outdoors is the walk from the taxi to the theater. But Arnie was really hot to go with this one. Mostly because his son is the mastermind behind it." She looked at me, arching an eyebrow.

I bit. "His son?"

"Yeah. Nathan showed up on our doorstep three months ago. Literally. The bell rang, Arnie went to open the door, and I hear 'Papa!' I guess the kid, Nathan—he's not really a kid anymore—was the result of some brief fling Arnie had with a dancer back in the day. Arnie never had a clue he was a father. Nathan's mom told him about his dad when he got older. Guess he tried to look for Arnie for a while, but this was pre-internet, and he gave up after a year or two. Then, coincidentally, Nathan buys this ghost town he wants to turn into a tourist trap, not a half hour from our place."

"Coincidentally?" I asked. My uncle had taught me there were very few coincidences in this world.

"That's what I thought too, but Nathan swears he had this all planned out. And he did have the place nearly up and running when he found Arnie."

"Which he did how?"

"Said he was reading the paper—"

"How old is this guy?" Most newspaper subscribers were over forty-five.

"Maybe forty? He said he was checking on an article about Gold Bug Gulch and happened to see a preview article for Desert Magic Dinner Theater right under it, with a quote by Arnie."

"Hmm."

"I checked the paper. The articles were on the same page, so he could have been telling the truth."

"But you don't believe him?"

"I don't know what to believe. This guy shows up out of nowhere, claims to be Arnie's son, and by the way, he's looking for investors in his newest venture."

"It does sound suspicious, but then again, the guy also sounds a little like Arnie."

"I know." Margie's voice grew warm. "You should see Arnie, grinning from ear to ear when he introduces people to 'his boy.'"

A blue sign ahead said, "Highway adopted by Gold Bug Gulch—where the Old West lives on!"

"It's another quarter mile or so on the left," Marge said. "So anyway, when Arnie asked, I said sure, we could invest a little money. Can't take it with you, you know." Marge tried to smile, but couldn't manage it. "God, Ivy, if anything happened to him..."

"I'm sure everything is just fine," I said, right as we turned a bend and saw Gold Bug Gulch. Couldn't have missed it. Not with all those flashing blue lights.

CHAPTER 3

I bumped the truck into the rutted dirt lot, steering around the knots of people who stood talking. Some were crying. I grabbed Marge's hand across the seat. "Don't worry. We'll find out what all this is about. I'm sure it has nothing to do with Arnie."

I parked as close as I could to the town's entrance, where "Gold Bug Gulch" was burned into a wooden sign that swung between two twenty-foot posts. I jumped out of the cab and ran around to help Marge. Those high heels of hers were going be a liability out here. I took her by the arm, and we headed toward the town

"Sorry, ladies." A uniformed state patrolman held up a hand. "Gold Bug Gulch is closed this evening."

"We're family," I said. "We got a call."

The cop shook his head. "How would I know—"

"I'm one of the owners." Marge somehow made herself look bigger, like she was facing a bear. "And I'm happy to take down your name and badge number."

"Yeah, all right." The cop waved us through. As I passed him, I said in a low voice, "Can you tell me what happened?"

"Guy got shot," he said, loud enough for the vultures circling above to hear us—wait, were those really vultures? "Killed."

At that, Marge dropped my arm and picked up her pace. Heels or no heels, she was headed like a shot to the clutch of people standing in the dirt road and milling around on the wooden sidewalks of the buildings on either side. I caught up with her.

I'd read a little about Gold Bug Gulch. Some entrepreneur from back East (Arnie's son, I guessed) bought the remains of an old mining town, planning to turn it into a "true Old West Experience." At one time, the original Gulch's population numbered a couple thousand, but once the gold mine was played out, the town dwindled to just a few desert rats. Arizona's dry weather must have preserved a lot of the buildings, which were strung out along the main dirt road. Wooden buildings with false fronts, like the ones in movies, lined the north side of the road. The south side sloped down a hill, bordered at the bottom by a stand of shivering cottonwoods. A couple of squat adobe-looking buildings—one with bars on the windows—crouched on the top of the southern side where the hill flattened out. The adobe structures and first couple of wooden buildings were all cleaned up and sturdy, obviously the backbone of the theme park. Farther down the road another dozen or so buildings awaited repair. And in the distance beyond the creek, an industrial, jumbled-looking platform—something to do with the mine?—stood black against the darkening sky.

"Arnie!" Marge shouted. "Arnie!"

No answer. The people in the street formed a ring around something. "Arnie," Marge called again. Nothing but the buzz of flies and worried people.

"It can't be Arnie. Remember? He said 'Oh my God' *after* the gunshot." Of course, they could have been his last words after he'd been hit, but I wasn't about to admit that.

Marge aimed for the clot of people in the road. I followed, elbowing my way through a mishmash of state patrolmen, paramedics, and people in old-fashioned Western garb. "Got him in the heart," I heard someone say. "The other guy was some shot."

"Ma'am." A uniformed officer grabbed my elbow.

"People," another state trooper said in a loud voice. "As I said just, oh, two minutes ago, everyone who is not law enforcement or medical personnel needs to wait inside in the saloon. The sooner we can get this sorted out, the sooner everyone can go home."

People began moving toward the saloon. Marge took advantage of the crowd's cover to creep closer to the body.

"You can't be here," the officer who held my arm said to me.

"I know. I'm trying to stop—" I pointed at Marge, who had somehow managed to get within a few feet of the shrouded body.

"Ma'am! You! Stop!" The officer waved his arms at Marge, releasing his grip on me.

I sprinted toward Marge—at the exact same time another guy did. We connected headfirst and *pow*—as Uncle Bob liked to say—right in the kisser. We both fell down in the dirt.

"Ow ow ow." I pressed my hand against my face and it came away bloody. "*Ow.*"

The officer who'd held me back glared at all of us, then planted himself in front of the corpse with his arms crossed, as if to say "serves you right." Marge stretched out a hand to help me up. At least my split lip had kept her from reaching the body.

The guy I'd head-banged scowled at me as he picked himself up. "Dammit, woman, why didn't you look where you were going?"

"Me?" I asked my unintentional assailant. "I was just trying to keep Marge from—"

"Me too. God, this is just what we need, two hysterical women—"

"Hey. There is no hysteria here. Even though there could be, with somebody dead and Marge's husband missing and blood running down my chin." I got to my feet and dusted myself off.

The guy reluctantly agreed with a grunt. I glanced at him. He wasn't a cop or a medic or a cowboy actor. Maybe he was...

"Nathan, meet Ivy." Marge proffered a Kleenex from her pocket. Nathan took it and dabbed at a tiny bit of blood under his nose. "Now, Nathan, for God's sake," she said, "tell me who's under the blanket."

"One of the cowboy actors, Mongo."

Marge closed her eyes. "Thank God." She opened them and looked at the blanket. "Sorry, Mongo." She looked at me as a drip of my blood plopped onto the dusty ground. "And sorry, Ivy, that Kleenex was for you. My last one."

"Here." Nathan thrust the used Kleenex at me.

Another drop of my blood trickled down my chin. Well...the Kleenex was *mostly* clean, only a little bit of Nathan's blood on one side. Better than nothing. I took it and held the clean edge against my still-bleeding lip. "His name was Mongo?" I said. That was one of Uncle Bob's favorite characters from *Blazing Saddles*.

"Real name was Michael Carver." Nathan bent down to rub the dust off his shoes made of some soft leather, which were way too nice for this kind of place. "God, I don't believe this." He wiped the sides of his face with both hands, maybe out of frustration since there wasn't anything on it except maybe moisturizer. Between his smooth face, fancy shoes, and the ton of product in his thinning hair, the guy couldn't have looked more out of place in this cowboy environment if he'd tried. "Just when we were starting get to a leg up, he dies."

"Doesn't sound like it was his fault. Now take me to my husband." Marge was her old take-charge self again.

Nathan shook his head and put his hands on his waist, or where his waist would have been. He was built square. Like Arnie.

"People." The trooper who'd spoken earlier stood behind us. "Am I not talking loud enough for you?" He pointed to one of the wooden buildings. "In the saloon. Now."

"I'm the owner." Nathan puffed out his chest.

I saw Marge open her mouth, then shut it again. She was an owner too, but maybe she anticipated the cop's next words. "I don't care if you're the ghost of Elvis." Well, she probably didn't anticipate those exact words. "Get inside, now."

The three of us walked toward the two-story building, under the saloon sign, and into a madhouse. The place was full of people and adrenaline and the booze was flowing. The combination made me nervous.

Marge grabbed Nathan's arm. "Is Arnie in here?"

Nathan jerked his chin toward a nearby table full of cowboys, then he headed to the bar where a woman sat alone, dressed in a shiny red-and-black-striped saloon girl's outfit. He put an arm around her and whispered something in her ear. Her shoulders began to shake.

We approached the table. Burly cowboys nearly hid Arnie, whose bald head was bowed. Uh-oh. He may have been alive, but he didn't look good. The cowboys vacated their seats with a nod to us. "Ladies," one said in acknowledgment.

"Babe." Marge hugged the gray-faced Arnie around the neck then swatted him on the shoulder. "You scared me half to death. Especially after Lass—" Arnie looked up at us without moving his head, sorrow in his eyes. Marge switched subjects. "Where's your phone?"

Arnie patted his pocket.

"Why didn't you pick up?"

"It's broken. I dropped it, then someone stepped on it." Arnie still didn't lift his head.

"Did you see what happened?" I asked, as gently as I could.

He nodded. "Mongo and Chance were performing their gunfight. It's always the same—they insult each other, then draw and shoot. Blanks, of course."

"And?"

"Mongo always dies in these gunfights, so when he went down we all applauded. Then he started to bleed. We were still clapping. We were clapping when he died. And it's all my fault."

CHAPTER 4

"What do you mean it's your fault?"

I was glad Marge asked. I hoped Arnie meant the clapping, not the killing.

"It's the curse—the family curse. Everything I do—everything my father did, maybe everything Nathan does—it's all ferkakta."

"All crap," Marge translated (or maybe replied). "Chickie, you know that's not true."

"What about Leroy?" Arnie said. Leroy was the departed alligator-wrestling star of Arnie's failed *Swamps are Fun!* theme park, who really should have remembered to feed the gator.

"C'mon, babe, you know there's no curse." Marge stroked Arnie's bald head. "What happened here was an accident."

Arnie shook his head and looked toward the corner of the saloon, where several uniformed officers stood talking to a young man in 1890s cowboy gear, rusty with dried blood.

"What exactly did happen?" I watched the cowboy talk to the cops. He'd swiped at his eyes, leaving streaks of blood mingled with the dust and tears on his face. "You said they used blanks?"

"Until today they did. Chance"—Arnie nodded toward the cowboy—"said he checked his gun, like always, a few minutes before the show. But when he fired..."

"Live ammunition," I finished. Chance slowly followed a policeman out of the saloon, another cop tailing him. He was young, maybe late twenties, but he moved like an old man. "But how could that happen?"

"Chance wore his gun most of the time, like a lot of guys around here." Arizona was an open-carry state. "So when he's not acting, he's got real bullets in it. They have a staging area here where they load the guns with blanks before the show. He thought he'd switched all the bullets for blanks, but he must've missed one. From the audience it looked like a regular show until..." Arnie hung his head again. "It's all my fault."

"Tell Ivy how the show usually worked." Marge gave me a look that said "keep Arnie talking about the facts so he doesn't go to a bad place."

"Right," I said. "How was the fight supposed to go before the...ending? Was anything different?"

Marge slid me a grateful look as Arnie raised his head. "The show starts off with each of them telling the other to step down. They're supposed to be fighting over a woman." Arnie's gaze drifted to the saloon girl at the bar. A broken black feather hung from her hair, snapped in two but still holding together—like a broken spine. "At the beginning it's almost silly. There's a bit where Mongo shoots a hole in a barrel—it's rigged to spurt water out of it—then Chance shoots the hat off Mongo's head. Then it gets more serious. Mongo shoots Chance, who pretends to take a bullet in the arm. Chance shoots back, and Mongo dies. Except he wasn't supposed to."

"So nothing was different this time."

"Nothing. Chance was the first one to realize something wasn't right. Said he could tell by the kick of the gun and by the shocked look on Mongo's face when he went down."

"But wouldn't he look that way anyway? As an actor who was supposed to die?"

"Mongo wasn't really an actor. He was a cowboy. The real deal. Grew up on a ranch not far from here. He did act in our gunfight, but mostly he was responsible for...Oh no."

"Yeah. I just thought of that too." Nathan had appeared behind his dad. "We're going have to find someone else to lead the horseback rides. Shit, and take care of the horses too. Yeah, the glories of ownership." He put a hand on Arnie's shoulder. "You want something to eat, Papa? Looks like we might be here a while. The police want to talk to us."

You couldn't miss the solicitousness in Nathan's voice. Also the fact that he didn't include Marge in the conversation.

"I'm not hungry," Arnie said. "You want something, babe?" Marge shook her head.

"Suit yourself," Nathan said. "Hard to believe, but I'm hungry enough to eat a horse." He laughed. "Guess I better not say that too loud around here, huh?" He patted Arnie on the shoulder and headed toward a door that said "employees only."

Marge looked after Nathan. "He's laughing? And he's gonna eat?"

"Shock?" I said.

Arnie put his head down on the table. "I can't believe this happened again. And Lassie..." His shoulders heaved and he snuffled into his hands.

"Listen." Marge gently took Arnie's head in her hands and made him look at her. "We're going to find Lassie. Right, Ivy?"

I nodded, not because I was sure, but because I needed to look sure, for Arnie's sake.

"And Leroy got eaten by the alligator because he forgot to feed him. Also he was dumb enough to wrestle alligators. This thing has an explanation too. I'm sure it was all an accident."

"But—"

"And I'm sure the police will check things out. But just to ease your mind, we could have somebody look into it. We do have a private investigator sitting right here."

I felt a little glow of pride, completely inappropriate given the situation. I gave my ego a mental kick and it retreated.

"I don't know about that. I wouldn't want Nathan to know."

"She could go undercover. You know, hush-hush." Marge knew that my uncle and I had recently finished an undercover gig on a cruise ship.

Arnie didn't look convinced.

"Listen," said Marge. "I'm not sure a few notes in a police report are going to make you feel any better about your supposed family curse. But Ivy could really look into things, let you know what's going on with everything at Gold Bug Gulch." She slid me a look. I was pretty sure she meant Nathan.

Arnie raised his head and regarded me. "It might work. You do make a pretty good detective. You even look like a private eye right now."

"I do?" I looked down at my paint-spattered jeans and yellow t-shirt.

"Yeah. Like you've been roughed up by the bad guys."

"Oh, kiddo." Marge patted my face. "Let's get some ice on that lip."

CHAPTER 5

A flashlight bobbed toward me in the dark. I stood up, brushing the grass from my jeans. The light came closer, carried by a lean figure silhouetted against the evening sky. Moonlight flashed off his glasses.

I walked a few paces toward him, and we met near a little flag that trembled in the faint breeze. "Thanks for coming." I felt a great relief, like a warm shower after a dusty day.

Matt smiled. "Why are we at a golf course?"

"Because it's romantic?" It wasn't the real reason, but now that he was here, it was true. The full moon shone in the water hazards, crickets serenaded us, and damp grass perfumed the air. The only thing that smelled better was Matt, the sweetness of his skin mingled with soap. He bent to kiss me, and the stars above him filled the sky and...

"Ow!" I jerked away. "Ow, ow, ow."

"What?"

"I forgot about my lip." I touched it gingerly and my finger came away wet. "Is it bleeding again?"

"Oh god, sorry. Couldn't see it in the dark." Matt came so near that I wanted to kiss him again, split lip and all. "It is bleeding, just a little." He looked closer. "Don't think you need stitches or anything though. Why didn't you tell me?"

"I can't see it, so I kind of forgot about it." I was a visual person. "If it'd been a cut on my hand, I would have remembered it."

"What happened?"

"Had a run-in with Arnie's son."

"Arnie's son did that to you?" I saw Matt's jaw clench.

"Not on purpose. We butted heads. I have the feeling he might do that a lot."

"I didn't know Arnie had a son."

"Neither did he." I filled Matt in on the newfound son, Gold Bug Gulch, and the gunfight incident. "I really hope it was an accident. Arnie and Marge aren't so sure. They want me go out there, see what I can learn."

"Do you need to play golf while you're there?"

"What? No."

"So we're on a golf course in Sunnydale at ten o'clock at night because..."

"Oh. Because Lassie ran off with a pack of Chihuahuas."

"That sounds serious," said Matt. "Did I ever tell you about the time I was attacked by Chihuahuas?"

"No." Matt and I had known each other a little over a year but had only been dating a couple of months. "When?"

"When I was just a kid. Our neighbors had a bunch. One day I was over at their house, and they rushed in from outside, running and yipping and...it was terrible. They licked my toes."

I smacked him, and he laughed, a big deep rolling laugh at odds with his slim frame. I loved that laugh.

"Seriously. I hate having my toes licked."

"Duly noted."

"Hey, you kids!" A man stood outside one of the houses that ringed the golf course, his face blue from the reflection of his lit swimming pool. "What do you think you're doing out there?"

"Making love in the green grass..." Matt sang softly.

I smacked him again. "I am not your brown-eyed girl." My eyes were green. "And I don't think making love in the green grass will go over well with the neighbors."

"Come on. These folks probably had Van Morrison's albums when they first came out."

"I could call the cops, you know," shouted the homeowner.

"Just looking for a dog," I shouted back. "Have you seen a black pug? Or a pack of Chihuahuas?"

"I've seen the Chihuahuas," he said. "Just yesterday they stole a couple of hotdogs off my hibachi. Little buggers."

"Thanks." I waved at him. "If you do see the pug, grab him. He won't bite. He's not wearing a collar, but you can call Marge Weiss—she lives here in Sunnydale. We're going to keep looking."

"Good luck." The guy raised a hand in farewell and went inside.

Matt and I spent another hour on the golf course. We saw a few tracks in the soft dirt around one of the water hazards and a gleam of eyes from beneath an oleander that turned out to be a cat. No dogs, but no coyotes either.

"Let's pack it in for the night," I said.

"Come back to my place?"

"I'm too tired."

Matt lived in Scottsdale, in an older condo off Camelback Road. My apartment was in central Phoenix, about a half hour closer to where we were right then in Sunnydale.

"Okay." He took me in his arms and kissed my head, then my forehead. I shut my eyes and he kissed them too.

"Mmm...maybe I'm not so tired, but...no, I have to be at Uncle Bob's for breakfast, then do some stuff for Arnie and Marge tomorrow—which might involve a trip to Gold Bug, and prep for that callback for *Annie Get Your Gun*."

"See you in a few days?" Matt released me, and I realized how cool the night had grown.

"I think so."

"You think so?"

"Not sure about this Gold Bug Gulch gig."

Matt was quiet.

"But it seems like they'd want me daytimes, so I should have some nights free."

"Unless you get cast in *Annie Get Your Gun*."

"Nah, rehearsals don't start for a month. Why don't you come over for a quick dinner before my callback Monday night? I should have an hour. Forty-five minutes at least."

Matt sighed. "You know, Ivy, between your schedule and keeping us—"

I kissed him before he could say any more, split lip and all. "It'll be okay. Better than okay. It'll be good. Everything will be good."

CHAPTER 6

Uncle Bob whistled as I walked into his kitchen the next morning. "What's the other guy look like?" He poured me a cup of the elixir of the gods and handed it to me.

"Yeah, yeah." I squinted at the neon green of his newest Hawaiian shirt and tried to figure out what the printed monkeys were tossing back and forth across my uncle's considerable mid-section. I sat down at the fifties-era Formica table and sipped at my coffee gingerly, trying to drink it without the hot liquid touching my fat lip. "I ran into someone face first. I'll tell you all about it after..." Another blessed smell wafted toward me. "Bacon? Is there bacon?"

"Yep. Staying warm in the oven, since someone is a little late."

"Where is Bette?" Bette was my uncle's girlfriend and the brains behind the investigative journalism site "All Bets Are Off." They'd met a few months earlier when we were all on a cruise ship (business, not pleasure). She lived in Colorado, but she was supposed to be here this weekend, hence this Sunday brunch.

"She had to extend her trip to Haiti through next week. Gonna interview some whistleblower for a supposed aid organization."

"So she's not late..."

"Sheesh, remind me never to send you out on anything important in the morning." Uncle Bob opened his refrigerator and leaned in. "Especially since you're usually late."

"Not always. And I'll be fine after my second cup of coffee. And some bacon. And...coconuts!"

Uncle Bob turned to me and raised an eyebrow. It had little gray hairs sticking out of it.

"On your shirt, I mean. Although I would eat some coconut if you had it. I'm starving."

"Then help with breakfast." He scrounged around in the fridge. "Put down your coffee, Olive." Uncle Bob always called me by my real name, which was Olive Ziegwart. Ivy Meadows was my stage name, my preferred name (wouldn't it be yours?), and the name of a subdivision off the 51 that lured people in with its promise of greenery, but was just another stucco-and-tile-roof development in the mostly brown desert. I had heard they had wrought-iron gates that looked like ivy. "And think fast." He tossed a can to me.

I caught it. "Cinnamon rolls! Aww, you know I love—"

"Popping the can open," we said together.

Best uncle in the world.

Over big plates of bacon and eggs and cinnamon rolls, I told Uncle Bob about the gunfight.

"That's a bad business."

"And bad *for* business, I bet. I think it's one reason Arnie and Marge want me to investigate." I got up and padded toward the Mr. Coffeemaker.

Uncle Bob shook his head. "Probably the opposite. Bet there are lots of people wanting to see where it happened."

"Oh." I stopped where I stood.

"What?" Uncle Bob must have known I just had a lightbulb moment, since I couldn't walk and think at the same time.

"Maybe Nathan *could* be involved. He sure didn't seem too upset about one of his employee's deaths."

"I don't know what you're talking about, but don't go there. If you're gonna investigate this—if you're gonna investigate anything— you can't go in with a preconceived idea based on a guy's reaction to sudden death. People react to tragedy in all sorts of ways. You of all people should know that."

I did know that.

I was eleven when my life changed on a frozen pond in Spokane, Washington. On a pond we *thought* was frozen. I was ice-skating with my girlfriends and annoyed that my mom made me take my little brother Cody with us. So I ignored him. Dissed by us, he skated away to the other side of the pond. I didn't even know he wasn't near until I heard the crack of the ice, the shouts that froze in the air, and the beating of my heart in my ears as I raced to the jagged hole where my brother had been.

Cody survived. Our family didn't. My parents blamed me for Cody's accident, for the brain injury he would have his whole life. I escaped into theater, where I could live in another world and create my own family of actors and stagehands and wardrobe mistresses. Outside the theater, Uncle Bob and Cody formed the nucleus of my family. And now, Matt too. Maybe.

"Who is Nathan anyway?" Uncle Bob's voice brought me back to the here and now.

I poured myself another cup of coffee and explained about Nathan and Arnie.

"And why not just leave this to the police?"

"Arnie and Marge think there may be more to the Gold Bug story than just this shooting."

"Ah. You said they're investors?"

"Right."

"Given the relationships involved, undercover seems the way to go."

"That's what Marge said. I need to call Arnie to figure out the details. Can I put him on speakerphone?" I was still really green with this detective stuff. Uncle Bob may have been a laid-back trivia buff who looked a bit like a beardless Santa Claus, but he was a crack PI.

He nodded. I grabbed my cell phone, a pen, and a notebook from the purse I'd slung across the back of the kitchen chair. I dialed Arnie's number and told him Uncle Bob was with us. Then I took a deep breath. "Lassie?"

"No sign." Just two words, but I could hear Arnie's voice begin to break.

"I'll email you the posters I made last night. Print out a bunch and post them everywhere. Did Marge call the pound this morning?" She'd promised to do that every morning and evening.

"Yes. No word." Arnie's voice still sounded strangled.

"We'll find him." I switched subjects. Maybe it'd make Arnie feel better. "You still want to go forward with this undercover gig?"

"I don't know..." If the catch in Arnie's voice was any indication, this subject was no better than the last one. "If Nathan found out and thought I didn't trust him..."

"You're doing this for Nathan." Marge's voice rang out in the background. "To make sure he's not getting himself into any trouble. Remember, chickie, this is a good thing you're doing."

Arnie snuffled into the phone.

"Right, Ivy?" shouted Marge.

"Right. Arnie, what's Mongo's real name again?" I remembered Nathan mentioning it the night of the shooting.

"Michael Carver." I made a note of it. "I think you mighta heard: besides doing the gunfight, he owned the horse ride concessions."

"You said he wasn't an actor. How'd they find him?" I slid a look at Uncle Bob, and he nodded in approval. I was getting better at asking the right questions.

"He's from the area, some big ranching family. His family owns most of the land around there, apart from the Bureau of Land Management. A good worker, but he had the reputation of disappearing for days at a time on a pretty regular basis. Nathan was trying him out but wasn't sure about keeping him on."

"How about the guy who shot Mongo?" I remembered the young cowboy at the saloon, blood and dust mingled with his tears. "What do you know about him?"

"Name's Chance Keeler. Nathan said he was a real find—an honest-to-God cowboy *and* an actor."

I wrote Chance's name down under Mongo's. "There was a saloon girl—woman—too, who looked awfully upset."

"Mongo's girlfriend, Billie Davenport. Theater background, bartender, et cetera, et cetera. She's worked at The Thirsty Vulture in Wickenburg for years. Hell of a gal."

"I think that's enough to get me started. So..." What else did I need to ask? I looked at Uncle Bob.

"How do you want to do this undercover gig?" he asked.

Yeah, that.

"I got an idea about a show," Arnie said. "Let me see if I can set it up."

"Okay," said Uncle Bob. "Anything else Ivy should know before starting the investigation?"

The burble of the coffeemaker was the only sound for a moment. Then Arnie said, "Nathan's my son, but..." The coffeemaker sighed. "I'm not sure he's on the up-and-up about the town's finances. I know he's got other investors besides me, but I've only met one of them, Josh Tate. He sold most of the town, kept his family house and the blacksmith's forge, and has a share in Gold Bug Gulch. He still lives on the property and works as a blacksmith. His family used to own the whole place, the mine and everything."

"Wait, I thought the big landowner there was Mongo's family." I flipped back through my notebook. "The Carver family. Are they and the Tates related?"

"Don't think so. Probably a bunch of families own property there."

"And the other investors?"

"That's part of my, uh, concern. The rest of the investors, the people who had to pony up the dough to buy the property from Josh...I've never talked to them, not even sure of their names. There's some group operating under an acronym listed in the incorporation docs, but Nathan gets real vague when I ask about them. And there's one more thing I should tell you. I've got a bad feeling about this. And I never get a bad feeling."

CHAPTER 7

I used Uncle Bob's computer (and his database access) to check Mongo's (Michael Carver's) background. From the articles I read in *The Wickenburg Sun*, the Carvers were movers and shakers in the area. They owned a big ranch, lots of cattle, and several big chunks of property throughout the state. Mongo had worked for his family's ranch outfit his entire life. Never been married, no kids, and no criminal record. His last address was listed as Wickenburg. I checked it against Billie Davenport's address. Yep, same one. I looked it up on Google Earth: a nice doublewide off a desert road, not too far from Gold Bug, not too close to anything or anyone else.

I went into the kitchen for more coffee and maybe some inspiration. "Pooh," I said to my uncle, who was whipping up his weekly batch of chili. "Just enough info to tell me Mongo existed. Not enough to figure out why someone might kill him."

"Darn," he said. I deduced he was being sarcastic, since Uncle Bob was not a man who said darn. "Guess you'll have to rely on outdated, old-fashioned investigative techniques, like questioning people who knew him."

Yep, sarcastic. But also right. "I'll drive out to Wickenburg this afternoon."

I headed west out of downtown around two o'clock. I knew what questions I wanted to ask about Mongo but had one problem: why would I—an actress working at Gold Bug Gulch—be questioning people about Mongo? Hmmm...an actress.

Ah. Yep. That would work. I got off at Bell Road and called Arnie. "Sure," he said. "Meet you there."

About fifteen minutes later I pulled into the empty parking lot for Desert Magic Dinner Theater. While I waited, I did a Google search on my phone to make sure my backstory worked. By the time Arnie got there, I had it all figured out.

I met him at the stage door. "Pretty smart, disguising yourself while you're in Wickenburg," he said. "Costume department's all yours." I walked the familiar hallway to the room, scrounged through the costumes hanging on portable racks, and found what I wanted. I changed into a nondescript blouse and skirt, tucked the rest of my disguise under my arm, and left, kissing Arnie on the cheek as he locked the theater door behind us.

Sunday traffic was light, so it was just forty-five minutes before I pulled off the highway and onto Wickenburg Way. I felt inexplicably happy. Wickenburg always did that to me. I loved its Old West-looking buildings with their false fronts, its neon-signed moviehouse with the plaster Saguaro on top, even the life-size fake bulls that decorated the shop roofs. Wickenburg felt a little like a Roy Rogers movie—not exactly the real Old West, but what you'd like it to be.

I parked on a street behind The Thirsty Vulture, looked around to make sure no one was looking, and slipped on the final pieces of my disguise. Then I got out of the truck, limping slightly (part of my new persona), and walked down a wide covered sidewalk, attracting a few curious glances from passersby. Oops, I still wore my cat-eye sunglasses. I quickly traded them for thick glasses from the costume department, pushed open the door to The Thirsty Vulture, and stepped inside.

The buzz of conversation in the dim room died as soon as I entered. Just as I figured it would. The bushy-mustachioed bartender cleared his throat. "What can we do for you, Sister?"

The nun costume seemed like the perfect disguise. Not only would people be more truthful when speaking with a nun (I hoped), but the veil, wimple, and thick glasses disguised me enough that no one would recognize me if they saw me later at Gold Bug. Couldn't have anyone telling folks I'd been asking around about Mongo.

I smoothed down my skirt. I'd used the nun ruse once before and had made the mistake of wearing a full habit (most nuns don't do that anymore), so I was proud of my choice of the serviceable but dull skirt and blouse. But you know what they say about pride.

"Yes," I said to the barman. "I'd like to—oh dear!" I found myself upside down, tangled with a vinyl-topped stool on the sticky bar floor. Too bad I hadn't considered the dangers of Coke bottle glasses.

A guy in a ball cap helped me up. I hoped no one had seen my red lace panties. Didn't seem very nun-like. I steadied myself against a long raised shuffleboard table in the center of the room. "Thank you so much," I said. "It's the dim light, you know. It always takes my eyes a while to adjust. It's the same when I step into our chapel."

"No windows in your chapel?" said another shuffleboard player, whose shirt sported two red vertical lines on either side of his barrel chest. "Not even stained glass?"

Why, oh why, couldn't I leave well enough alone? "Our chapel is...underground. Like a grotto. So much cooler, you know." Were they buying it? I wished I could see their faces. I pulled myself up to my full five-foot-four height and tried to look serious. "I'm a friend of Michael Carver. I was hoping to speak to his widow."

"You mean Mongo?" said the guy with the shirt and red lines, which I now suspected were suspenders. "He wasn't married."

"And the Carvers aren't Catholic," said the fuzzy outline of another man. He made a *thock* noise that was either setting down his beer or some sort of shuffleboard move.

"Oh dear," I said. "It seems Michael may have not been truthful with me. Or with you."

"What do you mean?" said the guy in the ball cap.

"He told me he was married to Billie, who I believe works here?" I knew she did, and I knew she wasn't working that day (I had Uncle Bob call earlier).

"They were as good as married." The bartender wiped a rag or a sponge or his sleeve across the bar top. "Been together for dog's years. Right nice of you to come see her." Ah ha. Answer number one: Mongo and Billie were well known as a couple. "But she's not here today. I mean, he just died yesterday."

"Oh, of course, how stupid of me. A few of us came into town to get some groceries, and I just thought...please convey my condolences to her." I waited, hoping someone would remembered that I'd said...

"You said he lied to us too?" said a voice from the vicinity of the shuffleboard table.

Bingo. "Mongo never told any of you about his spiritual conversion?"

"Never knew Mongo to be religious," said a low smoky voice I hadn't heard before.

"He recently had a spiritual experience," I said, "that led him to our community. He'd been on several retreats with us."

"Where's that?" asked the shuffleboard voice. "Your community?"

"Near Tonopah." At least that's what my Google search said. I hoped that no one had been there. Or that the convent really did have an underground chapel.

"So that's where he went all those times he took off," said the bartender. Answer number two: No one really knew where Mongo went when he disappeared.

"On an underground chapel retreat?" said Suspenders.

"We used to go underground and pray when we were kids," said Smoky. "Don't you remember?"

"No," Suspender said.

"Called 'em bomb shelter drills."

I let the guys have their laugh, then said, "I believe Mongo had an...argument, or a misunderstanding, with a friend that preceded some sort of epiphany and led him to seek a more spiritual path."

Silence.

Wickenburg being a small town, I figured that people would know each other's business. And that Mongo had argued with someone sometime. Was I wrong?

"You know," Suspenders said slowly. "He *was* worried about backing out of that business deal."

"Business deal?" I said.

"It was business, but he also said something about not wanting to crap in his own nest. That sounds like it mighta been a friend."

"I thought that 'crap in your nest' saying was about someone you were dating," said Ball Cap. "Like Billie."

"He did seem kinda upset about it. Unusual for Mongo," said the bartender.

Ah. Answer number three: Mongo was worried about a business deal with someone he knew.

"Hey," said the fuzzy outline by the shuffleboard table, "You don't think what happened out at Gold Bug had anything to do with—"

He was cut short by a slice of sunlight that swept that across the room from the open-and-shut door. "Hey, fellas," said the newcomer, who either wore a cowboy hat or had a very strangely shaped head. "What's the news—oh." His eyes must have adjusted enough to see me. "Hiya, Sister."

"She's here about what happened at Gold Bug," said Ball Cap.

"Terrible thing," the newcomer said. "Though anyone coulda seen it comin'."

"Really?" I said, at the same time as the bartender said, "Now, Earl..."

"Everyone knows he's got a hell of a temper. Just simmering beneath the surface, like a pot about to boil over."

"Earl," the bartender said again, "Just 'cause you had a beef with him..."

Ah. Could this Earl be the suspect I was looking for?

"And his temper got way better," said Ball Cap. "He changed. We all could see that."

"Part of his spiritual conversion, perhaps?" I said.

The cowboy snorted. "Yeah, he'd have you believe he went all Buddhist and shit."

Uh-oh. Maybe I made the wrong costume choice. "Michael never said anything about Buddhism."

"Michael? Oh, Mongo. Sorry, Sister." The man tipped his hat in apology. "I thought we were talkin' about Josh Tate."

CHAPTER 8

"Buddhist or not, perhaps I should ask this Mr. Tate if he'd like to attend one of our retreats." I wanted to ask him a lot more than that. "Thank you very much, gentlemen. And please convey my condolences to Mrs. Carver—Billie." I headed toward the door.

"Will do," said the bartender.

"Before you go, though, I got one question for you, Sister," said Suspenders.

"Yes?" I hoped it wasn't something about nun-ness. I hadn't had time to Google that.

"Do all nuns wear sexy underpants?"

I beat feet out of the bar while the guys were still yukking it up, hoping they would think I was just a naughty nun and not a spy.

By the time I reached Sunnydale, city lights were flickering against a deep purple sky. I dropped off the nun costume at Arnie and Marge's house, but I didn't stay. I needed to get home to work on the songs and scenes for my callback the next day.

I drove out the side entrance to Sunnydale and turned onto a road that skirted a patch of desert, undeveloped because it was a floodplain. Not as unusual as you'd think for southern Arizona, where most rivers were dry until the rains came. The open landscape let the night sky take stage, showing off a bounty of stars even through the glow of city lights. Since I was stargazing, I nearly missed the movement in front of my headlights.

"Shit!" I stomped on the brakes so fast I banged my split lip against the steering wheel. By the time I reoriented myself, the last of the Chihuahuas was slipping into the desert. "Lassie!" I yelled out the window. "Lassie!"

I jumped out of the truck and ran to the side of the road. "Lassie!" I could have sworn I heard a little pug snort, but I couldn't see the dogs in the dark. I turned back to my truck and there they were.

Two coyotes, noses to the ground, silently following the trail of the Chihuahuas.

"Shoo!" I ran at the coyotes, waving my arms and looking as scary as I could. They turned their heads just a fraction, looking at me as if I were an interesting piece of garbage blowing in the wind, then loped into the desert after the dogs.

"Lassie!" I ran after them, the gravelly dirt crunching beneath my feet. Sensing a chase, the coyotes ran faster, but I could still see them— and caught a glimpse of movement ahead of them too. The Chihuahuas. I upped my speed, keeping everyone firmly in sight, which is why I didn't see the cactus until it was right in front of me. "Eeeyahhh!" I twisted away so I wouldn't fall face first into the fiendish barbed thing. My maneuver worked. I sat in it instead.

The coyotes yipped like they were laughing and ran out of sight.

I picked myself up gingerly. The cactus I'd landed on was a cholla, which propagates itself by breaking off in pieces, falling to the ground, and re-rooting in its new spot. Everyone called this kind "jumping cholla" because the pieces seemed to leap onto you and thrust their sharp spines into your skin. Of course this cactus didn't need to jump at me. I just sat in it.

The cactus spines were wicked enough to penetrate my jeans, so the ones that poked through my t-shirt pierced even deeper, lodging themselves into my back like so many acupuncture needles. I picked a piece of cholla off the bottom of my jeans. It stuck to my fingers. And I mean stuck, a tiny barb working its way into the flesh of my thumb like it had been inserted with a hypodermic needle. I got the dang thing off me and dropped it on the ground, where it would spawn more devil plants. Oh well, I had bigger things to worry about. Like how to drive home when my entire backside was covered in cactus.

I pulled my cell phone from my pocket and dialed. "Marge? I'm so glad you're still awake. Could you please meet me outside Sunnydale's east entrance?...Great. Oh, and bring a flashlight. And some pliers."

CHAPTER 9

"You've been watchin' too much TV," Uncle Bob said as I walked gingerly into the office the next morning. "Most of us real PIs don't get beat up on a regular basis."

"Guess I'm just lucky." I sat down carefully in my chair, still feeling every puncture wound from the cactus spines.

"How'd you incur the damages?"

"I was attacked by a jumping cholla. Had bits of it all over my backside."

"Don't lean back," he said, as I, yep, leaned back. I bolted upright. He jumped out of his chair (he was surprisingly light on his feet for a heavy guy) and walked over to my "desk," a wooden TV tray in front of the window, nearly blinding me with a hot pink Hawaiian shirt with dancing flamingos. "Let me see." I obliged him by pulling up the back of my t-shirt. I decided not to tell him about the ones stuck to my behind. We were close, but not that close.

Uncle Bob tutted as he examined my back. "Might be too late, but...you got your duck tape with you?"

"Sure." I always carried a roll. Duck tape was so named because it kept WWII soldiers' ammo dry (like water off a duck's back), but I'd found it handy for everything from repairing my car to making temporary handcuffs. I dug it out of my bag and handed it to my Uncle Bob, who tore off a piece with a *rrrriiip*. I loved that sound. It was the sound of things being fixed.

"The problem with cholla—and prickly pear—is that they have what they call glochid spines." My uncle knew *everything*, maybe because he was a trivia buff. Or maybe because he was brilliant, in his low-key kind of way. "These type of cactus spines come in multiples, usually hundreds of spines in each entry point. How'd you do this?"

I gave him the short version of the Lassie/Chihuahua/coyote story.

"You say Marge used pliers?"

"Needle-nose ones." I felt the cool stickiness of duck tape on my back. "By flashlight."

"Nice try, but...it looks like a bunch of the spines have worked their way into your back."

The piece of tape sucked at my back as he pulled it off. Uncle Bob looked at his handiwork. "Yeah. We can get a few more off this way."

"Duck tape is magic. Probably could have used it to butterfly my split lip."

Uncle Bob leaned around to look at my face. "That's looking better."

"Good. I've got that callback tonight. Hoping to go for the 'just been kissed' look as opposed to the 'just been smacked in the face' one."

Uncle Bob worked on my back, and I told him about my trip to The Thirsty Vulture.

"A nun?" he said. "Bold choice, but I guess it worked." He patted my back. "Think that's all I can do for your back."

I pulled down my t-shirt. "Before you get back to work, could you sit in on a short call to Arnie?"

Uncle Bob squinted at the clock on the office wall. "If we can do it right now." He came over to stand near me. I put the office landline on speakerphone and rang Arnie. "Ivy and Bob here," I said. "Checking in about that undercover idea you had."

"Yeah," said Arnie. "We're all set. There's a small theater in Gold Bug Gulch, the Arnold Opera House. I'll hire you to act in our melodrama. I already told Nathan and asked Billie and Chance to be in the show too. Chance is really happy, since the police called off all gunfights until the investigation is finished."

"That means he's not carrying a gun, right?"

"Yeah. We'll use a prop gun for the melodrama."

I'd make sure of that. "When can I start?"

"Rehearsals begin tomorrow. We'll open on Saturday."

"Saturday?" I squeaked. "As in this Saturday?"

"It's just a one-act. You can do it. You're a pro, after all."

Right. I was. "Okay. Sure. But..." I couldn't put my finger on what wasn't right.

"How's she going to investigate the rest of the town offstage?" said Uncle Bob. "You've got a bunch of people and buildings out there, don't you?"

Yep, that was it.

"Oh..." I could almost hear Arnie's gears turning. "Yeah...what if...what if we...trained Ivy to be a history guide too?" He picked up speed. "We could offer walking history tours. She'd have to know everything and everyone. I'll see what I can do."

Uncle Bob looked at me and I nodded. "That'd work. And Arnie," I said gently, "are you sure Nathan is...Are you sure he's your son?"

"Well, the story he told me makes sense. I was going with his mom, Gabby DiRienzi, for about a year back in the day. She was a dancer, a chorus girl, from Philly but trying to make it in New York theater."

"She never told you that you were a father?" I asked.

"We had kind of a messy breakup. She was foolin' around with a guy named Tony. Maybe that's why she never contacted me."

Or maybe it's because Tony was the father, I thought.

"Have you done a paternity test?" asked Uncle Bob.

"Nah. I mean, Ivy, he looks like me, right?"

"Kind of."

"And besides, he's got entrepreneurship running through his veins. Just like me."

Flimsy evidence, but I could tell he wanted to believe it, so I let it be. For right then, anyway.

"Okay. Olive, you got any other questions?"

"How long do you think this will take?" I knew it was a stupid question as soon as it left my lips. Of course you never could tell with an investigation. It took as long as it took. But Arnie mentioning theater had got me thinking about my acting career and..."I might have an acting job starting in a month." Once you started a stupid question, I believed you needed to go through with it. Commitment made it sound less stupid. I thought.

I didn't look at Uncle Bob as I waited for Arnie's answer. I was pretty sure my uncle would not look pleased.

"Let's start with a month and see what we get," Arnie said.

I hung up soon afterward and immediately said, "So we do a paternity test, right?" Not only did it seem like a smart idea, I didn't want Uncle Bob haranguing me about my dumb actor question.

"Didn't sound like Arnie was up for it." Uncle Bob walked back over to his desk. "But we can do one without his knowledge, as long as we don't want to use it in court."

"Okay. What do I need to do?"

"Get DNA samples from both him and Nathan. Gum works pretty well."

"Arnie's not a gum chewer. Don't know about Nathan."

"We can also send in dried blood, nail clippings, Kleenexes they've blown their noses on, and Q-tips with ear wax on them."

"Eww."

"No one ever said bein' a PI was pretty."

CHAPTER 10

"Wow." Matt tried to look serious, but a smile tugged at the sides of his mouth. "Do I even want to know?"

Dang. I'd hoped to finish my little operation before Matt arrived at my apartment for dinner. Instead I sat on a kitchen chair, naked from the waist down. Oh yeah, and I was sitting on several strips of duck tape.

"If that's a fly trap, I really don't want to know."

I swiped at him, but missed since my butt was sort of stuck to the chair. "I'm trying to get leftover cholla needles out of my ass." I arranged my tunic top so I was mostly decent from the front. "Just give me a few more minutes."

"Nah." Matt knelt down next to me. "This is the best problem I've had to solve all day. Stand up."

You know you've got a good man when he spends half an hour picking cactus needles out of your behind.

"It's an amazing opportunity," I said as Matt and I finished up a pre-callback dinner of tuna mac and cheese, courtesy of a box and a can in my cupboard. "I've never gotten this far with Arizona Center Stage before. Hardly anyone I know has."

Arizona Center Stage brought most of its talent in from out of town. Local actors might get to play a small role or fill in the chorus, but the fact that I was called back for the lead in *Annie Get Your Gun* was nothing short of miraculous. It might have had something to do with a scathing *Arizona Republic* article about the theater's dismissal of the local talent pool. Or the fact that Marge knew the assistant director. Or that it was just a callback.

Matt put down his fork. "But you still haven't read the play or seen the movie?"

"I did pick up a side from the theater"—a side was a copied section of the script— "and I've been listening to the cast album. The music's by Irving Berlin, and there are some amazing songs, especially 'Anything You Can Do' and 'There's No Business like Show Business.'" I sang the last line with gusto, channeling Marge (Arizona's Ethel Merman, remember). "What do you think? Marge is teaching me to belt. I'm not a powerhouse yet, but I think I can sell them with my sass and spunk."

"You do have sass and spunk, but don't you think you should have read the script?"

"I tried, believe me. But I couldn't get hold of it. See, theater scripts aren't like books. They're proprietary. Samuel French and Dramatists and the other script publishers don't want everyone picking up copies and putting on shows without paying royalties, so they make them hard to get. I couldn't find a copy at the library or online. There was one on eBay, but the seller was from New Zealand. Didn't think it would get here on time."

"Isn't there a movie you could watch, at least?"

"Yeah." I cleared our dishes, walking the six steps from my eating nook to my tiny kitchen. "I have a hold on a copy from the library, but whoever has it right now hasn't turned it back in. I even asked the librarian if there was a way to contact them, but nope. Luckily Marge said the script is pretty fluffy, that it's the singing and attitude that matter."

"Sass and spunk."

"Exactly." I kissed him on the top of his curly head as I walked past him to the couch. I grabbed my duffel bag, which held my purse, the side from the script, and two pairs of shoes: soft-soled jazz shoes and character shoes, those chunky-heeled Mary Janes ubiquitous onstage. "Walk me to my car and kiss me for luck?"

"You look great," Matt said as we headed down the Astroturf-covered stairs outside my second-story apartment. I wore a form-fitting red t-shirt, black leggings, and a short flippy black and red skirt—easy to dance in. "But..."

"Are you still worried because I don't know the play?"

"I can't help it. I'm a student at heart." Though Matt worked at my brother's group home, he was on track to graduate with a Masters in Social Work in a few weeks. "I would want to know everything I could before committing to something that would take months of my life."

"Don't worry." I unlocked the cab of my truck. "I may not have been able to read the script, but I did read everything I could find about Annie Oakley. She was an amazing woman."

"Then you're perfect for the part." Matt held my face in his hands and kissed me tenderly on my split lip. For a moment, I wanted to stay right there for the rest of my life, in a hot, dirty parking lot littered with candy wrappers and full of Matt-ness. But…"I have to go," I murmured into his ear, forcing myself to pull away. "The stage calls."

"The force is strong with this one." Matt was a bit of a nerd—one of my favorite things about him. He kissed me again. "May the force be with you. And break a leg."

CHAPTER 11

I stretched in the hallway of the Berger Performing Arts Center, a multistage facility that housed Arizona Center Stage, along with several other companies. "Don't think we've met before," I said to the actor next to me. "Are you from out of town?" He nodded. "You Equity?" I asked. He nodded again.

In order to get into Equity, the actors' union, you had to earn points by appearing in shows produced by theaters that worked under Equity contracts. I had enough points to audition with the big dogs but hadn't joined the union yet. I wasn't sure what to do about that. Equity status was a bit of a double-edged sword in a place like Phoenix. It certainly had its pros: it showed everyone that you were a professional who considered acting a career, and you'd never see a non-Equity lead with the bigger companies. But it had its cons too: mostly the fact that there were just a handful of female Equity roles in town each season, and once you got your card, you were pretty much prohibited from accepting non-union work. If you wanted to make a living in the theater, you'd have to travel or move to a bigger market.

"I'm just eligible," I said. "Don't have my card yet."

The guy gave me a look I interpreted as "How the hell did you get in here?"

"I know. It's crazy that I'm even here." The guy was now stretching his other leg, his head turned away from me. "By the way, I'm Ivy Meadows. Stage name, of course. Hey, did you know that Annie Oakley was a stage name too? Her real name was Phoebe Ann Moses. Or maybe Mosey. The historical record is unclear." The actor looked at me, which I took for a sign of interest. "She had a nightmare childhood. Her dad died after being caught in a blizzard, and then her mom couldn't afford to raise the family, so she sent Annie and her sister to a poor farm."

It looked like he nodded ever so slightly, so I went on: "The poor farm sent her to live with this horrible family, who treated her like a slave and abused her so badly that she ran away back to the poor farm. Then, while she was still just a girl, she singlehandedly lifted her family out of poverty, even paid off the mortgage on her mother's house so her family could all live together again. Know how she did it?"

He shook his head and stretched his back. "All this time she was trapping and hunting—had been doing it since she was eight years old. She began selling the game and pretty soon was making a good living."

The actor raised his head to smile at a slender man in an untucked button-down shirt and jeans who had stopped to listen. "Is this Annie Oakley you're talking about?" said the second man.

I nodded. "She was amazing. Really changed the world's idea of what a woman could do."

"But she couldn't get a man with a gun," said Button-down, smiling.

"What? Oh, the song." I'd heard "You Can't Get a Man with a Gun" on the cast recording. "I haven't figured out why Irving wrote that song. After all, she did."

"She did what?"

"Well, she won that shooting match with Frank Butler. Ha! Can you imagine? I mean, he was a famous marksman, and she was only fifteen." The actor beside me stared at me intently, as if trying to convey some message. "No wonder Frank was smitten. He wooed her, really pursued her, you know, until they married."

"*He* wooed her?" Button-down's smile had slipped. "Pretty sure it was the other way around."

"Nope. He was definitely the woo-er. And they had a long and incredibly happy marriage." I couldn't figure out why Button-down looked annoyed, or why the actor was now clearing his throat. "So I'd really love to play her in this musical. Show the whole world what a strong, smart woman she was."

"We'll see," said Button-down, and he disappeared through a door that led backstage.

"We'll see?" I said to the actor. "I don't get it."

"Don't think you'll get the role either." He had a surprisingly high voice. "That was Larry Cooper."

"The director?" My chest began to get tight.

"The director. Who flew in from New York to do this show. Who fancies himself an expert on musicals. And who hates to be corrected."

CHAPTER 12

I knew what hell was. It was cold and dark and filled with things that rushed out of the darkness, screaming as they careened past, their breath fouling the air and rocking your pickup truck.

"There can't be this many eighteen-wheelers in the whole country," I muttered to myself as another rig blew past me, kicking dust in my face like some big bully. "Why are they all on this stretch of road at the ungodly hour of five o'clock in the morning?"

Yes, five o'clock. In the morning. The last time I was up at five o'clock I was still awake from the night before. "Not a morning person" was stamped heavily on my DNA. But I'd heard that the pack of Chihuahuas was most active in the early morning and late night. I didn't have a chance to get out to Sunnydale last night after callbacks, so I bit the bullet and got up way too early after a sleepless night.

I hadn't recognized Larry Cooper precisely because he was such a big shot. Like a lot of big theater companies, Arizona Center Stage held season auditions, where actors performed songs and monologues in front of theater personnel—often the artistic director. For my audition I performed a monologue from a great one-act called *Graceland* and sang "I Cain't Say No" from *Oklahoma!*, hoping those choices would help the theater's people see I was perfect for Annie. They did see something in me, because I was called back, where I performed again in front of the theater's assistant artistic director. Last night was a second callback, with the field whittled down to only a few of us actresses, onstage for the first time in front of the show's actual director. I sang with as much spunk and sass as I could, but even so, I didn't hear anything except, "Thank you. We'll let you know," from somewhere in the darkened theater.

I got off the freeway, headed down Bell Road, and went through a Jack in the Box drive-through. I took a big swig of coffee as I pulled back into traffic and promptly burnt my tongue. Even that didn't wake me up entirely. I drove until I came to the spot where I'd seen the Chihuahuas disappear into the desert. I eased my truck onto the gravelly shoulder and scanned the desert, now charcoal gray under the lightening sky. Nothing.

Even so, I put my plan into action. I got out of the car with my two big Jack in the Box bags. I took a wrapped-up kiddie hamburger from one bag and threw it as far as I could into the desert. I had a pretty good arm, so the burger made it forty feet, rattling a desert broom bush as it touched down. I lobbed another one a bit closer to the road, then another, until I had a Hansel-and-Gretel trail of burgers leading to the road. Before getting back in my truck, I carefully placed the piece de resistance—a bacon ultimate cheeseburger—on the shoulder near my truck. Lassie loved cheeseburgers. And he loved me. I figured if I could get him this close, his cheeseburger-and-Ivy love would be strong enough to overcome his yearning for a pack, and he'd leave the Chihuahuas and come with me.

I waited in the cab of my truck with the window rolled up, partly because the pre-dawn morning was chilly, but mostly so the dogs would smell hamburgers instead of me. I sipped at my cooling coffee and watched the sun rise over the desert, its long fingers painting the desert gold.

The desert broom near the first burger shook. I watched carefully, but I couldn't see any animal. Then again, Lassie was black and the Chihuahuas were short. Another nearby bush trembled. Definitely something there. I eased open the car door a crack so I could call Lassie when he got near. I watched the brush along the hamburger trail shiver as the dogs got closer.

Wait, what was that rumbling noise? Not thunder. No clouds in the sky. I heard it again, a low growling noise. Oh, sheesh. I took the lone breakfast sandwich out of the Jack in the Box bag and bit into it. Ugh. Cold egg and sticky cheese. At least it could keep my grumbling stomach from scaring the dogs away.

Or was it my stomach? No. Another growl, definitely from outside the truck. And closer. I slid down so most of me wasn't showing and peered out the dirty window. Two figures slunk close to the dirt, gray and tan bodies blending into the indistinct shadows thrown by the rising sun. They came closer, and yes, they were growling. The noise made the hair on my arms stand up. So I did what any human being would do. I jumped out of the car.

"You better not eat Lassie!" I yelled at the surprised bobcats, whose ears flattened against their heads when they saw me. "If you do, I'll come for you. And you owe me twenty bucks. Hamburgers don't grow on bushes, you know."

CHAPTER 13

High noon. There I was, alone on a dusty desert road, standing on the exact spot where a man had died. All traces of blood had been cleaned up, or maybe dried up and blown away on the wind that swept down the street. A hot wind for November. It kicked up little dust devils, blew sand in my face, and knocked against the iron tools that hung on the outer walls of the building so that they sounded like Marley's chains. Maybe this is what they meant by an ill wind.

"Hey! Girlie! We're closed, and this is private property."

Yep. Ill wind.

Nathan strode toward me, arms windmilling as he shouted, "What are you, deaf or something? Or just blonde?"

Being an actor has its benefits, like being able to act calm and professional and say, "Why, hello, Nathan. I believe you were expecting me," when you really want to smack someone. "Arnie said you'd introduce me to Josh. So I can learn about Gold Bug's history for the tour?" I'd gone over to Arnie and Marge's after the burger/bobcat incident, and we worked out the whole set-up.

"Oh." I swore Nathan's face fell when he realized there'd be no confrontation. "Yeah. I didn't recognize you."

Really? I had on a t-shirt and cowboy boots just like the day we'd met. Only difference was I wore a denim skirt instead of jeans.

"You should always wear skirts." Nathan ogled me from the waist down. "Yeah. I'll make sure your costume has a short skirt."

Normally I don't mind showing off my legs—they are two of my best assets—but the skeevy way Nathan looked at me, sort of "sex mixed with dollar signs," made me feel creepy-crawly.

"What era is Gold Bug Gulch supposed to reflect?" I kept my tone and language overly formal. Maybe if I sounded like a professor, he'd treat me with more respect.

"We're going for the town's heyday, around 1889."

"Then no short skirts, I'm sorry to say." I was not sorry at all.

"Yeah, sure."

I made a show of looking at my watch. Never figured out why so many people don't wear them anymore; watches work great as real-life props. "I'm supposed to meet Josh for a tour of the town." Today's meeting would be all about the town. I wanted to get Josh on my good side before asking him about Mongo or any business deals.

"Follow me. I've got to talk to him anyway." Nathan started down the road ahead of me, toward the chimney smoke that rose from a building on the edge of the renovated town. I studied him from behind as he walked. He was built like Arnie, short and square, but where Arnie exuded joy and a sort of childlike excitement about pretty much anything, Nathan's energy was all closed up tight and nervous—like a skunk who was deciding whether to spray you or not.

Huh. Arnie...Nathan...Oh. Right. "Want a piece of gum?" I offered him a stick from a pack I'd just bought.

He shook his head and kept walking. No DNA today.

"I'm so sorry about Mongo."

Nathan shrugged.

"How do you think it happened? The shooting, I mean?"

"Chance just forgot to switch out bullets for blanks."

"Could somebody else have done it? Switched the bullets?"

"They didn't."

"But they could've? I'm only asking because I get a little nervous around guns."

Nathan stopped and turned to me. "The guys used to load their guns with blanks over there." He pointed to a small area across from the saloon bounded by a short wooden fence and gate marked "no trespassing." Inside the area was a counter. A wooden wall at the rear of the space held pegs, and "Justice of the Piece" was hand-painted above them. "But from now on, no more hanging guns there—blanks or no blanks."

So the guys had left their guns there. And someone could have tampered with them.

Nathan turned and began walking again. We finally stopped across the street from a corral, empty now but for one horse. The adobe building in front of us had a big open entrance and an iron gate instead of a door. Metal letters mounted on the front wall spelled out "Smithy." Something glowed inside.

We walked through the entrance. Electric fans whirred, hefty and rusty-looking metal tools lined the walls, and a brick forge hulked in the middle of the dimly lit room. With its chimney and small oven-like opening, the forge looked like a built-in barbecue, but the smell of the coals was not the familiar friendly scent of charcoal briquettes, but an acrid metallic one I could taste in the back of my mouth. The blacksmith stood with his back to us, using tongs to hold something in the fire. Josh was tall and lean, with a full head of dark brown hair and a sweat stripe down the back of his chambray shirt. He cranked a fan with his free hand, and the coals changed color from orange to magenta.

"Josh!" yelled Nathan.

Josh tensed, a near jump. He caught himself quickly, his muscles relaxing. He didn't turn and kept his eyes on the coals. "Nathan. I've told you not to do that." His voice was tight, and I recalled what the Wickenburg cowboy said about a pot under pressure. "Liable to get a hot horseshoe in the face someday." He looked over his shoulder at Nathan, whose face still had that tight skunky look. "Might improve your looks."

"Ha ha, very nice. Here's the girl—"

"Ivy," I said.

"—that Arnie hired for the melodrama. Some sort of actress."

Hello? I was standing right next to him.

"And she's supposed to give a tour or something. Hey, do you think we could give her a short costume, show off those legs?"

"No." Josh and I both said together. I smiled at his back.

"I know all about it," said Josh. "I was ready for you, ma'am, but one of the horses threw a shoe. Thought I'd have time to get one ready before you showed up. My apologies."

"Speaking of horses," said Nathan. "You thought any more about my proposition?"

"You want to discuss that now?" Josh nodded toward me.

"She's just an actress," Nathan said.

Funny how you could be pissed off and thankful to be underestimated at the same time.

Josh took the molten horseshoe over to an anvil. He picked up a big hammer-type tool, held the shoe with the tongs over the anvil, and started to pound on the shoe, which glowed orange in the semi-darkness of the room.

"So?" Nathan said. "What do you think?"

"If I take over the horseback rides, I get Mongo's cut, is that it?" His hammer beat out a steady rhythm.

"That's the deal."

With each strike of the hammer, the orange horseshoe sloughed off small sheets of darkened metal, like a snake shedding its skin. "Do I get the horses too? And the land the corral's on?"

"What, are you crazy?" Nathan looked like he regretted the words as soon as they were out of his mouth. "We'll have to wait for Mongo's will before we know anything about that," he backpedaled.

"He didn't have a will." Josh turned the horseshoe on the anvil. His rhythm never let up. "Thought he'd live forever. I want the horses."

"Like I said, we'll have to wait—"

"I want the horses. And the land. If he did leave them to someone, make them an offer. Then sell them to me."

"Oh. Well..." Nathan actually rubbed his hands together like a greedy cartoon character.

"For five bucks."

"What?"

"All right, ten. The horses aren't worth much, and you of all people know that the land isn't either." Josh slipped the shoe into a vat of water and a cloud of hissing steam obscured his face.

"This is ridiculous. Like I couldn't find some cowboy with a few horses to take the tourists on rides."

"Sure, you could. Lots of cowboys out there. 'Course they'd need to know the terrain, where the rattlesnakes like to sun themselves, where the ground squirrels dig holes that can break a horse's leg. You'd need to make sure they were polite and friendly—"

"Like you?" Nathan grumbled.

"That they treated their horses well. That their horses were trained to let jittery tourist types ride them." Josh took the horseshoe out of the water and examined it.

"I see your point, but—"

"And that they don't come to work drunk. Actually, that they show up at all."

"You got me over a barrel. Okay, but not for five dollars. Five hundred."

"Fifty." Josh kept his eyes on the horseshoe.

"Two fifty."

"One hundred." Josh still didn't look at Nathan.

"All right already." Nathan threw up his hands. "One hundred. Can we offer rides this weekend?"

"Sure." Josh turned toward us for the first time. He pushed his plastic safety glasses up onto his head, and smiled. "I'm all yours."

CHAPTER 14

After Nathan left grumbling about highway robbery, Josh took a few minutes to clean up, and I took a few minutes to check him out. He appeared to be around forty, though it was hard to tell. His blue shirt, damp with sweat, clung to the powerful muscles in his arms and chest—a physique a twenty-year-old would envy. But he'd spent enough time outdoors that his face was lined, with deep crow's feet at the corner of his eyes from squinting into the sun. I reminded myself to wear sunglasses.

He wiped off his hands with a towel, though it didn't seem to do much good. They stayed charcoal gray, with black lines etched in the calluses. I felt gritty too. Just standing near the forge had left me covered with itchy grains of black dust.

"Ready, ma'am?"

"Yep." I swiped at my face and followed him out the door and into the street.

He stood and looked toward the saloon and other renovated buildings, then turned and looked the other way at the ramshackle structures that lined the rest of the road.

"Not sure what it is exactly you want to know, ma'am."

"Please, it's Ivy. And I don't know either. Let's just start at the beginning."

"All right." He eyed the sun, which was almost directly overhead. "I might paraphrase a little." He cleared his throat. "In the beginning, God said, 'Let there be light,' and there was light. He saw that the light was good, and he separated the light from the darkness." He looked at me sideways, a half smile on his thin lips.

"I don't think we have to go that far back."

"All right. How about separating the gold from the earth?"

"That'll do."

"In the beginning, my great-great-granddad said, 'Let there be cattle.' He was a cowboy who'd saved himself some money and bought a ranch over there." Josh pointed to a spot that looked just like the rest of the desert. I could barely make out the outline of what used to be a building. An old house, maybe?

"He, and later some of his kids, built up the ranch 'til it became one of the biggest in Arizona. We had water from Gold Bug Creek." Josh nodded toward the stand of cottonwoods I'd noticed on my last trip. "Pretty much a treasure in these parts. But my great-granddad inherited the ranch when his dad died, and the water and the cattle and the ranch weren't treasure enough for him. He had gold fever, big time. And when he discovered gold on this land, that was it. The family was done for." Josh stared into the near distance. I followed his gaze to a falling-down structure, a sort of cross between a fire tower and an oil rig. The dark shape I saw when I first came to town. The mine.

"I thought the gold mine was what built the town up."

"Built the town up, tore the land down. Messed up the pastureland we had, so we couldn't run as many cows. And the gold brought in a bunch of people, transient types who didn't care about anything except getting rich quick. Then when the mine played out, everyone left.

"At its height, Gold Bug Gulch had a school, a church, and a jail. It also had four saloons, three whorehouses—'scuse me, *bordellos*—and a hanging tree." Josh pointed at an enormous half-dead cottonwood. On cue, the wind rattled the tree's barren limbs, which clutched at the sky like a dying man.

"Gold Bug had a population of over five thousand people back then. But from what Grandpa told me, the town died in just five years. It took my family a little longer." Josh's nostrils flared. Huh. I would've expected sadness rather than anger. I remembered what Earl at the bar had said about Josh's temper.

"The mine dried up right about the same time as a big drought. It could've been that that killed off most of our remaining herd. It could've been something in the ground—they used cyanide to separate gold from dirt, you know. Or it could have been the Carvers." Another nostril flare.

"Carver? Wasn't that Mongo's last name?"

Josh's expression didn't change, but a tendon in his neck jumped. "How do you know that?"

I didn't want him to know I'd been snooping, so I said, "I read it in the paper."

Luckily Josh didn't know about the reading habits of my generation, so he bought the lie. "You read about the shooting?"

"Yeah. I'm really sorry about Mongo."

Josh didn't say anything.

"I was even here right afterward." I saw the body again, the wind tugging at the sheet that covered it. "I'm a friend of Arnie's."

"Terrible accident," said Josh. "But at least Billie'll be safe now."

CHAPTER 15

I wanted to ask. Oh, I wanted to ask. But I also had the feeling that Josh wanted me to ask, and that didn't feel right. Instead I stayed silent—until I could call my uncle.

After leaving Josh at his blacksmith shop, I walked to the saloon and stood on its porch out of the wind and where I could see anyone who might be coming. "PI question," I said when Uncle Bob picked up the phone. "If someone does that thing where they say something leading so you ask a question about it, should you?"

"Could you rephrase that?"

"You know, that thing where somebody wants you to ask a question—do you?"

"Have you eaten today?'

Uncle Bob was really telling me that I sounded a bit scattered. I sometimes got that way from not eating. "I had a breakfast sandwich this morning." At six. And nothing since. "Oops, I think you may be right. But still, this guy said something about Mongo's death keeping Billie safe, and then paused like he wanted me to ask why."

"And you didn't?"

"No."

"Why not?"

"Because he wanted me to. Seemed like he was trying to lead me to some conclusion."

Uncle Bob sighed. "You can always ask later. But think about it, what would you have learned if you asked?"

"Um, why he thought Billie was safe. Or Mongo was dangerous."

"And how would that info hurt your investigation?"

"It...wouldn't. I feel sort of stupid." I heard a growl. Bobcats? No, this time it was my stomach.

"Sheesh, was that you?" said Uncle Bob. "Don't worry about it and go find something to eat."

Easier said than done.

I walked back to the saloon. Maybe I could get something to eat, maybe even sneak a look into Nathan's office wastebasket and grab a used Kleenex or something. The door was locked, but voices floated out through an open window. A woman said, "We're even then. This is all I owe you."

"For now." Nathan's voice, I realized belatedly as I knocked. Also realized too late that this may have been a conversation I wanted to hear. Yep, still pretty green, PI-wise.

The voices ceased. I knocked again. "Just hoping to make a sandwich or something," I called, but no one answered. I peered through the window just in time to see a door marked "Office" close.

My stomach rumbled again. Dang. I only had a half hour until rehearsal, and Wickenburg—the closest town—was about twenty minutes away. I couldn't make it into town and back in time, and I was feeling spacey from hunger. I went back to my truck, scrounged around, and found a half-eaten bag of old peanuts in the glove compartment. At least it was protein.

I scarfed down the peanuts. They didn't make me less hungry, just thirsty. I dug into my duffel bag, found my water bottle, and drank all of the ickily warm water it contained. I felt better. Maybe I could fill up on water until I got back to Phoenix after rehearsal.

I grabbed my duffel and headed back into "town." The Arnold Opera House stood next to the saloon. From the front, it looked like most of the other buildings, two-story with a square false front, but without any windows on the second story. I stepped onto the wooden sidewalk that connected the saloon, opera house, and reptile house. Reptile house? Oh yeah. Marge had mentioned something about that. Probably was a big draw for families with kids. Not so much for me. The theater was my place. I opened one of the double doors to the opera house and stepped inside.

The Arnold Opera House was designed to reflect the opulent European opera houses of the era but on a much smaller scale. The orchestra level held about fifty seats. There was also a balcony tier so small that only one row of seats fit, and those had so little legroom that

I didn't think anyone over five-seven could possibly be comfortable in them.

But what the theater lacked in space, it made up for in decor. An ornately carved railing ringed the balcony. Gold-tasseled red velvet drapes swathed the stage. Hurricane lamps with electric candles lined the walls. It looked a little like the theater on a Dickens-themed cruise ship I sailed on a few months prior, but in miniature and without all the money. In short, it looked like a Victorian theater with a Napoleon complex.

The two people I'd seen in the saloon after the shooting sat in the first row, their backs to me. I didn't think they'd noticed my arrival. The young man, the one who had shot Mongo, kept leaning into the woman, who twisted away. Even though I couldn't hear what they said, the tension in the air was palpable, like the air before a thunderstorm.

I walked silently down the aisle, hoping to hear a bit of their conversation.

"But now you can," said the guy, who wore a black cowboy hat. Was he in costume?

"It doesn't work that way," the woman replied, her voice low and emotionless. Was she the one I'd heard talking to Nathan? Could have been. The saloon was right next door to the theater.

"Why not?"

"Oh, for God's sake, Mongo hasn't been dead a week and—"

A board in the wooden floor squeaked under me. Damn authentic building techniques.

"Hi," I said brightly. "I'm Ivy Meadows, here to report for duty." I gave a little salute, hoping that it and a bit of ditziness would make them forget I'd overheard their conversation. Also I still felt a little spacey from lack of food. "This is sooooo cool. I've never opened a theater before, you know, done the first show? Maybe we'll get our names on plaques or something."

The ditz role seemed to have taken over, but what the heck. I'd only worked undercover once before but found it tough, since I basically had to lie to the people I worked with. Maybe playing a role was a good way to get around that ethical dilemma. Besides, it was kind of fun. "OMG." Yes, I said the letters. "Is this the cutest theater, or what?"

The pair of them stared at me open-mouthed, like silent film actors directed to look surprised.

"So you must be Chance and Billie. Arnie told me. He said you're like, sooooo good."

I flopped down in a seat next to the guy, who studiously avoided my eyes. He had a broad, even-featured face and close-cropped blond hair, from what I could see under his hat.

My stomach growled again. "Oops. Hey, can I get some water somewhere?" Maybe more water would quiet my stomach. And maybe Billie and Chance would continue their conversation.

"There's a water dispenser in the lobby." Billie pointed toward the back of the theater. She wore her wavy strawberry blonde hair tied back in a ponytail. I couldn't tell how old she was, mostly because she wore heavy makeup: thick foundation, purplish eyeshadow, and lots of mascara.

I scooted up the aisle, filled my water bottle from an old-fashioned-type water cooler on a stand (the kind with a jug and a spigot), and put my ear to the theater doors. No conversation. I got back to my seat within two minutes. It was a very small theater.

I plopped down in my seat, continuing to play the ditz role. "I only got my script this morning, so I don't have it memorized yet, but I will. I'm a quick study." Doubt wrinkled Billie's forehead. "One question: Arnie said it'll just be me and Chance onstage, but the play has four characters, two men and two women."

"Chance plays all the male roles and you play all the female ones," said Billie.

"Cool!" I gushed. "I mean, I've played floozies and ingénues before, but never in the same play." Billie's forehead wrinkle deepened. I felt slightly mean, worrying her this way, so I dug in my duffel bag and handed her my headshot and résumé. "Oh, here you go, just in case Arnie didn't send it."

Billie's worry lines relaxed as she read. I was still building up my résumé, but it was decent enough.

I turned to the guy, who was fixedly staring at the stage—in defeat it seemed. "So, Chance, are you an actor or a cowboy?" Arnie had said he was both, but it was an unlikely combination. Chance didn't say anything. Great, a strong, silent type.

"Chance grew up on a ranch in Montana, but acted in college," Billie said. "He's multi-talented."

Chance looked at Billie with gratitude...and something else. Affection? Pride?

"Let's get this show on the road." Billie stood up. She had an amazing figure, the voluptuous type that's out of style in magazines and in style with men. Her Marilyn Monroe-ish bust strained at her white t-shirt, and her Wranglers defined a derrière that looked high and firm, especially for a woman in her...forties? Like Josh, her face was a bit at odds with her figure, tanned and lined, but still attractive. All the makeup she wore actually aged her. Maybe she thought she was covering the sun and wind damage that came from years spent outside in the desert sun. But...no. It wasn't her skin or makeup that made her look older: it was the touch of sadness that dusted her face like powder. Oh.

"I'm so sorry about the other actor, the one who died?" I toned down the ditz a bit. "It must have been awful for you. I mean, there are just a few of you out here, so you must have been a pretty tight group, right?"

"Yeah." Billie ducked her head. "But we don't really want to talk about it. Giddyup and get onstage."

I'd never heard anyone actually say giddyup before, but it sounded right coming from Billie.

The one-act we rehearsed was about thirty minutes long, a basic melodrama script. I played Rose the ingénue, the daughter of a rich man who died and left his fortune (and her) in the clutches of an evil older man, Neville Blackheart. I also played Fannie the saloon girl, who worked for Blackheart and who tried to distract the hero (Ernest, a clean-cut cowboy) from saving me. Billie directed, but she was also going to be at the performances. Someone had to hold up the signs for the audiences, which said things like, "The next day, at Neville Blackheart's mansion," and "Meanwhile..." and of course, "Boo!"

Chance was a fine melodrama actor, his hero strong-voiced and straight-backed, his villain a tight ball of miserly meanness. I was having fun too, sashaying across the stage as bad girl Fannie, and perfecting the art of lip trembling and eyelash fluttering as Rose.

We wrapped up after two and a half hours, which was good

because I'd also drunk two and half bottles of water. I sprinted to the restroom. Instead of filling my water bottle, I flipped up the toilet lid. Yellow "do not cross" tape stretched across the toilet bowl. A sign taped to the inside of the lid said, "Temporarily out of order." Dang.

I rushed out of the bathroom, or tried to. Hard to rush when you're keeping your knees together. "Where's the nearest bathroom?" I said to Billie, who was following Chance out the front doors.

"Guess they're still working on connecting this bathroom to the septic system. But everything else is locked up tight right now." Billie held open the door, a slice of harsh sunlight across her face. "I live down the road about fifteen minutes, if you want a lift."

"Thanks, but..." I meant to say there was no way I'd make it in fifteen minutes and didn't want to pee on her car seat, but I was distracted by the way the light illuminated Billie's face—and the black eye she'd tried to cover up.

CHAPTER 16

I hated peeing outdoors. First of all, there was the whole thing of trying to keep your underwear pee-free. Then you had to make sure you were on a slope so everything ran downhill. Peeing outdoors in the desert was worse. Not much you could use for cover except scrawny bushes, which were usually covered in thorns. Yep, the only thing worse than peeing outdoors in the desert was being caught with your pants down. By a stranger. Midstream.

"Hey there, Missie," said a gravelly tenor voice attached to a pair of feet clad in new hiking boots. "Didn't see you crouching there in the bushes. Almost fell right over you."

So much for the pee-free underwear.

The boots turned around, facing away from me. "But don't worry, didn't see anything except the top of your head, and I'm not lookin' now."

I dragged my eyes from the rocky ground and looked up. About three feet from me stood a man in his sixties, a little on the short side—maybe five eight, with bony legs in new-looking cargo shorts with lots of pockets. His back was toward me, and he wore a hat, not a cowboy hat, but a khaki fabric one that made him look like a kangaroo hunter.

Good thing I wore my jean skirt. The guy really couldn't have seen much, and the only thing I had to do to get decent was to pull up my underwear, which were around my ankles. I did so, but dang, there was a little pee stream near my feet, and I really didn't want to step in it and...oops. I toppled forward and had to make a split-second decision: fall toward the man or into a thorny-looking bush. I chose the man.

"Well, hey there," he said as I grabbed his back. "Didn't expect this type of welcome."

"Sorry, it's just—"

"Guess you saw that rattler, huh?"

"What?" I nearly fell over again.

"Just joshing you." The man had startlingly blue eyes, like Paul Newman (if Paul had been a scrawny, tanned desert-rat-looking guy), and a crooked nose. "I'm Frank." He reached out to shake my hand. "And you are..."

"Ivy Meadows."

"You must be the new actress they hired." Frank's hand was bony and dry. It was like shaking hands with a mummy. "Ivy Meadows. You get that name from that subdivision?"

"Wow. You're the first person who's ever figured that out."

"Picketed that development before they broke ground on behalf of the Acuna cactus. Endangered." He kicked at the dirt. "The cactus lost."

"I'm sorry." I didn't get out to the desert all that often, but I loved it. Except for cholla.

"Figured it was a long shot. And the Acuna cactus may have been rescued." Frank's eyes crinkled. "By somebody somehow."

"Nice. So you work here?"

"God, no."

"How'd you know they hired a new actress?"

"I keep my ear to the ground, at least where this place is concerned. I live just over the hill. Have for years."

"Were you here when the mine was open?"

He laughed. "Just how old do you think I am?"

"Sorry, not thinking." I really needed to eat something.

"I have been here almost forty years, though. Know just about everything there is to know about this place. Like all the best places to pee. I suspect the buildings are all locked up—that Nathan is afraid somebody's going to steal a bar of soap or something—but you coulda gone to Josh's."

Josh's. There was the forge, the anvil, a few worktops, but..."I didn't see any place for a bathroom in his shop. Do you call it a shop?"

"Sure. Or a forge. Or a smithy. And no, he doesn't have anything there, but he probably woulda let you in his house."

"Where's that?"

Frank pointed down the main road. "See there, at the bottom of the hill?" Standing off by itself, shaded by a few old trees, was a small white wooden house with a river rock foundation.

"Huh. When Josh was showing me around town, he didn't say anything about living here."

"Why would he?"

"Because he was supposed to be telling me all about Gold Bug Gulch. I'm training to be a historical guide." I stared at the little house, annoyed that I'd missed the fact that there was a habitable house in the midst of all the semi-shacks.

"Josh does like his privacy, 'specially where it concerns his house. But you being a guide and all, he shoulda told you. Probably shoulda told you a lot of things. Tell you what. Meet me here tomorrow around noon. Bring some cheese sandwiches, Fritos, and a couple of beers. We'll have lunch and I'll tell you the real story of this town."

CHAPTER 17

"Got an hour to spare?" I asked Arnie over the phone. Then I shouted, "A burger, onion rings, and a Diet Coke, please."

"You mean I should feed you in that hour?"

"No, sorry. Just getting a little dinner. Oh, wait," I shouted again at Dairy Queen's speaker. "And a Peanut Buster Parfait."

"When do you want to come by?"

"Now?"

"In that case, could you add two Dilly Bars to your order?"

About fifteen minutes later I sat at Arnie and Marge's kitchen table. "I thought you got ice cream too," said Arnie.

"Already ate it." I polished off my burger and started in on the onion rings. Good thing I got a large.

"How'd your callback go?" Marge asked.

"I don't know. I think I talk too much when I'm nervous."

"So dinner doesn't take an hour." Arnie finished his Dilly Bar and sat back in his chair, his eyes at half-mast. "What's up?"

"I thought maybe we could do a little double duty. You and Marge can come with me to look for Lassie." At the mention of the pug, Marge's lip trembled. "Who I'm sure is fine," I said firmly. "And while we're driving, you can tell me a little more about Gold Bug Gulch."

Arnie blew his nose on a paper napkin. "Not sure how two old people will be any help looking for Lassie. And didn't you meet with Josh today?"

"Um..." I was distracted by this perfect opportunity to get Arnie's DNA sample. I jumped up from the table and grabbed all the Dairy Queen trash, clearing the table as it were. "Yeah, but you know us PIs."

I dumped the trash into the can under the sink—all except for Arnie's napkin, which I slipped into the pocket of my jean's skirt. "We want everyone's version of the story. And as far as Lassie—"

"We'd be happy to help." Marge stood up and gave Arnie's chair a gentle kick. "Come on, chickie."

I drove carefully down the streets of Sunnydale, not because it was dark or the streets were curvy, but because I drove Arnie's Audi. My truck didn't have room for the three of us, and we wanted to have room for Lassie too. "So I know part of the town's history," I said, "and can do some more research regarding the mine and everything, but I'd really like to know how the whole idea of the new Gold Bug Gulch came about."

"You should talk to Nathan about that," Arnie said.

"I will, but—"

"Come on, chickie, you hired her," Marge said from the backseat. "Why not talk to her?"

I threw her a grateful look via the rearview mirror.

Arnie looked out the passenger window, which he'd rolled down. "I just feel disloyal or something."

Marge met my eyes in the mirror again. She shrugged.

"Don't worry, Arnie. Nathan will never know about this." I scanned the front yards of the houses we passed. No dogs and nowhere to hide in the raked gravel yards. "Besides, you're just trying to protect his investment, right?"

"Yeah. Right. Okay."

"Why don't you start with how Nathan came up with the idea and go from there?"

"Well, he's always been a big fan of Westerns..."

"Really? I'd never have guessed." With his soft Italian leather shoes, over-gelled hair, and in-your-face attitude, Nathan seemed the epitome of the back-East city boy.

"Yeah. He's crazy about the West. So he was messing around on the internet, looking at ghost towns, I guess, when he came across one for sale."

"The whole town was for sale?"

"Yeah. He flew out and looked at the place. He'd seen a ghost town theme park somewhere in Nevada and liked the idea of doing something similar. He's got big ideas, that boy." Arnie chuckled.

Marge gave me a "see what I'm up against?" look in the mirror.

"Gold Bug Gulch looked like it'd be perfect for that type of set-up," Arnie continued. "It wasn't too far from Phoenix, had a bunch of buildings, a couple that needed only minor renovations, and Josh needed to sell quickly so the price was right."

"Josh owned the whole town?"

"His dad had already sold the mineral rights to the mine to some corporation, but Josh sold everything else to Nathan with the stipulation he'd be a part owner."

"His dad sold the mineral rights? You can do that—sell them separately from the land?"

"Sure. Happens all the time. Mineral rights give you ownership of whatever's underground: gold, oil, that sort of thing. Separate from the ownership of surface land."

"Okay." I turned onto a road that skirted the desert. "Keep your eyes on the bushes, see if there's any movement."

"You know old people got bad night vision, right?" said Arnie.

"Just look," said Marge. "And seventy-one isn't so old."

"So Nathan bought the whole town himself?" I asked.

Arnie frowned. "Not exactly. I think some of the investors were in it from the beginning. But he had this genius idea—"

Marge huffed in the backseat.

"You hear something?" Arnie peered out the window.

"Just the wind," I said. Marge grinned.

"Anyway, he's got this genius idea where he sells pieces of the place to investors. They can buy whatever building and business they want and run it the way they want. I—we—bought the opera house."

"Of course."

"And the photo booth in the jail."

"Right."

"And the reptile house."

"Really?"

"Nathan said it'd be a hit with the kiddies, and it was pretty easy to stock."

We'd pretty much cruised the entire desert perimeter of Sunnydale, so I swung back into its residential streets. "So you basically bought those buildings from Nathan? How does he make any money?"

"He owns the saloon. Biggest moneymaker there. Plus he has a deal where each of the investors pays a monthly fee."

"I thought you bought the property." I pulled alongside one of the many golf courses that crisscrossed Sunnydale.

"Like Nathan says, think of it like a condo fee. He manages the place, takes care of the infrastructure, the security, that sort of stuff. The marketing too."

"It does sound like a pretty good deal. Hey! Chihuahuas!" I squealed to a stop and jumped out of the car. "Wait here."

My cowboy boots weren't the best for running, but I took off after the pack of dogs. Wait, was that a black curly tail in the midst of all those skinny rat tails?

"Lassie!" I yelled. "Hey, boy. It's me—"

"Crap," I heard behind me, then something that sounded like a pillow fight—"oofs," soft stuff making contact, that sort of thing. I looked over my shoulder. Arnie and Marge were in a heap on the ground. They didn't wait in the car. I probably wouldn't have either.

The little dogs disappeared into the dark.

I turned around. "You okay?" The couple still lay tangled together on the grass.

"Yeah," said Marge. "It's kind of romantic down here, lying on our backs, gazing at the stars."

"She's just trying to make me feel better," said Arnie. "'Cause I think I broke something."

The EMTs thought it was a broken ankle. I did too, given the unnatural way Arnie's foot twisted. "I can't believe you're so calm."

"I've got my love to keep me calm," he sang, clutching Marge's hand. Painkillers must have kicked in.

"Anyway, don't you two worry about anything," I said. "I'll find Lassie. I'll see if anything untoward is going on at Gold Bug, and I'll make sure Nathan doesn't know a thing about it. Okay?"

"Thanks, kiddo." Marge blew me a kiss from the back of the ambulance.

"I will weather the storm," sang Arnie. "I've got my love to keep me calm. Hey," he asked Marge as the EMTs shut the ambulance door, "shouldn't that rhyme? I coulda sworn it used to rhyme."

CHAPTER 18

"Isn't it a little early for Christmas?" Uncle Bob asked me the next morning when I came into the office.

"The stores have had up Christmas decorations since Halloween, if that's what you mean."

"No, it's..." He waved in my direction, his speech stymied by the maple bar he was eating. He swallowed. "You."

"Me?" I checked my outfit—just my denim skirt, a purple t-shirt, and..."You mean my boots?" My cowboy boots were red and sort of fancy.

"No, it's that song you're humming."

Arnie's song from last night was still in my head. Must have come out my mouth too. "It's a Christmas song?"

"Sure. 'I've Got My Love to Keep Me Warm.' Great version by Ella Fitzgerald."

"You should have heard Arnie's version last night." I told him the story. "So we hung posters, Marge is calling the shelters, and I've looked for him myself. Any other ideas on how to find Lassie?"

"I wish I knew," Uncle Bob said. "I think Pink knows someone who specializes in lost pets." Pink, or Detective Pinkstaff, as he was known at the Phoenix Police Department, was one of Uncle Bob's best friends. "I'll ask. Hey, did you hear about that dog they found? The one who fell off that guy's fishing boat?" Uncle Bob grinned. "He survived five weeks on an island. Guess he ate mice or something. The dog, I mean."

I loved my uncle.

I sat down at my computer. "Okay, for now I'll try something easier than a lost dog. How do I find out who owns a corporation?"

"I thought you said easier."

Uh-oh.

"You know what state the business is incorporated in?"

I shook my head.

"Well, once you do, you can start with the Secretary of State and the Corporation Commission."

"They'll have the info?"

"They'll have *some* info that might be able to start you down the right path. This for the Gold Bug case?"

"Yeah. I want to find out who the backers are." I told him what Arnie had said about the individual investors and Nathan's vague reference to other backers.

"It's going to be tough trying to find those guys—or gals—first," Uncle Bob said. "If I were you, I'd start with the sale of property and the people you know are involved."

I did. I found that Josh Tate sold fifty-five acres of property in Maricopa County to Gold Bug Gulch, LLC, for a million dollars. His dad, Luke Tate, sold the mineral rights to the mine two years earlier to Acme Arizona for $65,000. Gold Bug Gulch, LLC was incorporated in Arizona. According to the Arizona Corporation Commission, the only members (owners/investors) were Arnie and a partnership corporation called GBaU. Nathan and Josh weren't listed. Weird.

I searched Arizona's records for GBaU, but didn't find the company listed anywhere. I tried Pennsylvania too, since Nathan had said he had some investors from Philadelphia. Nothing there, either. Must have been incorporated in another state. I called the attorney listed as the corporation's agent, but her administrative assistant said she was unavailable. And Acme Arizona...

"I can't find any incorporation records for it here in Arizona," I said to Uncle Bob, "which is kind of weird, given the name. Nothing comes up when I Google it either."

"Huh." He came over to my desk and peered over my shoulder at my laptop screen. "Maybe the name is supposed to throw people off. Interesting. Tell you what, I'll take a crack at it a little later."

Since I was on the corporation commission's website, I plugged in Josh Tate's name. Nothing came up. If he planned to start some sort of business, he hadn't got very far.

No go with any corporations, at least for now. But I could start investigating Nathan...Oh, right. I took a baggie with the napkin out of my purse and gave it to my uncle. "Guess what? I got Arnie's DNA last night."

"Nice," he said. "See if you can get Nathan's ASAP."

I nodded. "I'm going out to Gold Bug today." I had to leave in about a half hour, but that was enough time to plug Nathan's name into the databases my uncle used for background checks. I found some info pretty quickly: Nathan had been born in Philly to a woman named Gabriella DiRienzi. He didn't have a criminal past, unless you counted taking people's money and losing it. Nathan had opened five restaurants, two gift shops, and a doggie spa, The Shiny Shih Tzu. Creditors and investors had taken him to court a number of times. Most of them had won their suits.

"So where did he get the money to buy Gold Bug?" I said aloud.

"You can conjecture all you want," said Uncle Bob. "Or you could just ask him."

Uncle Bob thought a lot of me. Too much. Sure, I was a good actor, but how in the world was I going to just ask someone where he got a million dollars after losing three times that much? Yep. Those were the figures. Nathan had lost three million dollars of other people's money, then somehow come up with a million for Gold Bug Gulch. But how to approach him? Maybe take the professional approach, ask like I needed to know for the tour. Yep, I decided as I pulled into the Gulch's parking lot. That could work.

I grabbed the small cooler I'd packed that morning and hopped out of the truck. I got stuck in traffic on the way out of Phoenix, so I had only fifteen minutes before my meeting with Frank. It'd have to do. I jogged over to the saloon. Arnie had told me Nathan's onsite office was there, and he was usually in Wednesday through Sunday.

The saloon had wooden swinging doors like you saw in old Westerns, with real doors behind them so the place could be locked up. The real doors were propped open this morning, maybe to catch the cool breeze that blew up from the cottonwoods fringing the creek. I pushed open the swinging doors, my cowboy boots making satisfying thuds on the wooden floors. "This town ain't big enough for the two of us," I drawled. I couldn't help it.

"Nice audition, but I think Arnie already hired you," said Nathan, who was not in his office but behind the bar pouring a cup of coffee from a coffeemaker. Then, he said, "ThoIwodnhave."

"What was that?"

"Nothing," he said, clear as a cowbell. He turned his back on me and blew his nose. Into a handkerchief. This DNA collection business was not going to be easy.

"Nathan," I said, in my strongest, most professional voice. "I'm still collecting all the information I need for the historical tour, and I'd like to speak—"

"Talk to Josh."

"I have and I will. Plus, I'm meeting with Frank in a few—"

"Crazy Frank? Oh, for God's sake, don't let him pull his sad bat crap on you, alright? That's all I need, some emowomatellpeopbatcra."

"I am not an emotional woman and I will not tell people bat crap." After years of living with my mother, passive-aggressive mumbling was my second language. "And I want to get the information correct, exactly the way you want it told. *So*, may I ask you a few questions about the inception of Gold Bug Gulch? Not the old ghost town but your new Western town."

Nathan made a big show of looking at the clock that hung above the bar. "You've got five minutes."

CHAPTER 19

It didn't take five minutes. Nathan got his money from investors. There was a group from back East who liked Westerns and thought this town sounded like a good idea.

Arnie and Josh were the only other investors, for now. There were a couple of other interested parties, but he wouldn't say who. Uncle Bob's confidence in my acting/questioning abilities was definitely displaced.

I took my pathetic PI self out to the place where I'd met Frank. He was already there.

"I do love a woman who's on time," he said.

Good thing I wasn't my usual ten minutes late.

"Thought we'd eat down by the creek. You been there yet?" I shook my head, and he started off downhill toward the cottonwoods, scrawny brown legs pumping. "Beautiful down there. You can hear the gods talk." Hmm. Maybe Crazy Frank's nickname was well-deserved. "Watch your step. It gets sandy pretty quick. Easy to twist an ankle. There's even—"

I didn't hear what Frank said next. We'd just reached the trees, and...ohhh.

Underfoot was soft grass. Grass. In the desert. And edging the small stream were honest-to-God bushes—not cactus or sage or desert broom, but soft-looking, autumn-yellow-tinged bushes. Statuesque cottonwoods stood guard, throwing lacy shadows on the ground while their leaves whispered overhead.

"The Hopis say that the sound of wind through the cottonwoods is the gods talking to us." Frank looked up and cocked an ear, as if he were listening. "Cottonwoods are sacred to the Hopis. They carve Kachina dolls from their roots."

I closed my eyes, the better to hear. It almost did sound like murmured conversation in the air above us.

A few rocks tumbled and splashed. I opened my eyes. Frank now sat on a fallen tree, parallel to the creek, in the shade.

"Our lunch seating, Madame." He took off his khaki hat and set it next to him. He had about seven hairs on his head, all sprouting from his ears.

I scrambled over a few rocks and joined him on the log. I opened the cooler and placed our sandwiches and chips on the log-table between us. I nestled the beers in the sandy shallows of the stream to keep them cool.

"Three beers?" he asked.

"Two for you and one for me. I've got my water bottle too." I didn't usually drink in the middle of the day, especially before a rehearsal, but...

"Good. Don't like drinking alone."

Yep. Got that one right.

"So..." Frank reached down and grabbed one of the beers. "How much did Josh tell you?"

"Not much. Mostly about how the town was big, then it wasn't."

"Yeah, Josh has a hard time talking about it. Tough to be at the tail end of a dynasty. You can get a lot of the official history of the town from the Wickenburg historical society. They can also tell you about some of the characters who lived here, the saloon owner, the teacher, the madam, those sorts of folks. And about the murders." He opened up his sandwich. "Praise the Lord—it's not American cheese. Can't stand the stuff. It's not cheese; it's chemicals. Oh, and there's mustard. Nice touch."

I was not about to be distracted by mustard and my fortuitous choice of cheddar cheese. "Murders?"

"This was the Wild West, you know. People shot each other over all sorts of things. Mostly the town's three most valuable commodities: water, gold, and women."

Two questions circled my mind. "Women were one of the top three? I would have thought cattle."

"Supply and demand. Way more cattle than women. If a woman was smart, she could make a fortune out here."

"By marrying a rich guy?"

Frank laughed. "Maybe. But I'm talking about working women."

I seriously doubted women came west to make their fortunes in prostitution, but wanted to ask my second question. "Where'd you go to school?" Though Frank's speech was mostly what you'd expect from a desert rat, it was also peppered with phrases like "valuable commodities."

"Berkeley. One of the first to graduate in Environmental Science. That's why I live out here. I'm protecting two of the most pristine desert riparian areas in the West."

"By living here?"

"I'm like a caretaker. I pay attention to the flora and fauna, notice what's doing well and what's struggling. I measure the groundwater and test the creek water. I pick up the crap that people leave behind. Like water bottles." He looked pointedly at my plastic bottle.

I gulped the last of my water and made a show of putting the empty bottle back into my cooler. "You said you were protecting two places?"

"Yeah, this one and...well, I don't know you well enough tell you the location of the other, but I can tell you it's in a little box canyon. The Hassayampa River surfaces there for a hundred feet or so. I did my spirit quest there. Really did hear the gods talk." He deposited his empty beer can in my cooler, slid off the log, and reached into the creek for his second one. "You ready for yours?" I nodded and he handed me a can, cool and dripping with creek water. "This here, Gold Bug Creek, is a tributary of the Hassayampa, you know."

"I didn't." This was interesting, but I was distracted by a thought fluttering around in my head.

"Bet you also didn't know that 'Hassayampa' means upside down. That's what the Apaches used to call it, since most of the river flows underground."

The thought flitted by me and I grabbed it. "Are there bats here?"

"There are bats everywhere. And good thing too. Keeps down the bug population. But I suspect you're asking because someone said something about me being batshit crazy."

"Not batshit crazy. Just bat crazy."

"We all got pieces of crazy in us, some bigger pieces than others." He took a long drink of his beer, his gaze on the creek studious and protective, like a really smart sheepdog. "Remember how I said I keep track of the animals around here? About a year ago, right after Nathan bought the place, I was doing some fix-up work on the reptile house. I worked past sunset that time and was just leaving when a bat swooped by me out of a nearby building. Something about it seemed different— its silhouette, I guess. So I stuck my head into the building, and there was a small colony just waking up. A colony of Lesser Long-nosed Bats, I later found out. Been on the endangered list for years. I started watching for them and discovered two more colonies, one in a building that hasn't been repaired yet. And a big one in the mine."

"Cool."

"It would be, if it weren't for the new Gold Bug Gulch. All those people are disturbing the bats."

"Don't they have to protect them? By law, I mean?"

"Sure. But first someone has to admit the bats are here. Someone has to fill out all the forms and such. Government moves slow these days, maybe always. And money talks. Oh, Nathan says they're going to do the right thing—if they need to—but it won't be enough. Used to be a big bat maternity colony in Colossal Cave down near Tucson. Until they opened it to the public."

"Can't Josh help? He must know everything about this place, since his family owned it for so long."

"Josh...let's just say he and I don't see eye to eye about much. Never have. See this?" Frank pointed to his nose, which veered off to the left. "Punched me right in the face during a protest about ten years back. His temper's better since he started working at the forge, smithing, but he's not exactly the Zen Smithy he pretends to be." He crumpled his beer can with one hand and put the empty in my cooler. "But that's not what you came here to discuss, is it?"

Actually it was. "I want to know everything," I said, "so I can help protect this place too." It wasn't a lie. Though I really wanted to know everything for PI purposes and to protect Arnie's investment, I wanted to make sure this oasis stayed pristine too. I hoped the goals wouldn't be mutually exclusive.

"Josh say anything about the Carvers?" Frank asked.

"That's Mongo's family, right? Josh said something about them maybe killing off his family's cattle."

Frank nodded. "Probably did. The animosity between the families goes way back. The Tates and the Carvers had ranches right next to each other, both big places and both along Gold Bug Creek. Started off fighting about rangeland right from the start, but water rights became a big thing during drought years. The Carvers owned the land upstream. When the creek started drying up, which it did at least some every summer, they'd dam it on their property. By the time the water made it to the Tate's ranch, their cattle got mostly mud. The Tate boys would sneak out at night and bust up the dams, and the Carvers would build them back up again."

"Wasn't that against the law or something?"

"Sure, but remember where you are and when it was. Back then, the law in Wickenburg had their hands full of real criminals who shot people. Things calmed down a bit between the two families in the middle of the last century, until one day in the seventies. Josh's dad and Mongo's dad were playing a high-stakes poker game in some back room somewhere. It'd been going on for a day and a night with everybody drinking the whole time, so it wasn't too surprising when Josh's dad did something stupid."

"He literally bet the ranch?"

"All his property except for this parcel the town's on."

"And the mine. He didn't bet the mine." I remembered he'd sold the mineral rights later, so he must have still owned them.

Frank shrugged. "The mine was played out. Not worth anything."

"It's like something out of a movie—Josh's family losing the ranch in a poker game."

"Not only that. Word is, John Carver cheated."

We ate in silence for a minute. Or I did. Frank chewed his Fritos noisily, with his mouth open. I got the feeling he'd lived alone for a long time.

"I can't believe Josh wouldn't want to hold onto what was left of his family's property."

"He had to sell. His dad left behind a ton of debt when he died. Josh needed money to pay off creditors."

Frank stopped talking, but it wasn't quiet. A mourning dove cooed softly to its mate, the creek sang to the rocks it skipped over, and the gods talked to themselves in the cottonwoods. I sat and listened, my heart full. I couldn't imagine what it must have felt like to lose a place like this.

CHAPTER 20

"Sure do appreciate this lunch." Frank belched. "And the beer. Nice to have a woman fix my meal."

"My uncle is a better cook than me." Not true, unless you counted chili cheese dogs, but I never did like the whole "women belong in the kitchen" thing. Always afraid it'd be followed up with "barefoot and pregnant."

"I do love a good cheese sandwich. Especially after all this years of surviving on mice."

"Mice?" I squeaked.

"Just kidding. I'm a vegetarian. Though I did eat a lot of weird shit for years—yucca, prickly pear, cholla buds. Mostly I ate—eat—beans, corn, and squash. Grow 'em myself."

Though the area around the creek was almost lush (almost; this *was* Arizona), the desert began not even a hundred feet away. I looked toward the place Frank had pointed out as home. Dirt and rocks and cacti. "Kinda tough to grow all that out here, isn't it?"

"I learned how. Tell you what, you bring me lunch again, and I'll show you my place. Got a meeting tomorrow, so let's make it Friday." He squinted at me, and his leathery face scrunched up, his blue eyes barely visible in the wrinkles. "Deal?"

"You bet."

I was a little early for the melodrama rehearsal (an unusual event, to say the least), so I sat on a bench on the wooden sidewalk in the sun until Billie walked up. "Hi!" I said, in my ditzy Ivy voice, then, "OMG, your eye. Did that just happen?" Of course I saw it yesterday, but figured the bright outdoor light gave me an excuse.

Billie held up a hand, as if to cover her eye from the paparazzi. "No." She unlocked the door to the opera house and stepped into the darkness.

"What happened?"

"Stumbled. Face first into a door. The knob caught me just right."

Uncle Bob had told me about some of his domestic violence cases. Billie's explanation sounded a lot like the excuses he heard all too often. I took a chance.

"Listen..." I steeled myself for the lie. "I had a boyfriend once who—"

"This was not a boyfriend." Billie pointed to her eye. "This was a door." She strode into the theater ahead of me.

"Sorry, sorry." I rushed after her. "I didn't mean—"

She turned to me, her eyes hard. "Alright. So you've heard about me and Mongo. It's not true."

"Um, actually, I didn't hear anything, except he was your boyfriend and..."

"Not anymore." Chance had entered behind us.

"Chance." Billie's voice signaled a warning. "Listen, Ivy. Let's get this out of the way. Mongo and I had been together for years. We lived together."

"When he wasn't out—"

"*Chance.*"

Chance, who seemed pretty macho to me, looked like a puppy who'd been told he was a bad dog.

"We have two hours to rehearse," said Billie. "Let's use them."

Rehearsal went pretty well, though every time we stopped saying scripted words and used our own, the air became thick with tension. Chance seemed especially strained, his voice slightly guttural and his words clipped. As an actor and a person, I was really uncomfortable. As a PI, I sensed an opportunity.

So when we were finished with rehearsal, I said to Billie in my ditz voice, "I really am so sorry about your boyfriend." Yep, Chance made a face as he bit off a reply. Definitely something there. "You two were, like, a long-term couple? My uncle and aunt in Utah are common-law married or whatever they call it," I fibbed. I knew Arizona didn't recognize common-law marriage, but I was curious about Mongo's estate.

Billie shook her head. "We're not."

"So you don't get any of his stuff? I mean, you won't have to move or anything, right? That would suck, big time." Again, I knew the house was in Billie's name, but I wanted to push things a little.

"He left her nothing," said Chance. "She deserves so much—"

"Chance," Billie said sharply. "The house is mine," she said to me. "And Mongo didn't leave a will. He was only forty-three. It's not like he left me out on purpose, he just...Listen, I really don't want to talk about this." She put her script into a paper grocery bag and picked up her purse off one of the theater seats.

"Sorry," I said following her and Chance up the aisle. "Hey, Frank took me down to the creek to listen to the gods talk in the cottonwoods. It was awesome. But I'm kind of surprised he's comfortable here. Said something about Josh breaking his nose during a protest."

"Josh has calmed down since then," said Billie. "But Frank deserved that punch in the nose."

"For protesting? Really?"

"Frank was protesting wolf hunting, just a week after all of Josh's wolf traps were sabotaged and he lost a bunch of cattle."

I wasn't sure what I thought of all that. I felt sorry for the wolves *and* the cows. The interesting thing was: "Frank sabotaged them?"

"Him or his buddies." Billie turned to me. "What were you doing with him, anyway?"

"I'm going to be a historical guide for the town. Frank said he'd give me the real story. You hear about that poker game?"

"What poker game?" Billie's face blanched. Hmm.

"The one where Josh's dad lost the ranch to Mongo's dad?"

Billie's face relaxed and the color returned to her cheeks. "Sure. Everyone knows about that."

"There's one thing I don't get. Don't gamblers usually bet the most valuable stuff last?"

"What do you mean?"

"Since Josh's family made their living off the ranch, it seems like his dad would have put this property up before betting the ranch. Or even just bet the mine."

"He was drunk," said Billie at the same time as Chance said, "There's gold in them there hills."

CHAPTER 21

I laughed. They didn't—at first. Then they both grinned and chuckled. Actors or not, they wouldn't have passed an audition.

"Chance likes to go prospecting," said Billie. "A hobby. In fact, he's going to run the gold-panning attraction as soon as he gets the money to invest in it."

"Saving up," Chance said.

I made a mental note to dig into the gold mine. Then I made a mental note to say that out loud to Uncle Bob. He loved puns.

"See you tomorrow," Chance said to me, tipping the black cowboy hat he always wore, indoors and out. "Walk you to your car?" he said to Billie. Annoyance flashed across her face before she nodded, but Chance either missed it or ignored it. I filed the exchange in my mental "what's up with these two?" folder.

Billie began to lock the doors. "Just a sec," I said. "I need to pee."

"Must still be out of order," she said. "They got a garden hose stuck in the toilet."

"Oh, pooh. Oh!" I opened my eyes wide like I had a genius thought. "Didn't Frank say there was one at Josh's house?"

"Yeah. Check the forge as you walk past. If he's not there, he's probably at the house. But make sure you ask him first. Josh likes his privacy."

The last light died as I walked toward Josh's shop. When I reached the forge, it was dark. The iron gate was pulled across the opening, so I hiked down the hill to the little white house Frank had pointed out. Once I got there, I stepped onto a wide front porch overhung by old apple trees and peered through one of the windows that flanked the door. No Josh, just a neat room with bookshelves lining the walls and an age-blackened fireplace crafted of the same river rock as the house's foundation. I knocked and waited. Nothing. I knocked again. Nope. No one home.

I tried the front door. It was unlocked. Should I? Even though this trip was mostly an excuse to talk to Josh, I really did have to go to the bathroom. But Billie had made a point that I should ask Josh. "He likes his privacy," she'd said. Didn't someone else say that too?

Seeing as how one man had been shot (maybe accidentally, I still wasn't sure) and remembering Josh's muscled arms, I decided not to chance it. I'd snoop from the outside instead.

I looked through the window again. An arched entrance on one side of the main room led to a small dining room. I could just see a sliver of a big old refrigerator in the kitchen beyond that.

I hopped off the porch and jogged around the side of the house. Now that I was down on the ground, the windows were almost too high for me to see through. Almost. I stood on my tiptoes. Nothing interesting in the dining room, except for the beautifully wrought iron chandelier that hung over an antique oak table. An open doorway led into the kitchen, which had a back door—one of those types with a window at the top. A perfect spying spot.

I went around the back. The yard was lush and wild, shaded by cottonwoods and covered with that long green grass I'd seen by the creek. I could hear water burbling. Ah. The creek must turn and run past the back of the house. That would explain the trees and grass.

Something rustled in the tall grass to my right. A snake? I jumped onto the steps leading to the kitchen door and stared at the place where I'd seen the grass shiver. Something jumped in my peripheral vision, to my left and...at knee height? That didn't make sense. Focusing on that spot, I caught another movement off to my right again. I felt like I was at the DMV doing that test where they check your side vision by flashing lights, but this felt way creepier, given the fact that I had no idea what might be in that long grass.

"What the hell are you doing here?" Josh opened the kitchen door.

"Aaaaaah!"

"That's not much of an answer."

"Um," I composed myself. "I have to pee."

"Still not an answer." He crossed his arms, and the sleeves of his t-shirt rode up, exposing his muscled biceps.

"I was at rehearsal."

"There's a bathroom in the opera house."

"The toilet's out of order."

"Still? Come on in." He pointed toward a closed door off the kitchen. "It's through there."

After using the facilities, I thanked Josh, who stood with one hand holding open the door to the backyard. A hint if I ever saw one. "How'd you know where to find me?" he asked.

"Billie told me." And Frank too, but that didn't help with my line of questioning. "Why didn't you tell me when you gave me the tour?"

"I don't want people to know. Don't want tourists tromping down here to take a look at the house."

"Yeah, Billie said you like your privacy. I was wondering—"

"Then she should have known better to send you down here, unless it was an emergency."

"It sort of was."

"You coulda gone outside."

What was up with this guy? He'd been friendly during our tour of the town. Why so hostile now?

The grass jittered behind Josh. The movement must have drawn my eyes for a second because Josh turned too. "What?"

"Just...the grass. Do you have snakes?"

"Where are you from again? This *is* Arizona." He closed the door. "Better go out the front way. And don't come down here after dark. It can be dangerous."

I followed him through the dining room into the main room. I stopped beside one of the bookshelves. *Zen and the Art of Motorcycle Maintenance*, a whole shelf full of Zane Gray novels, some Stephen King...No business-type books. "Dangerous?" I asked, mostly to distract him so I could snoop more. "Don't snakes mostly come out during the day?" *Leaves of Grass, Walden Pond, Of Mice and Men...*

Josh raised his eyebrows, surprised that the city girl knew anything. "Yeah, you rarely get trouble from snakes at night, but there are lots of holes from them and ground squirrels, that sort of thing. In the dark, it'd be easy to miss them. You could fall."

Ooh, perfect opportunity to ask, "Like Billie? Oh, no, that was into a door, right?"

"Billie fell into a door?"

"That's what she said caused her black eye, but I remember you saying something about her being safer since Mongo was gone. I was hoping that was true because, well, she and Chance seem awfully close and I was hoping it wasn't him."

"Billie 'fell' into something a couple times a year. Swore it wasn't Mongo, but she's not that clumsy."

"She said they lived together, but Chance said something about Mongo being out a lot? Out where?"

"No one knows. Mongo used to disappear pretty regularly. Pretty sure he was out drinking, maybe gambling like his old man, but he'd never say anything. Don't even think Billie knew."

"And her and Chance? Seems like something's going on there."

Josh sighed and ran his fingers through his dusty hair. "Listen, I don't like idle gossip, but you're going to be working with them. Billie told me that the last time Mongo took off for a while, she and Chance...got together. Ever since, he's been following her around like a lovesick calf."

Why was it baby animals—calves and puppies—who were lovesick? Shouldn't it be grown-up animals that fell in love? I dragged my brain away from that tangent and instead said, "I hate to say it, but that brings up another question, one that concerns Billie's safety again..."

"I know. Could Chance have shot Mongo on purpose? It's been on my mind too."

"And?"

"It's possible. People do all sorts of things for love."

CHAPTER 22

"Hello, my baby, hello, my honey, hello, my ragtime gal," Arnie sang when he picked up the phone the next morning.

"Did they give you Percocet?" I asked.

"Maybe. Marge!" He yelled so loud I had to hold the phone away from my ear. "Ivy's on the phone." Then in a normal tone of voice: "She wants to take all the calls right now."

"Imagine that."

"Send me your love by wire," he sang. "Baby, my heart's on fire."

"I'll take it from here, chickie." Marge must have picked up the other line. "Bye now." There was a click.

"So he's doing okay?" I said.

"He's not so good on crutches, but the man can sing."

"Just wanted to check in with you. I'm digging a little at Gold Bug Gulch, but haven't found anything concrete. And as far as Lassie..."

Marge sighed. "Yeah. I figured if you'd found him, you would have told me first off."

"But I'm going to go talk to a pet detective today—get some pointers. We'll find Lassie."

"I thought firemen found lost cats and dogs." I sat in a comfy chair in the home office of Joy Rogers, pet detective.

"Where'd you get that idea?" Uncle Bob entered the room, his hands full with two large bags from Filiberto's, redolent of chilies and pork and whatever it is that makes Mexican food smell so great.

"Um...*Leave It to Beaver*? Or maybe *Father Knows Best*. There was a fifties marathon on TV last night."

"I think you may have seen a fireman getting a cat out of a tree," said Joy.

"That was it."

"Not sure if they really do that." Joy stood up from behind her desk and took one of the bags from Uncle Bob. Late forties or so, she had dark springy hair and a wiry body. She looked way more comfortable up and moving around than she did behind her big wooden desk. "Thanks for bringing lunch."

"Thanks for meeting with us. Pink says you're the best." Uncle Bob pulled a couple of wrapped burritos out of one of the bags and handed me one. "Ivy here would like to ask you a few questions." He sat down in a chair next to me and tucked a paper napkin underneath his shirt collar.

"You heard about the pack of Chihuahuas in Sunnydale?" I asked Joy.

"Who hasn't?"

"Well, my friends' dog Lassie joined the circus, so to speak."

"Really? Big dogs don't usually take up with the little guys."

"Lassie's a pug."

"That makes more sense." Joy nibbled on her shrimp taco as I filled her in on the details and how I had tried to find Lassie. "All right," she said. "You've done a good job. You know this dog at all?"

"Yeah." My throat began to close up. I swallowed hard.

Uncle Bob must've seen I was struggling. "She used to, uh, dog-sit Lassie."

I found my voice. "I love him."

"Sorry. That'll make it harder on you, but it might increase your chances of finding him, since you might be able to predict his behavior. If you had to fit her...Lassie?"

"Lassie, and he's a he."

"Like all the real Lassie actors in the movies," added Uncle Bob. Sometimes he couldn't help showing off his trivia knowledge.

"Lassie the boy pug." Joy smiled. "Okay then. If you had to place him in one of the following personality categories, would he be, A) Gregarious, B) Aloof, or C) Fearful?"

"A," I said. "Definitely gregarious."

"Good. You'll have a better chance of finding him, because he's more likely to respond to people. And people will be more likely to try to catch him since he's a cute little pug. Lots harder to convince folks to pick up pit bulls. But..." Joy leaned back in her chair. "That could also be a problem. People are more likely to pick him up and keep him, unless he's wearing a collar."

"He's not. He likes to jingle it, and it can make you crazy, so they only put it on him when they take him for a walk. He's never gone out of the yard before without Marge or Arnie."

"The pack mentality can be strong. It's like a really great party is sweeping by your front door. Pretty tough to not join in," Joy said. "So, no collar and gregarious. First of all, make sure people know his name and that he belongs to someone."

I thought of the posters we'd put up. "Yeah. Done that."

"There are a couple more things you can try. Since this is the desert, you can watch for the pack by places that have water."

I'd done that too but kept quiet, hoping for more.

"You might look for tracks..."

Done a little bit of that.

"And you can buy wildlife cameras, set them up in areas you think the dogs might frequent."

Ah. Hadn't done that.

"The cameras have motion sensors and will take photos of whatever moves, stamping them with dates and times."

"That's a great idea." I felt encouraged for the first time.

Joy held up a hand. "They're pretty expensive, and if the pack is traveling, they might move from watering hole to watering hole."

"Right. I bet my clients would buy one or two though." Not only did Arnie want to find Lassie, he loved gadgets.

"Hunters use those cameras, right?" Uncle Bob said between bites of his enormous burrito. "To track game?"

"Yeah," said Joy. "Seems a little unfair to me."

"Hunters..." Uncle Bob said. "I don't even want to ask this, but there are coyotes and cougars out there and..."

"And I hate to say it," said Joy. "But yeah. Lassie's chances aren't great."

"Is there anything else you would do?" I tried to keep the pleading tone out of my voice.

"Yeah. I'd bring out my secret weapon. Sam!" she called.

The click of toenails on tile floors announced Joy's secret weapon. The enormous bloodhound padded over and leaned against her. She scratched one of his floppy ears. "Meet Sam Spade, my certified trailing and decomposition dog."

"Decomposition?" I put down my burrito.

"We're pretty good about finding lost pets—a seventy-five percent success rate. But it's a big scary world filled with cars and cougars and coyotes, and some of the pets—too many of them—we find...later."

CHAPTER 23

Funny how the word decomposition makes you not want to eat a burrito filled with mushy brown stuff. Instead, I fed little bits of tortilla to Sam the bloodhound. Not the beans. That would be mean.

We talked more about dogs as we finished up lunch. Then Joy stood up and stuck out a hand. "It's been great to meet you, and I wish you the best of luck." She handed both of us business cards. "Since you know Pink, I'm happy to have given you a few pointers. But you should know, this is my business. If you need to hire me and Sam, well, you'd have to *hire* me and Sam. And I charge two hundred dollars an hour."

Uncle Bob and I managed to keep from saying anything until we were outside the front door. "We are in the wrong business," he said.

"I don't know. If I had to find people's mostly dead pets, I think I'd charge that too." I kissed my uncle on his stubbly cheek and hopped into my pickup. According to the dashboard clock, I had just enough time to make it to Gold Bug Gulch in time for afternoon rehearsal.

When I got there, Billie was waiting for me outside the opera house. "Ivy!" She waved as I climbed the steps to the porch. She seemed awfully excited to see me. "You know, that top suits you. Really brings out those green eyes."

"Wow. You think so?" I said in my ditz voice. What else would an airhead say? "Maybe it's my new mascara." Yeah, that would work. Except I wasn't wearing any. Oops.

Billie didn't seem to notice. "Come on inside out of the sun. Don't want to ruin that pretty skin of yours." She hopped off the porch and beckoned me to do the same. "Let's go around to the backstage entrance."

When I got back down to the dirt street, Billie slung an arm around my shoulder and walked us around the side of the building. Being a theater, there were no windows and only one door: the stage door. Billie unlocked it and held it open for me. "Got a couple of costumes for you to try on. They'll look great on you. Gonna have to beat off the men with a stick."

Billie had called and asked me to come in early for a costume fitting. That didn't quite account for her effusive manner. I wondered why she'd turned on the charm. Oh, stop it, Ivy. Sometimes I didn't like the way that PI work made me question everyone's motives. Maybe Billie was just being nice. Maybe she was happy to have a woman to talk to. Maybe she really liked costume fittings.

I did. Especially when the costume looked like the first one she handed me. "Wow. Did you make this?"

Billie nodded. "You know us theater folk. Best to do a little bit of everything in order to stay employed."

"This is amazing." I fingered the ankle-length dress, white lawn and lace with a high Victorian collar. I was just about to ask her about the row of Velcro that split the costume up the front when she said, "Chance won't be able to take his eyes off you. He loves the whole lacy girly look."

Okay, that was weird. "Aren't you two, you know, like a couple?"

"Not really. He's way too young for me." She sighed and sat down in a wooden chair. I sat in one that was conveniently placed next to it. Given the carefully positioned seating, the just-the-two-of-us costume fitting, and Billie's over-the-top friendliness, I was beginning to think I was being set up. Did she want to tell me something? What?

"I should have never slept with him."

Oh, that. But why was she confiding in me? Was she afraid that Chance didn't shoot Mongo by accident? Or did she know it for sure and was throwing Chance under the bus? "Why not?" I asked.

"I was Mongo's woman."

Maybe it was guilt over her infidelity.

"We'd been together over ten years. But I was getting pissed off at Mongo. He was...unreliable."

"Didn't Chance say something about him taking off?"

"Yeah, he'd go off for a week at a time. Sometimes more."

"Do you think he had a drinking problem? Or gambling?"

"No." Billie bit the word off, like she wanted to end that line of thinking right there. "But I always wondered if he had another woman. One time I found..."

"Strange panties?" I did need to keep up the ditz role.

Billie wisely ignored me. "I don't know if it was letter or a poem. But it was romantic. I found it when I was putting away some of his laundry, stashed in the back of a drawer. I put it back, hoping he'd show it to me sometime. But he never did, so..." She shrugged. "The last time he took off, I took up with Chance."

"Revenge sex, huh?"

"Maybe. Mostly I felt sorry for him."

"Really? Chance seems like a pretty tough guy."

"He's not what he—never mind."

"What do you mean?"

"Ivy," said Billie, "you're young. You're going to figure out eventually that no one is who they seem." She stood up. "Speaking of which, you can drop the airhead routine."

"What do you mean?" I said again in the highest, most breathless voice I could.

Billie laughed. "Overkill, darlin'. I can tell you're not stupid. Can see it in your eyes. I know why you're playing the role, but you can drop it around me, okay?"

Oh no. How did she figure out I was a detective?

"I've played that role too. It's helpful. You got to give men what they expect. Don't want to rock the boat when they own the sea. But when it's just us women, you can be yourself, smart and all."

"You played that role too?" I used my real voice but treaded carefully. After all, Billie might be trying to catch me off guard.

"Sure. It's just one version of the two parts we women get to play in life."

"Two parts?"

"Now come over here and try on this other costume." Billie held up a saloon girl's dress. The top was green satin with a low square neck trimmed in black lace. The bottom half was green and black striped satin—and too short by about a foot and half.

I held it up. "This doesn't fit the period."

"It's what the boss man wants."

I wrangled myself into the stupid, ridiculous, woefully inaccurate costume and finally got it on. "Too tight," I said when I could breathe again.

"Nah. It's gotta be form-fitting to fit under the other costume." Form-fitting my ass. This was form-sucking. I felt like I'd been Press-and-Sealed. Billie picked up the white Victorian dress. "You wear this one over it." She ripped open its Velcro front. "It's a tear-away, see? You just step offstage and pull it off when you change from Rose to Fannie."

I looked at myself in the full-length mirror. Yikes. The top was cut so low I'd have to use double-stick tape to keep it in place, and the skirt was, well, we'd have to rethink some of the blocking if we wanted to keep it a family show. I'd worn my share of revealing costumes before, but this one looked like gratuitous sex in a B-grade movie. "Can we please fix this one?"

"Nope. Came down from the top. Better get used to it, Ivy. It's kinda like life. Like I said earlier, you get two choices: Madonna." She held up the white ingénue dress, then pointed at my ridiculous saloon girl's outfit. "Or whore."

CHAPTER 24

"If you had to choose, would you prefer white lace panties or black crotchless ones?"

Matt chewed thoughtfully. "Actually, I like boxers."

I swatted him with a napkin. "On me."

"I bet you'd look pretty good in my boxers." He stood up from the table. "Let's see. Right now."

"Are you trying to get me naked when I want to have a serious conversation?"

"A question about black crotchless panties precedes a serious conversation?"

"This time it does." We were sitting at my kitchen table, finishing up one of my fancier bean suppers, white Cannelloni beans with mushrooms and garlic. Ooh la la.

I told Matt about my conversation with Billie that afternoon. "Do you think men divide women into two groups?"

"No. It's an awfully black and white view of the world. That said, the question you just asked was black and white too." He smiled.

That was one thing I loved about Matt. Sometimes I was too satisfied with life's easier answers. He made me dig a little deeper. It was good for me as a PI, and as a person. "Okay, do you think women have fewer choices than men?"

"Absolutely. Women aren't even allowed to go to school in some parts of the world."

"Do you think things are getting better?" I had my own opinion, but I wanted to hear a man's point of view. Well, Matt's point of view.

"Well, in the last hundred years or so, women's rights have come a long way."

I saw in his eyes that he wasn't done thinking about the question. "But?"

"But things aren't equal. We still have a pay gap, for instance. Twenty-one percent."

"Twenty-one percent? You're kidding."

He shook his head. "Read it last week in the *Wall Street Journal*. How old do you think Billie is?"

"Forties?"

"Where did she grow up?"

"Not sure. Somewhere here in Arizona, I think."

"Depending on where and when she grew up, in what type of household, community, religion, etcetera, those two roles may have been the only options presented to her."

"But things are different for woman in the twenty-first century in a city the size of Phoenix, right? They're different for me?"

"Sometimes. I suspect there are times when you're treated differently from men."

"I certainly have to wear scantier costumes than they do."

"But to me," Matt reached a hand across the table and enclosed mine, "you aren't Madonna or a whore. You're the one and only Ivy Meadows, and I am lucky to be your man." He squeezed my hand. "But since we're having a serious conversation..."

Oh no. "Are you done with dinner?" I tried to grab his plate with my free hand.

"Yes, but..." Matt moved his plate out of my reach. "Ivy, I get the feeling that our problem—"

"It's not a problem. And even if it is, it's just temporary."

"—that our problem has more to do with you than Cody."

Confession time. Though Matt and I had been friends for a couple of years and dating for nearly four months, I hadn't told anyone. Not Cody, not Uncle Bob, not Arnie or Marge. Not only had I not told anyone and sworn Matt to secrecy, I didn't want us out in public as a couple. Not yet.

"It's only while you're still working with Cody." I dropped Matt's hand and stood up, placing my silverware on my plate. I walked the few steps to my kitchen sink. "You'll graduate in two weeks. Isn't that soon enough?"

Matt had been studying for his Masters in Social Work and already had a job lined up after graduation.

"It is, but I still think Cody could handle the news now—could have handled it earlier if we'd told him." Matt followed me to the sink with his dirty dishes. "He's an adult, Ivy. He understands, and I'm pretty sure he'd be happy for us."

"That's just it. I don't want him get all excited and then..." I turned on the water, too hard. It splashed me, and I backed away into Matt, who stood behind me.

"Then what?"

"I don't know." I turned the water down. "And then it doesn't work out."

"Ivy." Matt put his plate on the counter and turned me gently by the shoulders. "Do you want this to work out?"

"Yes." Why was my heart beating so fast? After all, we were already lovers.

"I do too. So it will." Matt kissed me gently on the lips. "It will."

CHAPTER 25

As Marge opened the door, I heard Arnie in the background: "Cookie, Cookie, listen while I sing to you…"

"I don't know that one," I said. "Is he singing to someone named Cookie or to a baked good?"

"Probably both." Marge let me in and closed the door. "You want one with some coffee? A baked good, I mean. I've got some rugelach. It's too early for cookies."

"It's too early for anything. Except coffee. And maybe a rugelach." It was not quite eight in the morning. I wasn't usually awake until nine, mostly because I had a hard time going to sleep before two in the morning. Actors' hours. But this morning I'd hunted for Chihuahua and pug tracks near the golf course water hazards. I did see some tracks, but they looked too big to be footprints of the little dogs.

I walked into the living room, where Arnie sat in a recliner with his leg propped up in front of him.

"You are looking good!" said a tinny voice. No one around except for Arnie, who brimmed with suppressed glee. "It's the clock." He pointed at a mirrored clock that hung on the wall. "Every hour, it says an affirmation. You want one for Christmas?"

"If I told you, then I wouldn't be surprised. Hey, I brought *you* something." His eyes lit up at the sight of the gift-wrapped box I placed in his lap. "I wish it was Lassie." The spark in his eyes extinguished. Dang, would I ever learn to think before speaking?

"It's okay." He smiled, but his bottom lip trembled. "I'm sure he's out there having a ball. Probably the big cheese with all those little Chihuahuas." Arnie opened his present. "Hey, this is great." He smiled for real now.

"It's an air-conditioned tie." I pointed out the little fan hidden in the tie's knot. "You charge it with the cable that's in the box. It plugs into a USB port. And sorry to follow up a gift with a request, but..." I explained how the wildlife cameras might help us find Lassie. Arnie agreed to buy four of them before I even finished my spiel.

"And did I tell you I've been peeing in a cup?" he said.

Oh no. "Are you having tests done or...?"

"It's to help lure Lassie home," he said. "Somebody told me about it. You put cups of pee around the borders of your house. He smells them, thinks of you, and comes home."

"I don't know," I said. "Seems like that would only work if you smelled like pee."

His face fell. Dang again, Ivy. "Hey," I said. "You want some rugelach?" It made him smile. Pastries usually did.

I left Arnie fiddling with his new tie and went into the kitchen, where Marge had arranged our treats on a plate. I told her about the pet detective and the cameras I was going to buy. "I think we might get somewhere that way. And I think you can skip the pee cups."

"Thank God." Marge handed me a cup of coffee. Ahhh. Marge's coffee was dark and rich, and she liked to add a little cinnamon. Almost took the pain out of morning. "Hey, is there any way I could work from here for a few hours? I want to get to Gold Bug a little before noon."

"Sure. No sense in you going all the way back to Phoenix and then having to turn around and come back out this way again. You can use the home office."

After I grabbed my laptop from the truck, I sat down at a desk under a framed poster of *The Sound of Cabaret* (the show where we'd all met) and dug into my investigation. I found out that everything Frank and Josh had told me was true. Lesser long-nosed bats were endangered. Josh's family had once owned the ranch, the town, and the gold mine. His dad transferred the deed to the ranch to John Carver (no mention of a poker game), and then right before he died, sold the mineral rights to the mine to Acme Arizona. There had been no recent applications for mine permits. If there was "gold in them there hills," as Chance said, no one was actively doing anything about it.

Josh later sold the town and remaining land to Gold Bug Gulch,

LLC. I checked similar properties and found that a million dollars was a fair price for the land. Might have been a matter of supply and demand. Gold Bug wasn't the only ghost town for sale, and I suspected that buyers for run-down towns in the middle of nowhere were few and far between.

I'd never heard back from Dawn Wayne, the attorney/agent for Gold Bug Gulch, LLC, so I called her again. "Oh, I am so sorry," her admin assistant said, "I forgot to give her your message. I got a call from my son's school right afterward and..."

"Is he okay?"

"He stuck gum in his ear."

"*In* it?"

"On a dare, I guess. We had to go to Urgent Care to have it removed. Anyway, I am so sorry about your message. Tell you what, Ms. Wayne is in between appointments right now. If you can hold a sec, I'll put her through."

She was as good as her word, and Dawn Wayne was accommodating too. "I'm happy to give you this information. For future reference, you can also get it through the Arizona Corporation Commission."

I didn't tell her I'd already tried. I wanted to hear what she said.

"The members of Gold Bug, LLC are Arnie Adel and an investment group called GBaU."

"Can you tell what the acronym stands for?"

Dawn Wayne cleared her throat. "The Good, the Bad, and the Ugly."

"Really?"

"Swear to God."

"Wow...What about Nathan DiRienzi and Josh Tate? It's my understanding that they're owners too."

"Only members owning more than twenty percent are listed in the public record."

Huh. It wouldn't be surprising if Josh had a small share, given that he also got the money from the sale of the land. But Nathan? He was the catalyst behind this whole venture. Surely he'd want to own at least twenty percent. "Back to The Good, the Bad, and the Ugly—can you give me any information about them?"

"I'd like their permission before giving out any further information. May I tell them why you're asking?"

"Never mind. It's not that important. Thank you." I hung up and leaned back in the desk chair. "The Good, the Bad, and the Ugly..." I said out loud to myself.

"You can meet 'em yourself."

"Aaah!" I about tipped out of my chair.

Arnie stood outside the office door, balancing precariously on crutches. "Oops. Didn't mean to scare you or eavesdrop, but I got good hearing on account of these." He pointed to his enormous ears. "Nathan's investors will be here on Monday. They're flying out for the first chuckwagon cookout. We're doing a dry run before we offer it to the tourists, work out the bugs. The *gold* bugs." He chuckled. I did too, just to make him feel good, since his joke made no sense whatsoever. "Wish we could go, but I think Marge is glad we got my crutches as an excuse. She's not crazy about horses."

"Not true," Marge said from behind him in the hall. "Don't we have a Kentucky Derby party every year?"

"That's so you can wear a fancy hat." Arnie winked at me. "Hey, why don't you invite your uncle? And your brother."

"Matt too?" Arnie and Marge had met Matt when he'd accompanied Cody to the theater. "He can bring Cody. Not sure I would have time to pick him up otherwise." Not a great lie, but Arnie bought it, so it worked. And it made me tired. Secrets were exhausting.

I called my uncle and invited him to the cookout.

"Sounds good," he said. "Can I bring a date?"

"Is Bette here now?"

"Not yet. She'll be here Wednesday. Just a few more days." Uncle Bob couldn't keep the anticipation out of his voice. I'd never seen him happier than since he'd met her, even though they lived in different cities and only saw each other in person about once a month. Or maybe because of that. Maybe that kept the relationship exciting. Maybe familiarity was the death of romance. Maybe Matt and I wouldn't make it once he really knew me. Maybe...

"But I do want to bring somebody." Uncle Bob's voice stopped my mind from wandering too close to that particular edge. "Your dad."

* * *

"Hey, Cody."

"Olive-y!" The joy in my brother's voice made me smile. I'd called him once I got out of the worst of the Valley traffic. Now there was just desert on either side, wide-open blue sky in front of me.

"You free Monday night?" I asked.

"Sure...But Mondays are dark."

"They are indeed."

I'd taken Cody to the theater these past couple of years, and he'd become a real fan. He saw every show I was in, accompanied me to previews, and learned that most theaters didn't perform on Monday. Their lights were off, so they were "dark."

"But we'll get to see stars in the desert," I said.

"Stars like Brad Pitt?" Brad Pitt was Cody's favorite actor, probably because people compared the two of them all the time. My brother was one handsome man.

"No Brad Pitt. Just yours truly, Uncle Bob, a few tourists, and a bunch of cowboys. And Dad."

"Olive-y..." A whine crept into Cody's voice.

I mentally kicked myself. Some people might find my beating around the bush a fun tease, a little puzzle, but to Cody it was like nails on a chalkboard. He needed me to be concrete so he could process things in a linear fashion. "I'm inviting you to a cookout in the desert— a cowboy-style party—at Gold Bug Gulch, that new western town. I'm working there right now."

"Cool. Did you say Dad was coming?"

"Uncle Bob wants to invite him. I don't know if he'll come." Until a few months ago, our dad saw Cody and me once a year at Christmas, even though he and my mom lived in Prescott—just an hour and a half from Phoenix. Recently though, Dad had begun tiptoeing around the edges of our lives—calling, mailing articles he'd cut out of the paper, and even coming to town and taking us out to dinner a couple of times.

"He'll come," Cody said. "He loves cowboys. Hey, do we get to ride horses?"

"Not sure. Wait, Dad loves cowboys?"

"Duh. Why do you think he named me Cody?"

CHAPTER 26

Something was in the wind when I pulled into Gold Bug Gulch. And it didn't smell pretty.

I followed my nose. Just downhill of the saloon was a puddle of brown sludge. I didn't need to ask what it was. The smell gave it away. That and the Pretty Good Plumbers truck parked in the dirt street outside of the saloon. A stout woman in a ball cap came out of the saloon, wiping her hands on her coveralls. "Yeah, we're going to have to pump this sucker, that's for sure."

"Just do it." Nathan stalked out of the building after her. "Do it now. We got people coming tomorrow. A couple of busloads of tourists, even."

"I'll do what I can, but..." The plumber waved away the stinky air. "This place isn't gonna smell like gardenias. Not by tomorrow."

"Nathan!" Josh strode up the road, yelling as he walked, his blacksmith's glasses pushed up on his head. "This is a riparian area. We can't have sewage flowing into the stream."

"Like that was my plan." Nathan ran his hands through his overly gelled hair. It didn't move.

"We've never had a problem with the septic tank in all these years," said Josh. "What in the hell happened? You install the new lines wrong?"

The plumber's face grew red. "We did everything by the book. The system flooded somehow. Too much water and *whoosh*—it all overflows into the drainfield before it's processed."

"Fancy way of saying it's still crap," said Nathan.

"Flooded?" Josh stood with his hands at his sides, like a cowboy about to draw. "And how exactly did that happen?"

"Got me." The plumber tugged on her cap. "Usually see this sort of thing when there's a flash flood, but..."

It hadn't rained in a month. Wait..."Could someone flood it with a hose?" I asked.

"What do you mean?" Josh said.

"Billie said there was a garden hose in the opera house toilet."

"That could do it," said the plumber.

"So somebody flooded the system on purpose?" Josh asked.

"Could have," the plumber said. "Did a real nice job of it too."

Nathan walked back into the saloon. I followed at what I thought was a respectful distance, but I must have been a little too close because I nearly ran into him when he whirled on me. "What? What now?" He had a little sweat moustache.

"Can I help? There's got to be something we can do. We don't want the tourists, or, omigod, the investors to get wind of this problem." I meant it literally. Pee-u.

"Yeah, sure, the plumber can't help, but you can, right? Make it smell like gardenias?"

"Gardenias...Omigod." I was so excited by my brainwave that I nearly did a little happy dance, but it seemed inappropriate given the raw sewage issue. "Maybe I can help. If I had a thousand bucks..."

"I'd pay double that to clean up this business."

"Are you serious?"

Nathan did something with his head that could have been a nod. "Now, I got work to do." He turned around and walked toward his office.

I followed him inside. "Wait. About the chuckwagon cookout on Monday: what time should I be there?" I snuck a look in his wastebasket for anything gross (i.e., anything that might have his DNA on it). Spotless. Must have just been emptied. "Do you want me to greet the investors? Maybe make name tags?" Lame, I know, but maybe, just maybe Nathan would tell me their names.

"Greet 'em, sure. God, that mess better be cleaned up by then. Gotta show these guys a good time. Hey"—he seemed to see me for the first time that day—"you can wear your saloon girl costume."

"No." I was not going to show anyone a good time in that costume. Not even if it involved tap dancing (I loved tap dancing).

Nathan's eyes narrowed. He did not seem like the kind of guy you said "no" to.

I thought fast. "This is a family-friendly event, right? Isn't that why I was supposed to invite my family?"

"Whosaidyoushouinvi—"

"Arnie wanted them to come."

"Oh. Well. Whatever." Nathan's expression softened at Arnie's name. He almost looked like a halfway decent guy. Almost. Then he went back into his office and slammed the door shut.

I pulled out my cell and called Arnie. He picked up without singing—a good sign, since I needed him to be clear-headed. I told him about the plumbing problem, then said, "I told Nathan I could fix it for a thousand dollars, and he said he'd pay twice that. Do you think he meant it?"

"Sure," said Arnie. "And if I'm wrong about that, I'll cover the costs."

I was hoping he'd say that. "Great. Maybe you can help me coordinate this." I told him my plan and we got everything mapped out.

CHAPTER 27

As I walked down to the creek to meet Frank, I thought about my response to the saloon girl costume. I was an actress in my twenties. I'd certainly worn revealing costumes before. Sometimes they'd even been helpful in my investigations, since getting information from men was often easier when they weren't looking at my face. So what was my issue? Authenticity? Maybe. My other costumes had suited whatever character I was playing. But there was more to my reaction, I knew. Just wasn't sure what it was.

But the whispering cottonwoods and the green grass and the musical stream worked their magic on me, so by the time I saw Frank perched on a log by the creek, I was positively chipper. He waved at me. "Want to eat here or at my house?"

"I only have an hour before rehearsal, and I'd really like to see your place, so let's eat there."

Frank clambered off the log. "Follow me." We crossed the creek and headed east. Within a few minutes, I had to look back over my shoulder to make sure the green riparian area wasn't a mirage. Brown desert and rocky mountains stretched to the horizon, broken only by cactus, scrub brush, and the occasional mesquite tree. We trudged about five minutes, the sun hot on our heads even in November.

"Home sweet home." Frank pointed up a hill toward something that looked like one of the un-renovated buildings in the ghost town. The shack had been cobbled together of mismatched lumber, the spaces between the wood sealed with tar and...maybe mud?

"Built it myself. Started construction, oh, back in '79, when I was fresh out of college. Wanted to live off the land, you know. And I did—*have*—ever since."

"I thought all this was BLM land."

"It is. But the Bureau o' Land Management, they don't bother me too much. It's not like it's good land. Anything nice about it is 'cause of me. Like these trees." Frank stopped underneath one of two mesquite trees. Its lacy leaves gave almost no shade. "Planted these babies too." He thwacked the mesquite tree fondly and pointed toward another one that struggled to provide shade to Frank's shack. "Plus the BLM was scared of me."

"Why?'

"I'm an environmental activist. You know *The Monkey Wrench Gang*?"

"Edward Abbey, right? Something about protecting the land through...eco-terrorism?" Like the wolf traps he had supposedly vandalized?

"Not terrorism. Just...mischief." He grinned. He did look mischievous, like a leprechaun who'd been left out in the sun too long. "Anyway, I figured out a really good way to keep the BLM away whenever they came poking around. I'd just stroll out to meet them buck naked, except for my shotgun."

That would work. Especially the naked part. Frank was the kind of scrawny where you could see every joint sticking through his skin, and that skin was tanned so dark you couldn't tell where his shins stopped and his boots started. Put that all together with a bit of man-chicken dangling between his legs—couldn't be a pretty picture.

"Want a tour?" Frank said as we reached the shack.

"You bet." My enthusiasm was not feigned. How often would I get to see how a true desert rat lived?

He opened the door for me, and I stepped inside. The interior was dark, only a few bars of sunlight coming through the windows, which were shuttered from the outside.

"Got to keep it shut up during the day to keep it cool, you know."

Cool was a stretch.

"I open the window and the shutters at night, or when there's a nice breeze. About twice a year." He laughed. "That's a joke. It's really not too bad for about half the year."

I wondered which half he was talking about. It was November—already into Arizona's cool season—and the interior of the place felt like it was ninety. If it hadn't been for the dust in the air (the cabin had a dirt floor), I could have sworn we were in a sauna.

Frank pushed a button on a battery-operated lantern that swung from a beam. "Nice, these long-lasting LEDs. Used to have to use a Coleman lantern or kerosene. Always felt bad about that. Not exactly environmentally friendly, you know. Tried to make my own candles for a while, but they never gave off enough light. Plus I was using tallow. You ever smelled it?"

I shook my head.

"Let's just say there's a reason they use soy for candles now." He pointed at an old iron woodstove that took up a large portion of the shack. "I cooked on that stove. In the winter, that is. Too hot in the summer. Then I cooked outside over a fire. At night."

"Did you say 'cooked'?" Did Frank mean to use past tense?

"Yeah, I'm a good cook. As long as it's beans."

Another bean aficionado. I knew I liked the guy.

"But that stove also kept me warm in the winter. It can get down to freezing every so often." Frank motioned to a twin bed shoved up against the wall. "I thought about building a sleeping loft," he said. "One of my buddies in Northern California had a sweet set-up like that; more space below and more privacy. But this is Arizona. Heat rises."

"Yeah." I wiped a trickle of sweat from my face.

"Oh, sorry. I forget that everyone's not as acclimatized as me." He opened the door and we stepped outside.

"Where's your garden?" The only green things around were the mesquite trees.

"It's up at my new house. Next stop on the tour."

A new house. That was why he'd used the past tense.

"Do we have time?"

"It's just on the other side of this hill."

Frank was quicker than me, so by the time I reached the top of the hill, he was surveying his kingdom proudly, hands on his skinny hips. "Built this one myself too. Well, I designed it and helped finish some of the inside. It's a beauty, huh?"

Wow. The view stole whatever breath I had left after my climb. The house at the bottom of the small hill was built in concentric squares. The largest one was the house. Its whitewashed walls

surrounded the second square—an interior courtyard full of plants—
and a small square pond in the center reflected blue sky.

"It's a straw bale house," Frank said as we walked toward it.
"Wait'll you feel the difference in temperature."

When we got to the house, Frank held open the front door, a
massive wooden one carved in a Spanish style. He patted it fondly.
"Reclaimed this beauty from a tear-down in Ajo."

I stepped inside. The interior was dark, but in a pleasant dusky
way, unlike the claustrophobic gloom of Frank's cabin. There was
Saltillo tile underfoot and wooden beams overhead. A beehive fireplace
graced one corner of the room, and candles filled niches carved out of
the two-foot-thick walls. The wall facing the courtyard was all windows
and sliding glass doors, visually enlarging the room and showcasing
the greenery-filled courtyard.

Frank slid open one of the glass doors. "Let's eat out here. It's
pretty cool right now, and you can see my garden."

We ate lunch on a stone bench. "I've got my fall garden going
now. Planting season is different in the desert, you know. Right there
are the three sisters." He pointed at a raised bed, where the tasseled
heads of corn rose above a mass of green vines. "When you plant those
three—corn, beans and squash—together, they all help each other. See
how the beans are using the cornstalks for support? And those big
squash leaves keep the ground cool, while beans put nitrogen back into
the soil. And over there," he smiled slyly, "is my cactus garden, which
may just have a few rescued Acuna cactus in it."

Frank talked about the garden and the house nonstop during
lunch, which was good because I was speechless. I'd thought I was
doing some poor old guy a favor by bringing him lunch, but from the
looks of this house, he could afford a lot better than cheese sandwiches
and cheap beer. Still, he scarfed those down, talking all the while.
"People come from miles around to look at the house. It's even going to
be on some green home tour in a couple weeks." Frank brushed the
crumbs from his lap and stood up. "Well, missie, about time for you to
get to rehearsal. Can I offer you a ride?"

I must have looked surprised, because Frank laughed. "Yeah, I got
a car. What'd you think, I walked everywhere?"

Yeah, I kind of had. I'd been thinking of Frank as some modern-day version of those crazy miners you used to see in old Westerns. I followed him back into the house and out a different door, where a Toyota Prius waited on the gravel drive. It beeped as Frank unlocked it.

"Nice car," I said as I slid onto the leather seat.

"First one I've had in years." So I wasn't that far off. "Came into a little money a couple years ago." He pulled out onto the dirt road that led to the Gulch.

"A pretty big change for you."

Frank laughed happily. "Yes, indeed. And no one appreciates it more than me." His expression abruptly changed. "Dammit." He scowled at something through the windshield. "I'll have to get back here later and pick up all this crap." We drove past the object of Frank's ire, the remains of a bonfire ringed with beer cans and plastic bags. "People," he groused. "Can't live with 'em, can't shoot 'em."

CHAPTER 28

Frank stopped in front of the opera house and let me out. I waved at him as he drove off and turned to go to rehearsal. Then the wind shifted.

Gluhhh. The plumbing truck was gone, but the odor was not. The sludgy brown pool had been covered with something that looked like kitty litter, but it didn't mask the sewage smell. Maybe we needed one more piece of ammunition. Hmm. I pulled out my phone, did a Google search, and found exactly what I needed.

I nearly skipped on my way into dress rehearsal. I loved making things right.

My mood darkened as I walked into the windowless theater. Weird. I loved theaters. Just being in the space usually made me think of exotic costumes and happy chattering audiences and the beautiful, beautiful sound of applause. Today, this theater felt oppressive, like a gloved hand too near my throat. I shook off the feeling and headed toward what was probably the root cause of the unease. Billie and Chance stood onstage. Their backs were to me, but it didn't take a detective to read their body language.

"Kaput," I heard Billie say as I got closer. "You've got to understand that." She turned, saw me, and gave me an actress's smile. "Ivy, go on back to the dressing room and get into costume." Chance was already dressed in a vest, neckerchief, and gun belt, his typical cowboy hat on his head. "Remember to wear both, the white dress over the green costume. You'll also find two wigs. Put on Rose's one—you'll be able to tell which is which—and bring Fannie's out with you."

Wigs were a good thing. I had a little hair dye accident this past summer and had to get most of my hair cut off. It had grown out some, but the longest layer barely reached my chin. Plus my mouse-brown roots showed through the blonde right now. It wasn't too bad—Matt said it gave me an edgy rocker look—but it certainly wouldn't have flown in the 1890s.

The dressing room door was open, and the two wigs sat on the counter, pinned to Styrofoam mannequin heads. One of them was a red up-do with a green feather pinned to it. The other, long blonde curls with a small straw hat fastened on top.

I squeezed into the saloon girl outfit, then put my arms through the white dress, and Velcro-ed it up the front. Pretty impressive, this two costumes at once business. The saloon girl outfit acted like sturdy undergarments and the white dress slipped right over it. I put on a wig cap, bobby-pinned the ingénue wig to my head, tucked the mannequin head with the red wig under my arm, and walked softly back to the stage, hoping I might overhear something more. And I did.

"Yes!" Chance yelled. "YES!" He grabbed Billie in a hug and whirled her around. I hadn't needed to be quiet. All of Gold Bug Gulch could've heard him.

"Thank God," Billie said. "Now put me down."

"What happened?" I used my ditz voice. After all, Chance didn't know I wasn't dumb. "Did they fix the toilets?"

"That too," said Billie. "But Chance is whoopin' and hollerin' on account of a phone call he got from the sheriff's office. They just ruled Mongo's death an accident."

"Seems awfully expedient to me." I sat in my truck in Gold Bug's parking lot, talking to my uncle on the phone and watching Billie and Chance walk to his pickup. She'd looked a little dazed all through rehearsal, while Chance had been almost manic.

"Yeah, but it would be pretty hard to prove it was anything except an accident," Uncle Bob said. "And sure, the decision was made pretty fast, but I've seen quicker. You have to remember that Gold Bug Gulch probably brings in a nice bit of money for the area, even just starting out. And then there's the fact that we're one of the most gun-friendly states in the union."

Chance opened his truck's door for Billie. She stood beside it for a moment, then got in. He shut the door behind her and ran around to the driver's side. Literally ran, like he was afraid she might get out again.

"And Chance could still be sued by the family," Uncle Bob said. "Or brought up on charges, most likely negligent homicide."

"Homicide?" Chance and Billie pulled out of the lot and onto the highway, toward Wickenburg.

"Yeah," said Uncle Bob. "He's not off the hook yet."

CHAPTER 29

"But you always say that a bad preview means a good opening night," said Cody, who had attended his share of bad previews with me. He sat on my couch next to his girlfriend, Sarah.

"But this was a bad dress rehearsal and we don't have a preview," I said. "I'm not sure that counts with the gods of theater."

"The gods of theater?" Sarah had dressed for her date with Cody in a flowered top and pressed jeans and let her dark curly hair hang free past her shoulders. My brother had spiffed up too, his blond hair and favorite blue shirt both freshly washed.

"That's just Ivy's way of talking about luck and superstition." Matt carried a big bowl of popcorn in from the kitchen.

"And fate," I said. "Don't forget fate. Like the fate I'm facing: having to be onstage in front of an audience tomorrow after today's disaster." Not only were Billie and Chance off during rehearsal, the melodrama was comical in all the wrong places, mostly due to our costume changes.

"Your wigs really fell off?" asked Cody.

"Both of them. Twice each. And my costume kept unzipping itself." The white dress fit a little too snugly, so every time I raised my arms, riiiiiiiip, the Velcro opened wide down the front. Billie promised to fix it before our opening show.

Matt sat the popcorn on the coffee table in front of the couch, slid the DVD into the DVD thingie, and joined me on the floor. My couch fit three people, but tightly, so it made sense that he sat next to me. Still, I made sure to keep an inch of space between us. After all, Cody was right there.

"*Cody*," said Sarah. I felt her pluck something from my hair. "Popcorn. Your brother," she said with fondness in her voice.

"Oops. Sorry," said Cody. The menu popped up on my TV screen. "Matt, you *bought* this movie for Olive-y?"

"Yeah..."

I jumped in. "I've had it on hold at the library for ages. I even checked with the library. They think someone took it."

"Maybe you should investigate," Cody said.

"Ivy Meadows, overdue book detective." Matt grinned at me. "I like it."

"It might be less dangerous," said Sarah. Cody had regaled her with one too many stories of my escapades.

"I don't know," Matt said. "Someone might throw the book at her."

"Omigod," I groaned. "You sound like Uncle Bob."

"I'll take that as a compliment."

"Did you get the part yet?" asked Cody. "Of Annie?"

"No word, but I haven't heard that they cast it." I crossed my fingers.

"You're auditioning for this part but haven't seen the movie?" Sarah asked as the credits began to roll.

"I know. I couldn't even get hold of the script—oh, duh." I slapped myself on the forehead. "I probably could have found the screenplay online. Oh well, doesn't matter now. And I did read a bunch about Annie Oakley. Did you know she was a Quaker? It's one of the reasons she always dressed so modestly. They tried to talk her into sexier costumes, but she wouldn't do it. Even sewed her own costumes. She could do anything...ha! That's a song from the play...do you know 'I Can Do Anything Better Than You?'" I asked Matt.

"I don't know, I do make a mean omelet."

"No, it's a song..." I stopped. Matt was smiling at me. "Oh. Ha!" Then I sang, "Any egg you can break I can break better, I can break any egg better than you..."

"Olive-y." Cody sighed exaggeratedly. "Can we just watch the movie?"

One hundred and seven minutes later, we sat silent as the end credits rolled.

"But..." said Cody.

"Yeah," said Matt.

"I thought you said Annie didn't wear sexy costumes," said Sarah.

"She didn't. She wouldn't. She would have never worn that strapless outfit." My jaw ached. It had been clenched for nearly one hundred and seven minutes.

"She was dumb," said Cody.

"She was *not* dumb. She may have been uneducated, but she was not stupid." I grabbed the remote and turned off the TV. "I am so pissed for her. If Annie saw this film, she'd roll over in her grave and shoot someone. Did you know she spent five years of her life fighting a false story about her in the newspapers? A Chicago paper said she was jailed for stealing a man's trousers in order to pay for cocaine. Turns out it was a burlesque performer who called herself 'Any Oakley.' The real Annie traveled the country and spent tons of money until she had her reputation back. She would have never stood for this...this drivel." I jumped up and walked the few steps to the TV.

Matt was reading the back of the DVD box. "It does say the film is loosely based on her."

"Loosely! It's the exact opposite of her—okay, of what I know of her." I took the offending DVD out of the player. "They made her seem dumb—"

"I told you," said Cody.

"And man-crazy," I continued. "When it was Frank Butler who wooed her."

"I'm sure they did it to create a good story," Matt said. "You know, like Eliza Doolittle getting made over?"

"Omigod, that scene where they decided to make Annie look 'pretty'? I thought I was going to scream."

"I didn't like that," said Sarah. "What's wrong with freckles?"

"Nothing." Cody took Sarah's hand.

"But worst of all was the way she decided to lose her marksmanship contest at the end, just so Frank wouldn't feel threatened by her. I can't believe it. They took this amazingly strong woman and made her a simpering husband-hunter who gave up her integrity for a man." I burst into tears. Wow, where did that come from?

Matt jumped up and hugged me. I let him for just a second—it felt so good—then pushed him away. "I'm sorry. I don't know why I'm so upset."

"Because you don't like people calling other people stupid," said Cody. "Especially when they're not."

"I think that's it," said Matt. "You do have a strong sense of justice. And this," he waved at the TV, "just seems unfair."

"That's it. It's not fair, especially to someone like Annie. But that said..."

"Yeah?" said Matt.

"If I'm being fair, I have to admit..." I wiped my eyes. "The music *was* pretty awesome."

CHAPTER 30

After stopping in Sunnydale to set up the four wildlife cameras I bought with Arnie's credit card, I drove out Gold Bug Gulch, pulling into the parking lot at six thirty. Yep, six thirty *a.m.* Even so, the plants beat me there. Several big panel vans were already in the parking lot. I pulled up next to the one that had "Alan Greensman" painted across its side.

A hefty guy in a green shirt got out of the van. "Mornin', Ivy." He sniffed the air and wrinkled his nose. "Phew. Looks like we have our work cut out for us."

"Hey, Alan. So you think we can do it?"

"I brought the most highly scented plants I could find: stock, gardenias, jasmine, a bunch of hanging baskets of sweet alyssum, and fragrant petunias, that sort of thing."

"And I," I waved at the back of my pickup, "brought backup air fresheners and battery-operated fans."

Alan's pudgy face creased in a smile. "You are just short of brilliant."

I nodded my thanks. "Let me show you where to set up." We walked toward the town.

I'd met Alan about a year ago on a film that was shot in Arizona but supposed to be set in Hawaii. He and his crew had transformed the landscape of the resort where we filmed from desert to tropical paradise, just by adding potted palms, hibiscus, and a load of other lush-looking plants.

"Only these few buildings are open." I pointed at the saloon, the opera house, and the reptile house. "The jail photo booth and blacksmith are also open, but I think they're far enough away from the septic tank that the smell won't be an issue there."

Alan rubbed the morning stubble on his face. "I don't think we have enough plants to hide that." He waved at the kitty-littered brown sludge pond down the hill.

"I was thinking more diversion than screening. Kind of like when someone is coming over to my apartment but I don't have time to clean, so I buy flowers on the way home. All anyone sees is the flowers."

"Ah ha. So you want us to put these plants along the front porches of the buildings, to draw people's eyes away from the mess."

"Exactly. It'll look pretty and they'll walk right into a good smell. I also have floral-scented air fresheners we can tuck into the plants and place inside the buildings too."

"Did you say something about fans?"

"That was my friend Arnie's idea. I bought a bunch of those small personal battery-operated fans. We can tuck them into the plants too."

"So the scent is blown toward the tourists."

"Right." The strains of "Maple Leaf Rag" floated out of the saloon. "The piano player I hired should distract folks too."

"Nice. But..." Alan looked at the sludge puddle. "You sure you don't want me put a few plants around that, to try and screen it?"

"Nah. I've got an even better idea."

"Look, Mama. Goats!" The little boy pointed down the hill where three goats grazed in the grass. "Can we go see them?"

"No." The boy's mom pointed at a sign I'd planted on the edge of the hill. "It says not to disturb them while they're working. Besides," she wrinkled her nose, "they're a little stinky. Let's go see the blacksmith instead."

"You're a genius," said Billie, who stood beside me on the porch of the Arnold Opera House underneath a hanging basket that hummed, thanks to one of Arnie's fans. "The flowers I get—though it's a damn good idea—but how did you ever come up with goats?"

"I was trying to think of something smelly that people still like. Sort of like stinky cheese." As if on cue, one of the goats gamboled in the grass, and the crowd said, "Aww" in almost one voice. "I'd heard that people rent them out to get rid of undergrowth. Sort of like organic lawnmowers."

"Hey!" Nathan strode toward us from the parking lot. "What is all this?"

"I tried to find you earlier," I began.

"Isn't it great?" said Billie.

"Who gave you permission?" Nathan got right in my face.

I stepped back. "You did, when we talked yesterday."

"Gondranmedry."

"No, I am not going to drain you dry. I kept the costs under the two thousand we talked about—"

"Two thousand?!"

"What the hell?" Josh steamed toward us like a freight train. "Get those goats out of there."

"But they're working to distract—" I said.

"They're eating the grass. This is a delicate riparian area."

"You sound like Frank," muttered Nathan.

"I sound like someone who gives a good goddamn about what happens to this land."

"Stillsounlifrank."

"Get them out of here, or there'll be goat on the grill tonight." Josh looked like he'd be happy to kill and butcher them himself.

"Okay," I said. "Sheesh. My phone is in the dressing room. I'll call the goatherd right away."

"Good." Josh turned and strode down the street toward his forge. Nathan stomped up the stairs to the saloon, mumbling something even I couldn't understand as he ducked under a bower of jasmine.

"How do you account for that?" Billie talked to me but watched the two men as they walked away. "Coulda sworn they were mad that you saved the day."

CHAPTER 31

"Save me!" I cried.

This was where Chance was supposed to, yes, save me. As Blackheart, he had tied me to a train track then dashed offstage. His change in the wings was pretty simple: he just had to take off his long black coat and trade his villain's black top hat for his hero's white cowboy hat. Then he would run back on and untie me. But instead he just stood there in the wings next to Billie, who had picked up the "Applause" sign.

"Save me!" I yelled again. The recorded train noise grew louder.

Chance just stared at the stage. Then he pointed at a spot about a foot from my face.

"Aaaah! Save me!" I wasn't acting anymore. "Help!" The biggest hairiest spider I'd ever seen crawled toward my eye. My *eye*. The audience screamed. I struggled with the ropes, but Chance had tied them tight.

"I've got you, my dear," said a strange-sounding voice behind me. Someone slid arms under my armpits and dragged me away from the spider. "Don't worry," Billie whispered in her real voice. She was wearing Chance's cowboy hat. Must've run onstage in his place. "Tarantulas are mostly harmless and really slow."

Looking sheepish, Chance walked on holding up the applause sign. The audience clapped—at first. "Look at that," I heard someone say. "Is it real?"

It was real, it was a Gila monster, and it was onstage with us too. "It's slow too," Billie said into my ear as she untied the ropes that bound my hands. "Just stay away from it, and we should be all right. It's poisonous, but it can't kill us. I don't think." The foot-long black and orange lizard padded center stage, paused under a stage light, and lifted its head. The audience burst into applause.

"Didn't know they could train those," someone said.

"Chance," Billie whispered, just loud enough for the three of us to hear. "Go get the guy from the reptile house." He was off like a shot. "And Ivy, we need to clear the theater before any of these critters make their way into the audience."

"All's well that ends well," I said to the audience. I couldn't improvise to save my life, but I could recite Shakespeare. "So thank you all for coming and have a safe drive home." Yeah. Really couldn't improvise. I headed toward stage left, away from the Gila monster. Billie followed a few feet behind. I was almost to the wing when I heard a collective gasp from the audience. Then, a rattle.

"Don't move," Billie said behind me. "Stay really really still."

"Is it...?" I'd only heard that rattling sound in the movies.

"A diamondback," she said quietly. "Crawled out from behind one of the flats." I began to turn my head to see. "Really." Billie's voice, though soft, was sharp. "Don't move."

I heard footsteps. They got softer as they moved away from me, leaving me alone onstage with a pissed-off rattlesnake. I wondered if shaking in my boots counted as moving.

Footsteps came back across the stage. The audience murmured. "Okay," Billie said. "Now I want you to take a few slow steps toward the wing."

"I thought it was dangerous to move."

"It is. But I need you to distract the rattler."

So I was bait. Great. But I took a slow step. The rattling intensified. "Ohhh," said the audience.

"Ladies and gents," Billie said softly. "I need you to be absolutely quiet. Go on, Ivy."

I took another step. The sound of my heart pounding was drowned out by even louder rattling. Then...

"Gotcha!"

I turned my head. Billie had pinned the snake with a broom. She reached down and grabbed it right behind its head. "Can't turn and bite me from here," she said. She picked it up, holding the rest of the snake's body with her other hand. "Okay, folks, please proceed calmly out of the theater, staying quiet. But you," she said to a tourist busy snapping photos with his phone, "take a picture of me, would you? Send it to info at goldbug.com."

"For posterity?" I asked as quietly as I could while keeping a good, oh, twelve feet away from the rattler.

"For ammunition. I want a raise."

"But you just started work here, right?" Gold Bug Gulch had only been open a few weeks.

"I only want what's right. Chance gets paid more than me. Mongo did too. Nathan says it's because they handle guns." She held the snake up and it flicked its forked tongue at her. "I think a rattlesnake wrangler should be worth at least as much."

CHAPTER 32

"All those critters crawled onstage?"

"Yeah. Why?"

"Seems like they'd be more likely to hide somewhere dark." Uncle Bob flipped a burger on the grill, and it sizzled and popped. I wanted to talk to someone after my overly exciting day at the Gulch. Matt was busy working on a big paper that was due on Monday, so I stopped by my uncle's house and was persuaded to stay for dinner. Truth be told, I'd been hoping for an invitation. The only thing better than a talk with my uncle was a talk with him in his nice green backyard over one of his big juicy burgers and a cold beer. "I s'pose they could have been drawn by the warmth of the stage lights. But not real probable if you ask me."

I got up from my folding chair and went to stand near him, the heat from the barbecue somehow comforting. "The guy who manages the reptile house told us the animals escaped. But you're telling me that..."

"I don't think they'd head for the stage. Unless someone helped them get there."

After burgers and beer and a bit more conversation about reptiles and such, Uncle Bob and I sat in his small backyard, enjoying the balmy, barbecue-scented November evening.

"So the police said Mongo's death was an accident?" Uncle Bob settled into his lawn chair with a second beer.

"Yeah, but between that and the plumbing issue and the reptiles, I'm beginning to think there's something else going on. That maybe someone doesn't want Gold Bug Gulch to succeed."

"Like who?"

"There's a guy named Frank, an old desert rat who wants to protect some bats in the mine. Seems like kind of thing he might do."

"The vandalism or killing Mongo? Those are two different animals."

I sighed. "I know. I can't see any of the people I've met being involved in murder."

"Anyone else who could be involved?"

"Not sure. The only other people I've turned up are investors and employees. Why wouldn't they want Gold Bug to work out?"

We sat in silence for a moment, thinking and drinking in the coolness of the plant-filled backyard. My green-thumbed uncle was quite the gardener.

"This is beginning to sound dangerous," said Uncle Bob. "Maybe you shouldn't—"

"Hey," I said, "there's something else I wanted to ask."

"What's that?" My uncle wasn't usually so distractible. Maybe it was his third beer.

"Did you know Dad likes cowboys?"

"Yeah. It's always been a dream of his to own a little land and a few horses. He was even saving up for a place when you all lived in Spokane. Had his eye on a few acres over the state line in Idaho."

"Really? How do I not know this?"

"Probably because he gave up on it. After Cody's accident."

"Oh." I felt like I'd been socked in the stomach.

"Not your fault, Olive. Don't even go there."

How could I not? I'd never even thought about how Cody's accident had affected my parents' dreams. Just mine.

"Olive..." My uncle was reading my mind.

"Okay. Okay." Now I wanted to distract both of us: me from guilt-tripping myself into a bad place and Uncle Bob from worrying about any danger in Gold Bug. So I said the next thing that came to mind: "What do you know about *Annie Get Your Gun*?"

Uncle Bob leaned back and stretched his legs out. He loved showing off his trivia knowledge. "I know that Ethel Merman made the role famous in the stage play, but Bernadette Peters, Reba McEntire, and Susan Lucci—that soap opera star—played Annie too. I know that Rodgers and Hammerstein produced the original show. I know that

Jerome Kern was supposed to write the music, but he died, so they got Irving Berlin. They had to make a few replacements in the film too. Judy Garland was slated to star but got mad at Busby Berkley and started coming in late, generally making a mess of things. Probably more about pills than the director, but anyway, Judy was replaced by Betty Hutton, and Busby was replaced by George Sidney.

"The film won a couple of awards, but Berlin hated it. Word was he never liked Betty Hutton in the role, and he made enough noise about copyright to keep the film out of distribution for years. It wasn't until its fiftieth anniversary in 2000 when it was finally released on video."

I slapped at a mosquito. They loved Uncle Bob's backyard. His was one of the few in the neighborhood that had actual green plants that needed watering (most folks had desert landscaping; i.e., gravel and yucca). "And what do you know about Annie Oakley?"

"She was a famous sharpshooter, one of the most famous women in the world at one point. Married to Frank Butler, another sharpshooter. Toured with Buffalo Bill Cody's Wild West—Cody didn't say 'Wild West *show*' so that the, well, show seemed more authentic."

I waited, but there was nothing more except the sound of Uncle Bob nailing a mosquito. "That's it? That's all you know about Annie Oakley?"

Uncle Bob cleared his throat. "Uh, yeah."

Alrighty then. I knew what I had to do. If Annie Oakley could change the way the world thought about women, I could change the way the world thought about Annie Oakley. At least I could try.

When I got home, I made a quick call to Arnie and Marge, then called Billie. "I've got a piece of good news and a proposition. You'll have to talk to Nathan about what he pays you, but Arnie is giving you a raise for your melodrama work. Same pay as Chance."

Actually it was Marge who'd make sure Billie got a raise. When she heard about the pay difference, she was furious that Arnie had just accepted the numbers Nathan had quoted him. "Just saving us some money, babe," Arnie'd said. I hung up pretty quickly after that. Marge could really project.

"That's great. Thanks. What's the proposition?"

I explained my Annie Oakley brainwave.

"Love it," she said. "But..."

"I've got it all figured out. I just need your help with few things."

"You got it. Not only do I owe you one, but after seeing what you did today with goats and flowers, I'm a fan."

CHAPTER 33

On my way to Gold Bug the next morning, I swung by Sunnydale to check the wildlife cameras. Nothing. Several pictures of coyotes drinking out of the water hazards, but no Chihuahuas. No Lassie.

Light traffic on a Sunday, so I made it to Gold Bug two hours early, as promised. The sewer stink had dissipated and the flowers looked great, but...

"I miss the goats," Billie stood in the open door of the opera house, reading my mind. "Cute little guys," she said as I followed her inside. "Maybe I'll get a couple. Mongo never wanted any animals, except for horses. 'They earn their keep,' he'd said."

At last. A way to ask the question I needed to know. "Was it a money thing? Somebody said something about Mongo trying to get out of a business deal."

"Who? Josh?"

"I shouldn't say."

"It better not be Josh. After all it took for Mongo to put aside that old feud. Besides, far as I know, he hadn't invested yet. He was still thinking about it."

"Invested? In what?"

"I don't know. Some big secret deal. And I don't want to talk about it." Billie wiped at her eyes. "It's not you, Ivy. I just can't...Can we focus on this new Annie Oakley thing instead?"

"Of course. I'm so sorry." I was. I knew one of the best ways to get information out of people was to catch them when they were emotional, but I didn't like doing it. That said, I did like the new Josh info.

"So," she said. "I found a costume that'll work great and revamped the melodrama script. Good thing it's in the public domain. Chance should be here any minute. We should have time to run the new bit at least twice before the show."

But Chance didn't show up. Billie called his cell, but it just rang and rang.

"Do you think he's okay?" I asked

"You know, I'm not sure which he felt worse about, actually shooting Mongo or being suspected of doing it on purpose. Now that everyone knows it was an accident, well, he was celebrating pretty hard last night. Let's you and I run through the script."

We did, and I got dressed and in makeup and still no Chance. Finally, five minutes before showtime, he staggered into the hallway outside the dressing rooms. He looked like hell, unshaven and kind of pale green, but already in costume at least.

"All right," Billie said. "Since you missed rehearsal, you're just going to have to wing this. We made a few changes to the script. You don't tie Ivy to the tracks any more. You're going to push her offstage, hold a gun on her, and say these lines." She held a piece of paper out to Chance. "Then—"

"No. Not without rehearsal." Chance's voice sounded funny, throaty and staccato. He didn't reach for the page Billie held.

"You're supposed to be a professional," Billie said. "Act like one."

"Doing this without rehearsal is not professional."

"You know, we can wait—" I interrupted.

"C'mon, Chance, after all, we both know what a great actor you are."

Between Billie's taunting tone and Chance's glare, I could tell this was about more than a rehearsal. I was a detective, after all. They must have had a fight after leaving yesterday.

Chance grabbed the sheet of paper and stalked off to wait in the wings.

"You really want to go through with this without any rehearsal?" I asked Billie. Chance was right. It was unprofessional.

"It'll be okay," she said. "Chance really is a great actor."

The beginning of the show went fine. My costumes stayed put and no critters crawled across the stage. But as we neared the new unrehearsed section, my palms begin to sweat. It didn't help that Chance had a crazed look in his eyes.

He pushed me offstage right, like he was supposed to. Then he said something he wasn't supposed to: "I've got you now, my pretty." Offstage, I ran through the cramped backstage to stage right, undoing my Velcroed costume and unpinning my wig as I went.

"Ever danced with the devil in the pale moonlight?" Chance was being a good actor, pointing a gun at the place where he'd supposedly left me as Rose. He was also completely making up the script.

"You, escape?" Chance laughed at the invisible Rose's naivety. "You underestimate the power of the Dark Side." I skidded into place next to Billie, un-Velcroed my white dress, and dropped it to the floor. Billie grabbed the wig off my head.

"Go on, test me," Chance said. "Someone did once. I ate his liver with some fava beans and a nice chianti."

"Dammit." Billie guided my arms into a fake buckskin dress. "Chance's movie stuff works better than the lines I wrote."

"Just try to escape," he said. "Go ahead, make my day."

Billie jammed a cowboy hat on my head. The two pigtails attached to it hung on either side of my face. She handed me a rifle. "I re-checked. They're definitely blanks. Now go. You're on."

I was sweating bullets (pun intended). It wasn't just the fact that we were unrehearsed, or that I was handling a real gun, but that Chance wasn't following the script. I sucked at improv.

I stepped onstage. Billie came on right behind me. She held up a sign and the audience read aloud, "Why, it's Annie Oakley!"

"Turn, you no-good varmint." I said my scripted lines and pointed my rifle at Chance. "I won't shoot a man in the back."

Chance faced me, pointing his long-barreled pistol at my head. "Oh look, it's a girl with a gun. How sweet." He may have run out of movie lines, but he still wasn't following the script.

"Run like the wind, Rose!" I shouted at the space offstage where the ingénue supposedly cowered.

Chance watched the disappearing Rose. "She won't get far. And I'll punish her when I catch her. Hmm, now where did I put my whip?"

"Boo," said the audience. Billie must've held up that sign.

"And speaking of running, shouldn't you run home now?" Chance said. "Someone's going to be awfully mad if you don't have dinner on the table on time."

"Boo," the audience said again, even though Billie wasn't holding any sign.

"Guess I'd better hop to it then, 'specially since I need to shoot dinner, skin it, and cook it." I cocked my gun. "Or maybe I'll just have liver with some fava beans." The audience roared. Ha. First good bit of improv I ever delivered.

"Think you'd better stick with beans," Chance said. "That's an awfully big gun for a little girl."

I pulled the trigger. "*Boom!*" Chance dropped his gun, as if it'd been shot out of his hands. Good. He may have been improvising his dialogue, but he obviously read this part of the script. "That's for all your villainous deeds," I said. I stopped myself from rubbing my shoulder. Even full of blanks, the rifle had a kick.

"*Boom!*" Chance hopped as if avoiding a bullet at his feet. "That's for Rose."

"*Boom!*" He jerked his head so his black top hat fell off. "And that's for calling me a little girl."

The audience erupted into applause before Billie could even get the sign up. I kept the rifle trained on Chance. "Now, I'd like you to get over here and apologize to me." Chance didn't move. "Did you know I can shoot the apple off a dog's head?" I sighted the rifle at Chance's scalp. "Too bad you ain't got no apple."

He scuttled over to me.

"Now, I want you to say, 'My apologies, Miss Oakley, for being a whoreson beetle-headed, flap-ear'd knave.'"

"I didn't write that," Billie whispered next to me. I shrugged. Sometimes Shakespeare just came out of my mouth.

"My apologies, Miss—"

"And I want you to curtsey while saying it."

"My apologies, Miss Oakley, for being a whoreson, beetle-headed, flap-ear'd knave." Chance curtseyed, spreading his black villain's coat like a skirt. The audience roared its approval.

"That's all she wrote, folks," I said to the audience, "but if you'd like to hear the real story of Annie Oakley, come up and see me after the show."

Chance bowed and Billie held up a sign that said, "The End."

But I wasn't finished. I don't know what came over me. Maybe it was playing Annie Oakley. Maybe it was all those times I'd listened to the *Annie Get Your Gun* cast album. Maybe it was the glow I had from my first successful attempt at improv. All I know is that instead of bowing, I opened my mouth.

"It's fun business, this gun business, like none business I know." The audience exploded. Everybody loves that song. And my new version all rhymed. Ha.

"Every gal can be a crack gunslinger..." I sang. So far so good.

"All it takes is spunk and sass and smarts," I belted, a la Ethel Merman.

"Every shot she takes can be a zinger..." Ack! What rhymes with "zinger"?

"Just pull her finger..." Oh no. Please tell me I didn't just say that...

"She farts." Wow. Guess seventh grade is never really behind you.

Despite my last line (or maybe because of it) dozens of girls lined up to hear Annie's story after the show. And dozens more after the next two shows. Around five o'clock, Billie and I stood in front of the opera house, still in costume. We waved goodbye to the last stragglers and watched Chance perform a few roping tricks in the road. "Loved your stories," Billie said. "And your Annie Oakley was amazing."

"It's you who's amazing. Coming up with that Annie Oakley costume and new script so quickly."

"Pretty good for an old broad, huh?" Billie held a hand up against the sun—which illuminated a bruise on her forearm. I instinctively reached for her. She grabbed my hand and shook her head.

"That's new," I said quietly.

She shrugged. "Maybe now everyone will believe that it never was Mongo."

"Is it Chance?" I asked as he lassoed a delighted little boy.

She shook her head. "It's just sore losers. You wouldn't believe it. I finally figured it out. I found out where Mongo was going. All those times. It's not what I thought at all. It was something good."

Did Billie shake her head because her bruise wasn't caused by Chance? But he was a sore loser, right? As if on cue, he narrowed his eyes at Billie, then caught me watching him, and looked away.

And what wouldn't I believe—that it wasn't Chance or the new information about Mongo? "So where was Mongo going?"

Billie smiled. "I'll show you. I'll bring it to the next show."

"'It'? Ooh, I love a mystery."

"Yeah?" said a voice behind me. I must've been awfully focused on Billie not to have noticed Nathan coming up behind us. "Then maybe you can solve the mystery of the cars with flat tires."

"Shoot, Nathan, did someone let the air out of your tires?" Billie clucked her tongue in sympathy.

"Not just mine," Nathan said. "All the cars in the lot. All of 'em."

CHAPTER 34

"Everyone had flat tires?" asked Matt. "Every single car?"

"Yeah." I lay on my couch cradling my cell phone close to me. I wished it were Matt. "Employees' vehicles were the last to be aired up. That's why I'm calling so late."

"It's okay. I'm going to be up for a few more hours working on this paper." Matt yawned. "Do you think the flat tires are connected to the sewer system vandalism and the escaped reptiles?"

"Seems like it. But I can't figure out how Mongo's death figures in. It seems like such a big jump from vandalism to murder."

"And why start with murder? Wouldn't you start small?"

"Me, the criminal mastermind?" I smiled at Matt through the phone line, or cell tower or whatever. "You're right, I'd try something less extreme first...unless Mongo's death gave me the idea to begin causing more accidents..."

We were both quiet for a moment, thinking. Matt yawned again. "Sorry. Late nights. So, still no word about *Annie*?"

"No...You're not hoping that I don't get cast, are you?" Arghh. I wanted the words back the second they were out of my mouth.

A pause. "You know me better than that."

"I know, I know. I'm sorry, it's just that..." What? What was my problem? "I'm tired." That wasn't it, but I was too tired to figure out why I was behaving like a twelve-year-old.

"You do know I'm crazy about you, right? And that I want you to be happy?"

"Yeah. I do. Thanks." I hugged the phone again. "I'm just a tired idiot. See you tomorrow? At the cookout?"

"You bet. Good night. Sweet dreams, Ivy."

"Good night." We hung up.

I lay back on my couch and studied the water stain on my ceiling. Sometimes it looked like a heart. Other times it put me in mind of a bloodstain. Tonight it was both. What was up with me? Was I really afraid that Matt didn't want me to succeed as an actor? Getting the gig would mean a lot of time away from him, since Arizona Center Stage always had performances in Tucson as well as Phoenix. And it could lead to more jobs that took me away from him. But he had never said anything about that. Well, he'd talked—maybe complained—a little about my schedule. Or had he? Maybe that was me projecting my feelings. Maybe I was afraid...

Next thing I knew sunlight was streaming in my windows, and I had a crick in my shoulder from sleeping the entire night on the couch. Great. I'd hoped to get out to Sunnydale early this morning, scope out the desert perimeter, maybe stake out the water hazards. Lassie had been gone for over a week. I didn't like to think what that meant.

I grabbed a quick shower and changed into a clean t-shirt and not-so-clean jeans. I made coffee in my French press, poured it into two big to-go cups (I didn't have a thermos), and hit the road.

I was too late to catch a glimpse of any night creatures, including Chihuahuas and pugs. I ran by all of the cameras, checking on photos. Coyote. Coyote. Coyote. Hey, was that a black curly tail? I peered at the small black-and-white photo displayed on the camera's small screen. Might have been a pug-butt or might have been wishful thinking. I downloaded the photos onto a flash drive.

On the way into the office, I pulled into the Whataburger drive-through for another cup of coffee and ooh...a honey butter chicken biscuit. I scrounged through my purse, already salivating. Almost enough money. I raised up in my seat so I could check my jeans pockets. Yes! A crumpled five-dollar bill and...

The Kleenex Marge had given me that first night at Gold Bug. With blood on it. From me—and Nathan. "Woo-hoo!"

"I'm sorry," crackled the drive-through speaker. "We don't serve Yoo-hoo. Would you like a chocolate shake?"

"Yeah, I would. And a cup of coffee and a honey butter chicken biscuit." What the hell. I was celebrating.

The meal was gone by the time I got into the office. Uncle Bob was out on a call, but he'd left a note on top of my desk. "Found Acme Arizona," he wrote. "Incorporated in Nevada. Looks like it's owned by another business, Acme Alabama, which is also incorporated in Nevada. My antenna is up. Lots of shady folks have companies there or in Delaware or Wyoming—easier to hide stuff in those states. Asked my buddy in Nevada to check into it." Huh. We might be onto something.

I was packaging the DNA samples to drop off at a quick-turnaround lab when my phone buzzed. A text from Arizona Center Stage. I squeezed my eyes shut for a second, then looked. "Please let us know if you can make another callback at 3 p.m. this Wednesday."

I called Matt immediately, even before responding to the text. "I have another callback!"

"Congratulations!" Matt's voice was warm and sincere. Yep, I'd been an idiot.

"I guess these big theater companies have more callbacks. Maybe because they have so many more people auditioning. Not sure." I'd never gotten this far with Arizona Center Stage before. Getting the first two callbacks was a coup. Getting the third one was nothing short of miraculous.

"It's fabulous, Ivy," said Matt. "And so are you."

I hung up, happy happy happy. I texted the theater back, then powered up my computer. I grabbed the flash drive from my bag, slipped it into the USB port, and scrolled through the photos, holding my breath and...omigod, what a day. "It's Lassie's butt!" I said when Arnie picked up. "Your new camera took a picture of Lassie's rear end. He's alive!"

After I hung up, I did a little happy dance. We had a lead on the Gold Bug case, my acting career and love life were on the rise, and Lassie was alive. The world looked pretty good.

Until that night.

CHAPTER 35

Five men in black hats took up the breadth of the street, walking slowly toward us, squinting in the late afternoon sun. The haunting strains of "The Good, the Bad, and the Ugly" hung in the dusty air.

"Installed those speakers today," said Josh, who stood beside me on the saloon's porch. "Love that music."

Nathan burst out of the swinging doors behind us and scuttled down the steps like a beetle. "Welcome to Gold Bug Gulch." He walked toward the group, who now stood still in the middle of the street, like a posse waiting for a hanging. "Glad you could make it for our Sundown Showdown cookout."

"Showdown?" I whispered.

"Nathan added a gunfight." Josh had swapped out his blacksmith duds for a tan Stetson, Wranglers, and a fitted Western shirt. He cleaned up nicely, but there was still something...untamed about him. Like a pet cougar. "We're supposed to be surprised by bandits. Well, one bandit in this case. Chance."

"One bandit doesn't sound like a showdown."

"I shoot him. And don't worry." He patted the pistol he wore on his hip. "I checked both guns. All blanks."

"Umm." I bit my lip.

"You can check this one." Josh handed me his pistol. "But you'll just have to trust us on Chance's gun."

I shook the round out of Josh's gun and into my hand. All blanks. It was pretty easy to tell: live ammunition has a projectile at the end of the bullet, while blanks are shorter, with the tips crimped closed.

Josh took the gun and put the blanks back in the chamber,

showing me as he did it. "Satisfied?" I nodded, though I really wished I could check Chance's gun too.

Nathan clomped up the stairs to the porch, followed by the The Good, the Bad, and the Ugly. Josh tipped his hat. "Howdy, partners." He stuck out a hand. "And I do mean partners. I'm Josh Tate. One of your fellow investors. Pleased to meet you." He turned to me. "This is Ivy Meadows, one of our actors. She'll be along for the ride tonight."

I was in costume as Rose, so I curtseyed and demurely lowered my eyes like a good ingénue. Through my eyelashes, I could see the men checking me out. Glad I'd said no to the saloon girl outfit.

Nathan held the saloon's swinging door open with his body, so he had hands free to greet the men. "Mario." He glad-handed a short portly fellow. "Great to see you again. Alfonso, how's your mother?" he said to another. After greeting all the men, he said, "Josh, why don't you join us for a minute?" Then to me, "I'll be out when we're finished with business. Don't bug me until then. If your guests arrive beforehand, they'll just have to wait." Nathan's face was bathed in a fine sheen of sweat, even though it was five o'clock and a very pleasant seventy-eight degrees. "Got it?"

I swallowed a smart-aleck reply about understanding simple commands and nodded. Nathan followed the investors into the saloon. I turned my attention to the horses, who waited patiently in the dirt road, tied to the porch railing of the jail across the way. They were all turned away from me, their tails twitching at unseen flies.

I knew nothing about horses. Never even been up close to one. Uncle Bob, Matt, Cody, and Dad wouldn't arrive for a little while, so I had a few minutes to appease my curiosity. I walked over to where the horses stood facing the building. Wow. They were so tall and muscular. "You all are so handsome," I said, creeping closer.

"Ivy!" My dad's voice. "Don't you know better than that?"

I stopped.

"Don't walk up behind a horse. You're likely to get your teeth kicked in."

I backed up a little and faced my family. "Oh, these horses know me," I lied. "Long as I talk to them, they're fine."

Why did I lie? I didn't know, probably something to do with not looking stupid in front of my dad, though from the look on his face he wasn't fooled. Uncle Bob swallowed a smile too. Cody just hugged me. "Olive-y. You look pretty."

"Thank you kindly, sir." I smoothed down my dress, which I suddenly realized was white and not exactly the thing to wear on a trail ride. Oh well. "Hey, where's Matt?"

"I told him he didn't need to come along, since I was in town and could pick up Cody," my dad said, making his way to the horses. "Nice of him to offer though."

"I wish he came," Cody whispered to me.

"Me too." I really did. Not just because I missed him, not just for moral support, and not just because I thought he'd have a good time, but because it was me who kept him in the role of Cody's caretaker rather than my boyfriend. My secretiveness screwed up his chance to be here. One more arrow in his "let's not keep our relationship secret" quiver.

"I wish Mom came too," said Cody. "She never comes."

"She's not much for horses." My dad stroked the nose of a tall brown one.

She wasn't much for her offspring either, but I didn't go there. Having Dad with us was miracle enough.

"You work here?" Cody looked around him, wide-eyed. "It's like a movie."

"Cool, huh? And yeah, I heard Nathan was just approached by a film crew yesterday."

"That should be profitable," Dad said.

"Maybe." I'd worked enough in the acting business to know that film stuff often fell through. "So what breed is this one?" I pointed to a small horse with a sad-looking tail. He also had ears that seemed a bit too big for his head, but a nice fuzziness the other horses lacked.

"That," said Uncle Bob, "is a Don King."

"Like the fight promoter?"

"A *donkey*." Cody laughed, but not at me. "Haven't you ever seen a donkey?"

"I thought they were smaller." This one was pretty tall. He did however, look like a donkey. And I looked like an ass.

"Ivy, you like Toby?" Josh joined our little group.

"Isn't he big for a donkey?"

"Sort of," said Josh. "Do you want to ride him?"

Toby looked at me with liquid brown eyes that seemed kind, in a donkey sort of way.

"That would be great," I said.

"All right, I'll get him saddled up." Josh looked at my outfit and frowned.

"I know. Hope this dress bleaches okay."

"And hope you can ride sidesaddle," said Josh. "I'll get you one in a minute. Anyone else see a horse they'd like to ride?"

My dad patted the tall brown one he'd been with the whole time. "I'd like this one."

"Okay, you take Jack. I think you might like Sassy," he said to Uncle Bob, giving him the reins of a whitish gray horse. "And you," he said to my brother, "should ride Cody."

"Cody? That's my name." My brother smiled so big he looked like he had an extra set of teeth.

Josh handed him the reins. "If that ain't a coincidence." He winked at my dad. Must have heard him say Cody's name earlier.

Josh showed each of the men how to mount with the help from a little portable set of stairs: "a mounting block," Josh called it. Then he traded the donkey's saddle for a sidesaddle. "Okay, Ivy, now you. See this here?" He placed his hand on a bit of the saddle that looked like two very sturdy rabbit ears, about ten inches high, mounted slightly to the left of center. "This is the pommel. You have two. The other saddles have just one."

"They're sort of like handles for us," Dad said, showing me the knob on the front of his saddle.

"That's right," Josh said. "But for you, they keep your legs steady."

"Does this mean I don't get a handle?"

"That's right. Let's get you up. Situate yourself so that your rear end is behind the pommel and both legs face me."

I used the mounting block to get onto Toby's back and did as Josh said.

"Now wrap your right leg around the pommel and bring it back to this side. Your left leg tucks under the other part of the pommel."

"The downward facing bunny ear?"

"Yeah. That's a pretty good description. I may use that."

I arranged myself—and my dress—around the pommel. The sidesaddle made me sit further back on my rear than the men, but the position was surprisingly comfortable. "Now put your left foot in the stirrup and grab the reins."

"I really don't get a handle?"

"You can hold onto the top pommel—"

"The one covered by my skirt?"

"And we'll go slow."

"It's okay," Cody said. "She's a dancer. She can do almost anything."

I loved my brother.

Josh stood beside his own horse, a shining muscled black beauty. "It's gettin' on sunset. Let's mosey on down to the cookout." He swung into the saddle in a practiced, effortless move, without the use of the stair thingie. "The others can catch up later."

"Do they know how to get on a horse?" Cody asked Josh.

"Nathan says he knows all there is to know about 'cowboy stuff.' We'll hope he meant it."

We rode slowly out of the corral. Toby and I were a head shorter than the rest of the crew, but I didn't care. Less far to fall, and besides, Toby's ears were so soft.

We headed down Gold Bug's dirt road and into the desert. Late afternoon light threw everything into high definition, creating shadows and depth that had been flattened out by the sun just an hour earlier. It was gorgeous and romantic and made me miss Matt.

As we rode, Josh told stories of the town and the desert. I listened for anything he hadn't told me, but it was pretty much the same story, maybe cowboyed-up a little for effect.

"Why do they call it Gold Bug Gulch?" asked Cody. Dang. I couldn't believe I'd never asked that question.

"The stream that runs through the property is Gold Bug Creek," Josh said. "Some folks say it's because of these big bugs we have in the springtime. They have a kind of iridescence, so they shine gold in the sun."

"And other folks?" Uncle Bob never missed a trick.

"Other folks say it's because they used to find gold nuggets the size of beetles. Maybe they did once upon a time."

"There was gold here?" Cody asked.

"Yep. In fact, we're coming up on the mine right now." The industrial-looking structure I'd seen from town now loomed out of the shadows at the foot of a rocky hill. Triangular and made of wood, it looked a little like the pictures of old oilrigs I'd seen, except that one of the triangle's legs went into a deep hole. "That's the headframe," Josh said. "It had cables that could raise or lower men or buckets."

Uncle Bob leaned over in his saddle to get a better look as we passed by. "Looks like that hole goes straight down."

"Pretty much. There are a bunch of horizontal shafts that lead off of it." Josh said. "It's deep too—about two thousand feet."

"I thought there was talk of giving mine tours." I couldn't imagine anyone wanting to step foot in that gaping black hole.

"Yep," Josh said. "But they're thinking about using the original entrance, right over there." In the side of the hill was a tunnel, framed by wood beams. "That's the hole where it all started, where my great granddad first discovered gold."

"That looks more like what I think of as a mine," I said.

"Better for tourists too, I think," Josh said. "They can walk right into this entrance."

"Can we go in?" asked Cody, beating me to the punch.

"Too dangerous," said Josh.

"'Cause it's dark?"

"Because its dark and you can get lost, or fall down a mine shaft, or wind up in a dead end where the gasses build up."

"Or run into bats," I added.

"Bats won't hurt you," Josh said.

"But maybe we'd hurt them. Frank said something to me about needing to protect the bats."

"Frank has bats in his own belfry," said Josh. "The ones in the mine are Brazilian free-tailed bats. Tons of them in Arizona. Most common ones around." He turned to Cody. "Tell you what. You can be one of the first people through when we start up the mine tours."

"Cool," Cody said.

"Seems like that might be a while," Uncle Bob said. "I mean, considering the age of that mine and all."

"Just takes money. And those guys behind us," Josh looked over his shoulder, "could take care of it like that." He snapped his fingers.

I glanced behind us. A little cloud of dust followed at a distance.

"Wait, do they own the mine?" I asked. "The investors from Philadelphia?"

"Yep. The mine and the land around it, but not the mineral rights. Some corporation bought those from my dad before he died. Who knows why—the mine's been played out for decades." We rode around the curve of the hill and could now see the chuckwagon, a campfire glowing next to it. "But here's the real question," Josh said, "are you hungry for gold or for steak?"

"Steak," Bob and Dad and I all said together.

"Gold," said Cody.

"Really?" I said. Cody loved steak.

He nodded and looked longingly at toward the mine.

"Gold makes some people crazy," Josh said. "Never felt it myself."

The smell of meat cooked over mesquite wafted toward us. "I changed my mind," said Cody. "Steak instead of gold. Definitely steak."

CHAPTER 36

"Grub's up!" Billie rang a big iron triangle affixed to the chuckwagon, startling all of us sitting around the campfire. Cody covered his ears. It was awfully loud. "We got beans, cornbread, coleslaw, and steaks, plus apple pie for dessert. To drink, we've got Budweiser, a local ale called Kiltlifter, and water. Come and get it." She stood behind a table made of an old door and two sawhorses, and in front of a makeshift kitchen setup composed of several propane barbecue grills and a couple of coolers. Though Billie was obviously the designated cook, she wore her saloon girl costume. Guess she didn't say no to Nathan.

We lined up in front of the table as she ladled out cowboy fare from cast-iron kettles and blue enamel pots. Our little group consisted of Josh, Nathan, my family, and the investors. I'd studied them during the mercifully short pre-dinner sing-along, by the light of the campfire and a few strategically placed lanterns. The men all had Philly accents, and their Western wear was new. They may have been going for a Magnificent Seven look, but ended up looking like Goodfellas who'd gotten stranded near a Saba's Western Wear. They all seemed nice enough, though a couple of them couldn't keep their eyes off Billie's breasts as she bent to serve the food.

"Put your eyes back in your head," she said to an investor wearing a brand new white cowboy hat.

"Just admiring what's on offer, Billie." He knew her? I didn't remember Nathan doing any introductions.

"Too rich for your blood, Mario," Billie said.

The investors went through the line first. Then Dad and Uncle Bob heaped their plates full and grabbed longnecks out of a cooler. Cody and I got our food, then filled blue enameled mugs with water from a big water jug with a spout. I was working, after all. We sat back down around the campfire on some logs that had been set up for seating. I balanced my plate on my knees and lifted my glass to my lips, thirsty after the long dusty ride. But something was off. Even over the smell of the mesquite fire and the grilled meat and the cornbread, I could smell...

"Stop!" I jumped up and knocked Cody's glass from his hands before he could take a sip, scattering food and water everywhere.

"What?" said everyone.

"The water. There's something wrong with the water."

"Seems fine to me." Billie sniffed at her cup. "Better be since I just drank two cups."

"Women," Nathan said to the investors. "Always making a fuss about something."

Was I wrong? I turned to my uncle. "I thought I smelled—"

Suddenly all hell broke loose. Gunshots rang out in the night and a figure appeared on the top of the chuckwagon.

"Give me all your gold," shouted Chance, pointing a pistol at the group.

"I don't have any gold." Cody had a big grin on his face, obviously delighted to be part of the show.

"Your valuables, then," said Chance. "Give them up, or you'll all be vulture food. And speaking of food, I want one of those steaks too."

No one moved. Cody giggled.

"Wait," I said. "I really think there's something wrong with—"

"Don't believe me?" Chance said. "Maybe this'll convince you." He squeezed off a shot aimed at Josh's feet. Josh kicked over the tin cup he'd set near his boot, pulled his gun out of its holster as he jumped to his feet, and aimed at Chance. *Pow!* The shot rang out in the desert air and Chance fell off the top of the wagon onto a carefully placed "sack of flour" (filled with foam).

"That'll teach any bandits to keep their grubby hands off my friends," said Josh. "And my steak."

Nathan led the applause, Josh took a bow, and Chance jumped up from his spot on the flour sack and tipped his hat. Everyone clapped.

Everyone except Billie.

She just lay on the ground.

CHAPTER 37

"Shit!"

I don't know who said it. I just know that Chance and Josh and Uncle Bob and I all ran toward Billie at the same time.

She lay in the dirt next to the chuckwagon, breathing rapidly, thrashing her arms and legs like she was having a seizure. Then suddenly she was still. Josh began CPR, while Chance backed off, wild-eyed.

"No one touch that water!" Uncle Bob commanded. "What did you smell?" he asked me.

"Bitter almonds."

"Cyanide." He didn't have to say more as we all looked at Billie, inert and pale in the moonlight. Cody hugged my dad hard. Nathan and the Philly investors huddled in a tight knot. Someone cried quietly.

"I'm calling 911." Uncle Bob dialed as he spoke. "How do they get here?"

Josh kept pounding on Billie's chest. "Tell them to take Gold Road. We're about a half mile northeast of the mine."

My uncle got through to 911, explained the route, and hung up the phone. "They're on their way."

"Did you say cyanide?" my dad asked. "Wouldn't Billie have smelled it too?"

"Only about half the population can detect it," Uncle Bob said. "Ivy must be one of them. And Billie," he looked sadly at the body in the dirt, "was not."

None of us spoke again for ten minutes. Josh kept doing CPR, even though we could all see it wasn't working. I knelt on the ground next to

Billie, rocks digging into my knees. Every few minutes I spelled Josh at
CPR, pounding on Billie's chest and breathing into her mouth and
hoping somehow that my will would bring her back. It didn't.

Finally Uncle Bob roused himself. "Help should be here soon," he
said. "In the meantime, let's get everyone out of here so the EMTs can
do their job. Josh and Ivy, you stay here with Billie. The rest of you can
use the steps of the chuckwagon to mount your horses. Chance, can
you help everyone saddle up?"

No answer. We all looked around. No sign of Chance.

"Maybe he went to be by himself?" I said. "He and Billie
were...close."

"Huh." My uncle stared into the darkness that surrounded us, lit
only by a sliver of a moon. "Alright then." He grabbed the reins of his
horse, led her to the chuckwagon steps, and eased his bulk onto her
back. "I'm going to look for Chance. Keith," he said to my dad, "can you
get the rest of them back to Gold Bug?"

"Sure." My dad approached his horse and swung himself into the
saddle with practiced ease. I stared at him. "Used to do a bit of riding,"
he said quietly to me.

"But earlier you used the..." He'd used the mounting box like
everyone else.

"Didn't want anyone to feel uncomfortable." Then louder, to the
group. "All right, folks, follow me."

"You know the way?" asked Nathan, whose hair stuck to his
forehead in spikes.

"Yeah," my dad said. "I know the way."

After the group had gone, Josh and I worked for another five
minutes in silence. Finally, he sat back on his heels. I put Billie's head
in my lap. I knew she couldn't feel the hard ground, but still.

The campfire turned orange and then red. Finally, just as the
ambulance appeared down the dirt road, the last glowing ember
flickered and died.

CHAPTER 38

"Smelled a lot of cyanide before?" a county patrolman asked me.

Josh and I stood in Gold Bug's dirt lot next to the officer's car, near the ambulance that held Billie, her face covered with a sheet.

"No, but..." I had to be careful. I'd studied up on poisons after a cruise ship death I investigated a few months ago. I could tell the police about that later, but Josh couldn't know I was a PI. I opted for a different truth. "I read a lot of Agatha Christie. She used cyanide in several of her books."

"We did too." Josh frowned. "I mean, the mine did. Use cyanide."

"What for?" I asked.

"Used it to separate gold from ore. Common practice back then— even today in some parts of the world."

"How long has the mine been closed?" asked the officer.

"Since 1942."

"Then the cyanide couldn't have come from there."

"Sure it could. Well, not exactly from the mine. When the town went bust, people just left crap behind. The company did too, left stuff or sometimes buried it." Josh kicked a rock and watched it tumble down the ridge to the dried-up sewage sludge puddle. "I've heard there are tanks of the stuff buried out here in the desert. Looks like somebody found one of them."

I called Matt on the way home from Gold Bug. He was pretty pissed. "If you didn't insist on keeping us a secret, I could've been there."

Along the highway shoulder, glass glittered in my headlight beams like the eyes of animals. "And you could've died."

"So could you. Ivy, I don't want to fight. I just want to be with you, especially if it's dangerous. I want to protect you."

"I can protect myself, thank you very much."

"What part of 'I don't want to fight' do you not understand?"

"Listen, I'm just calling to tell you why Cody might be upset for a few days."

"I hope that's not the only reason you're calling."

"Of course it's not. In a completely selfish way, I wish you had been there. I wish you were here right now."

Matt's voice softened. "How about I be there in an hour? Stay over at your place tonight?"

"Yes." I found myself close to tears. "Yes, please, yes."

The next morning Matt left for the group home. A half hour later, I did too. I wanted to be there at breakfast to make sure Cody was okay, given the past night's events.

"Why did Billie die?" Cody stirred the Rice Krispies in his bowl, never lifting the spoon to his mouth.

"She was poisoned by the water."

"That I almost drank."

I nodded.

"I almost died?" asked Cody.

I didn't want to think about it, so I didn't answer. Matt jumped in. "Good thing Ivy was there." He poured me a cup of coffee, placing a hand on my shoulder and letting it graze my cheek before taking the coffeepot away. "She saved you."

Last night I'd asked Josh who had access to the water. "Besides all of us at the cookout?" he said. "Pretty much everybody else too. We set up the chuckwagon early in the day. Billie brought the food out later, but we had the water there from the get-go bein' as how this is the desert."

Was it Chance who tampered with the water? Did he run off because he was guilty or because he was broken up about Billie? Uncle Bob never did find him. Were the police looking for him? And how was Billie's death—Billie's *murder*—connected with the accidents and Mongo and—

Cody interrupted my thoughts. "But why would someone kill Billie?"

I'd asked myself the same question. Was Billie really the target? Anyone could have drunk the water. It was just luck that all the men (except for Cody) had opted for beer. Or was it?

"Why?" Cody asked again.

"I don't know," I said, "but I'm going to find out."

CHAPTER 39

"Was Billie a drinker?" I asked Nathan. I'd called him on my way to check the wildlife cameras in Sunnydale.

"Damned if I know. Can't believe this shit is happening again," he muttered. "Gonclosusdown."

"They'd really close us down?"

"I don't know. Maybe. They're going to study our water, make sure it's not all contaminated. But goddammit, that means we can only serve bottled water."

"That's not so bad."

"We can also only use bottled water to wash dishes, clean the place, everything. Even need to use it in the bathrooms. You know how much this is going to cost me? Crap, I forgot to order that Purell stuff. Need a shitload of it."

"So you don't know if Billie drank?" His lack of concern about Billie's death did not endear him to me.

"She probably did. You can ask Chance when he turns up."

"Probably did? Why do you think that?"

"I've never known a gambler who didn't drink."

That seemed like a generalization, but it also seemed like a good bit of information. "Billie was a gambler?"

"A gambler? Hell, Billie was the house."

I made my rounds of Sunnydale's golf courses and our wildlife cameras. Nothing except a few coyotes, but I still felt encouraged from the photos the day before, like Lassie was just out on a tear and would come home when he was done. Some may have called it denial. It was one of my personality traits.

I stopped over at Marge and Arnie's afterward. After knocking I heard, "Come in—door's open."

"Should you really be leaving the door unlocked?" I asked Arnie, who was propped up on the living-room couch.

"It's Sunnydale," he said. "What's going to happen?"

I could have reminded him about the guy who nearly killed Marge last spring, but I kinda liked having a fellow denier. "Where's Marge?" I said instead.

"On the phone with her agent. He's trying to talk her into doing a show she's not crazy about."

"Marge is a Broadway legend. Why would she need to do a show she didn't like?" I wondered if it was about the money. She and Arnie must've sunk a bundle into Gold Bug Gulch.

"He says she needs to keep her name out there; that if she doesn't, she'll go from legend to has-been pretty quick."

Aargh. The agent was right, and not just about Marge. I hadn't been onstage in the Valley since *The Sound of Cabaret* last spring. I'd had a few commercials and an independent film role, and played Nancy in *Oliver! At Sea!* onboard a cruise ship, but Phoenix audiences had not seen me for a good six months. *Annie Get Your Gun* would be great in terms of money, prestige, and my résumé, and it would fill the blank spot in my acting calendar perfectly. I needed to nail this callback. Maybe I should go home and practice...

Nice, Ivy. Your friend was killed *last night* and you're thinking about your acting career. I shook my head at my shallow self and focused on what really mattered: "What do you know about Billie?"

Arnie shook his head. "Such a shame. She was a nice woman. Don't know much about her, though. Lived not too far from the Gulch, in a trailer out in the desert somewhere near Wickenburg. With Mongo. When he was hired on, he mentioned to Nathan that Billie had a theater background. She was working in a bar at the time, cooking and pouring drinks. Nathan figured he was killing a bunch of birds with one stone."

Just Arnie saying "killing" brought back the feeling I'd been trying to shake all day—Billie's head lying in my lap, her body cool to the touch...No. The best thing I could do for Billie now was to find out what happened. "Did she drink?" I asked.

"Dunno. The few times I met her, she was working."

"Ever hear anything about her gambling?"

"Oh," said Arnie, "you're asking about the game."

"Sure," I said. "The game."

Arnie sat back on the couch and hooked his arms around a couple of cushions, in full storytelling mode. He even took the cigar out of his mouth. "The way I heard it, this Gold Bug poker game has been going on—off-and-on—for forty years."

"Forty years? How is that even possible?"

"You know how I said Billie worked in a bar? The place has been around forever, has a nice little back room. Years ago, a few guys started playing a friendly little game. They never stopped, took Sunday and Monday nights off, but that was it. After a while the game got bigger and it got less friendly, so someone needed to step up and organize it. That was Billie. She's the hostess—takes care of the money and takes any heat there might be."

"Has there been? Any heat, I mean?"

Arnie shrugged. "Nothing I ever heard about. Local law enforcement looks the other way about the gambling—I think some of them even sit at the table. I guess there were fights every so often. Billie broke them up. She was one tough cookie."

Ah. The sore losers behind Billie's bruises.

"This is all hearsay, you know. I've never played there. Too rich for my blood."

"Did Billie play?"

"I don't think so. She was..." Arnie shook his head. "God rest her soul, Billie was what you call 'the brush.' Collected and paid out the money."

I remembered one of the investors calling Billie by name. "Do you think Nathan's friends from Philly might've played?" I wanted to ask about Nathan too, but decided against it.

"I think Nathan did say something about it. But, listen, you want to know more about the game, you should talk to Josh about it."

"Josh? Is he part of the game?"

"No, but his dad was. Word is that's how he lost the family ranch."

CHAPTER 40

I drove back into town, parked on the street, and climbed the stairs to Duda Detectives. I was dragging from lack of sleep and the emotional wallop of Billie's death, until I opened the office door. Ah, liverwurst and onions—the smell of a happy Uncle Bob. I inhaled deeply.

My uncle sat at his desk, flattening a white paper bag. "Got you a roast beef with horseradish." He gestured toward a paper-wrapped sandwich on my desk. As we unwrapped our sandwiches, we commiserated about Billie's death.

"You hear any more about Chance?" he asked.

"Arnie said no one has seen him yet. I wonder why he took off. Guilt or grief?"

"Could be either. Or both. Maybe he felt responsible somehow. Or maybe he didn't understand exactly what the cyanide would do." Uncle Bob grimaced. "That was a pretty horrible way to go."

"Yeah, it was." The medical examiner had arrived last night right before I left the Gulch. He was pretty sure it was cyanide, something about Billie's skin looking flushed. He also said cyanide was a quick but incredibly painful death. I didn't like to think about it. "There are a couple different ways to look at it. Billie's love life was complicated— that could be a motive. It seems more likely that the poison wasn't intended for Billie—she was just the unlucky one to die. After all, I smelled cyanide in my water too."

"About that," said Uncle Bob. "This whole thing is beginning to smell. I'm not sure—"

"That's just your liverwurst."

"Olive."

"I'll be careful. Cross my heart." I needed to distract my uncle or he would try to make me quit the investigation, and I really wanted to find out what happened to Billie and Mongo. "There's another interesting motive, but I can't quite figure out how it works." I told Uncle Bob about the game.

"Forty years," he said. "Too bad it wasn't continuous. Would've given the one at The Birdcage a run for its money."

Uncle Bob was launching into a story. Good. That meant my distraction worked, and I'd have time to start eating that roast beef sandwich. "The Birdcage?" I said, just to edge him into full trivia geek mode.

"The Birdcage was a saloon and theater in Tombstone. Still is, but it's sort of a tourist attraction now. And it's the home of the longest continual poker game in history."

"How did that work?" I took a bite of my sandwich. It was perfect. Sourdough bread, spread with a little cream cheese and horseradish, a few thin slices of cucumber, and mounds of rare roast beef. I had a brief moment of survivor's guilt, enjoying a sandwich like that.

"The game was played 24/7 for eight years, five months, and three days. Doc Watson was one of the players, Diamond Jim Brady, and Bat Masterson too. They all lost boatloads of money."

"But somebody must've won." I took another bite of my sandwich. Whoever realized that roast beef and horseradish went together was a genius.

"Sure. Somebody must have. But the biggest winner was the house. It kept ten percent."

I put down my perfect sandwich and took out my cell phone. "Arnie," I said when he picked up. "You know that poker game we were talking about yesterday? Do you know if Billie made any money as the bank?"

"You bet." Arnie chortled. "Get it? You *bet*?"

"Uh-huh. Was it very much?"

"Ten percent," he said. "She got to keep ten percent for herself."

I hung up. "Billie got ten percent too. Seems like she would've made good money. But she didn't wear expensive clothes, drove an old Ford pickup, and lived in a doublewide. If she had money, she sure didn't spend it."

"So where did all her money go?" My uncle put down his liverwurst sandwich. He loved a puzzle.

"Maybe she was a gambler too?"

"Could be. Have to be a pretty bad one to lose all that money. Let's see if maybe she put it somewhere else. Let's look for companies, trusts, that sort of thing." Uncle Bob told me which database to use, and he logged into another one. For twenty minutes there was no sound but the tapping of fingers on keyboards and the occasional chew and swallow.

"Got it!" Uncle Bob said. "There's a nonprofit. Billie was the only director and signer. It's called The Golden Girls."

"A non-profit..." I tossed my empty sandwich wrapper in the trash and Googled the foundation. "Huh. No website—that's unusual. Do you think she was hiding her money there?"

Uncle Bob chewed the last of his sandwich thoughtfully. I could tell he was thinking because liverwurst doesn't require much chewing. "Wouldn't be the best place to do it. The IRS is pretty sticky about nonprofits. In fact..." He tapped at his keyboard.

"The Golden Girls..." I mused out loud. "Huh. The *Golden* Girls. You know, I still haven't found out who's behind Acme Arizona, the corporation that owns the mineral rights to the gold mine. Could Josh's dad have lost the deed to Billie in a poker game? I mean, that's how he lost the town to Mongo's dad."

"Ah!" Uncle Bob peered at his computer screen. "Love the internet. So, The Golden Girls have over five hundred thousand dollars in assets..."

"Any chance mineral rights are one of those assets?"

"Can't tell."

"Hmm. Nonprofits have to have a mission, right? What's theirs?"

"'We will strive to collaboratively morph feminine mindshare into economically viable opportunities.'"

"Really?"

"Really."

"Is there any contact info?" I jumped up and went over to Uncle Bob's desk.

"Billie's listed as the contact again."

I looked over his shoulder at his computer screen. "Yeah, that's her address and phone number too. Oh well...Wait. Go back to that screen you were just on."

"The one that lists donors?"

"Yeah."

He clicked back to the previous screen. "Scroll down...Stop." I leaned in for a better look. There it was. Josh, who was so broke he had to sell his family's home, contributed $10,000 a year for the past three years—ever since his dad's death—to The Golden Girls.

CHAPTER 41

"You think it could be blackmail?" I asked my uncle.

"Maybe. It could also be that he likes the organization."

"But Josh has no money, and besides, he doesn't seem like the type to donate to an organization whose mission is feminine mindshare..."

"He could be an ally. You shouldn't make assumptions."

My phone buzzed. Marge. I picked up. "Hi. Hey, we may have found something. You ever hear of The Golden Girls?"

"TV show with all the old broads, though they're not lookin' that old to me now."

"Is that you, Arnie?"

"Haven't replaced my cell phone yet, so I'm using Marge's. Why you asking about a TV show?"

"It's also a non-profit founded by Billie."

"Never heard of it. Hey, I'm calling you on this phone for a reason. Nathan left a message when I was in the shower. Wants me to call. I thought about taking notes when I talked to him, but then I remembered how you put Bob on speakerphone sometimes. How 'bout I do that with Nathan so you can hear the whole conversation? I already got you on speaker on this line, and I can call him on the landline. Neat, huh?"

"Sounds good."

I listened to Arnie dial. "Hi there," he said to Nathan. "Sorry I missed you earlier...What's that? Can you speak up?"

I suspected Arnie said that for my benefit. I listened hard, but still couldn't hear Nathan. Probably because Arnie forgot to put him on speaker. Oh well. At least I could hear Arnie's side of the conversation.

"That's bad...Yeah...He hasn't been to his apartment?...How 'bout the bars?...You know, Ivy could look for him...Why her? Uh, they're close...Sure...Yeah, love you too."

I surmised three things from Arnie's end of the conversation:

1. I was going to look for someone, probably Chance.
2. I was now supposedly "close" to this someone.
3. Nathan must have said "I love you" to Arnie.

Though none of the three pieces of information were expected, it was the last one that threw me. Nathan didn't seem like an "I love you" kind of guy.

But maybe, I thought as I drove to Gold Bug to—yep—look for Chance, maybe my general bad feeling about Nathan was actually jealousy. I loved hearing the joy in Arnie's voice when he talked to his son. It also made my heart ache. I didn't hear it in my parents' voices. My dad had floored me when he said, "I love you" this past summer after years of no affection. And though he was beginning to show his love in small ways, Dad hadn't said the words again, as much as I'd wished for them. It was no use even thinking about my mom.

I rolled down my window and let the wind blow those thoughts away. I needed to find Chance. He'd been missing since last night and his truck was still in the Gulch's parking lot. Nathan had called around to Chance's usual haunts (and I suspected the police had too), but no one had seen him. Since Chance hadn't taken his truck, he was probably on foot somewhere in the vicinity of Gold Bug. That's where I'd look.

I needed another caffeine hit, so I grabbed a Frappuccino at a drive-through on the edge of town, then hit the highway. I pulled into the Gulch's parking lot about a half hour later. Chance's pickup was still there. I scrambled out of my truck, slapped on some sunscreen, and slung a water bottle over my shoulder (it had a strap). Carrying my half-empty Frappuccino, I walked down the town's road, which seemed doubly empty in the bright sunlight. By the time I saw Josh's smithy, I was already regretting my choice of footwear. Sketchers were great for bopping around town, not so much for hiking down a dirt road. Wouldn't be great in the cholla-filled desert either. So when I saw that Toby was tied to a post in front of Josh's shop, saddled up and everything, I took it as a sign from God.

"Josh!" I yelled. No response. The iron gate was still drawn across the forge's open door and locked. "Josh!" I yelled again. No way he would ride Toby, I told myself. Josh was way too tall. So it wasn't like I was borrowing his mode of transport. More like taking his pet for a walk.

Still, I should leave a note. I patted my pockets. No pen or paper. Hmm. I found a stick on the side of the road. "Back soon - Ivy," I scratched in the dirt in front of the forge. Toby stuck his tongue out at me. I wondered if it was a comment on my choice of writing paper. No. He was licking up the last of my Frappuccino, which I had set on the ground.

"That's okay." I patted him on his fuzzy head. "Everyone needs a treat now and then."

I decided to saddle up from the ground. After all, Toby was short, and I was a strong flexible dancer. Nope. I tried mounting from the other side. Nope again. Toby looked at me with his kind eyes (and a little Frappuccino on his whiskery mouth), then looked back over his shoulder at the porch on a building across the street. A three-foot-high porch.

"Are you a mind reader or just really, really nice?" I said to Toby. "Come on, you donkey-angel or whatever you are." I led him to the spot he'd shown me and used the porch to mount.

"All right, Toby," I whispered into his soft ear. "Since you're obviously more than just a donkey, maybe you can help find me Chance. Let's giddyup."

CHAPTER 42

I was glad I'd chosen Toby as my form of transportation on this particular trip. Walking in the desert looks easy from the road. It's pretty flat and you can see far into the distance. But once you're actually in it, you have to watch for cactus, snake holes, and the slithery creatures themselves, who occasionally sun themselves on rocks. But with Toby carefully picking his way through the desert, I was able to scan the horizon for any sign of Chance.

The night Billie died, Chance had worn a white thermal-underwear type of shirt and a red kerchief, so he should have been pretty easy to spot. But no. Nothing. Toby the angel-donkey and I kept at it until sunset, then I turned him home. It was easy to recognize the Gulch, even in the dying light—the cottonwoods that lined the creek beckoned like a green heaven. When Toby saw we were going home, he picked up his pace. He also panted a little.

"Sorry, boy." I stroked his soft ears. "You're probably thirsty. We'll stop at the creek for you."

The sun had just set, so the desert wasn't dark yet. Then we reached the trees.

What was I thinking? I pulled on the reins as the canopy closed over us. "Let's go back to the road." I tugged on Toby's reins, but he must have smelled water, because he was having none of it. I could smell it too, that peculiar mix of damp soil and greenery that gladdens a desert dweller's heart. What the heck—we must be pretty close to the creek, and Toby knew the way to go.

But something moved—jumped?—in the grass near us. Toby stopped. The something jumped again. I couldn't tell what it was, too dark, but I heard the shush of the tall grass and glimpsed the movement. I nudged Toby in his ribs. "Let's get out of here," I said as the grass on both sides of us rustled with movement.

But Toby wouldn't move. Not forward or backward. I slid off his back, grabbed him by the halter, and tried to turn him around. I couldn't even get him to turn his head. Finally he took a step toward the glimmer of water in the near distance. Okay then. We could cross the creek and go up the hill on the other side to Gold Bug.

We had just taken a few steps when the grass near us exploded with movement. Toby didn't have to be nudged. He took off running. I couldn't keep up. The reins slipped out of my hands. I ran after him. Who knew donkeys could run so fast? I almost got hold of him when he slowed down near the creek, but at the last moment he veered left past an old snag and—

"Stop!" A man's voice came out of the darkness. "Don't take another step."

"Or you'll shoot?"

"You've been watching too many Westerns," said the voice I now recognized as Josh's. Toby must have heard his master's voice, because he trotted up behind me. I could feel his breath on my arm.

I took a step toward Josh. I could see him now—him and two other men—standing at the edge of another grassy area on the other side of the creek.

"Don't! I mean it. You're about to step in quicksand."

"Right, quicksand in the desert." Why didn't Josh want me to come nearer? And who were those two men with him? I took another step toward him.

"Goddammit. What did I tell you?"

He had told me the truth—there was quicksand in the desert. My left foot was now stuck tight in it. "Is this like the stuff in the movies?" I tried to keep my voice from shaking. "That swallows you whole and suffocates you to death?"

"No. This doesn't suffocate you. Just grabs your leg so you can't move. You die of exposure while waiting for help."

I kicked at the sandy mud.

"Stop." Josh had put on a calm voice, but it didn't fool me. It was the sort of voice people use when they tell you you're all right when you can see the blood spurting from the deep gash in your arm. Still, I stopped what I was doing.

"Now, relax."

Yeah, right.

"What shoes are you wearing?"

"Um, Sketchers. The slip-on kind."

"Good. Reach back and hold onto Toby. Don't let him get any closer, but grab him around the neck."

I did. His donkey warmth made me feel a little better. A little.

"Your other foot isn't stuck?"

"Right." I picked it up.

"No," Josh said. "Put it back down exactly where it was."

"Okay." I did.

"Use Toby to steady yourself. Now, staying relaxed, wiggle your foot—the one that's stuck—out of your shoe. Wait. Stop." Josh must have been able to see pretty well in the dark. "Move your stuck foot and leg as little as possible. Just small circles. Use your good leg to do all the locomotion."

I held onto Toby's warm neck, bent my knee, and pushed against the ground. Then relaxed. And moved my leg in little circles. And pushed. And did it all over again. And again. After several hours (okay, probably minutes, but looong ones), there was a *schluup* sound, and my foot was free of the mud. And my shoe.

"Now push against Toby so he backs up."

I did, but Toby wouldn't budge. "C'mon, Toby," I pleaded.

"Dammit," Josh said. Toby moved.

"Wish I'd known the secret word," I said as Toby and I backed away from the stream.

"Now you do. But after you get Toby back where he belongs, you better not use the secret word—or him—again. They used to hang folks for rustling, you know."

"What were you doing out there anyway?" Josh caught up with me in the parking lot after Toby was safely back in his corral. The two shadowy men were not with him.

"Looking for Chance."

"Any sign of him?'

"No. What were you doing there? Who were those men?"

He crossed his arms. "Not a good idea to be poking your nose into other people's business."

Was that a warning? A threat? Josh's face gave nothing away.

I turned away and got in my pickup. Josh didn't leave, just stood outside my door until I rolled down my window. "Why were you looking for Chance?" he asked.

I remembered what Arnie had told Nathan. "We're, um, close."

"You too?" Josh shook his head. "Women."

CHAPTER 43

I was out at Sunnydale at six a.m. the next day. I really hoped I would find Lassie soon. I loved the little bugger, but these early mornings were wearing on me.

But getting up early also meant that by the time I made it into the office, I had almost a half-day before my three p.m. callback. I put on a pot of coffee as soon as I got in. Uncle Bob was out, but I was pretty sure I could drink the whole pot by myself. As the coffeemaker filled the air with the best smell in the world, I checked my Duda Detectives email. Hey, an email from the lab. They weren't fibbing about their quick turnaround. I scanned the attached results. Huh. Nathan was definitely Arnie's son.

I got up and poured myself a cup of coffee. I guess this meant that Nathan was telling the truth, at least in part. There was nothing in his background that really seemed suspicious either. Failed businesses weren't a crime. I called Marge on her cellphone. First things first: "Did Chance come back?"

"Not yet."

"I'm sure he's just licking his wounds. He's a cowboy-type. Probably finds solace in the desert," I said, as much for me as for Marge. "I have some news..." I told her the paternity results. "No history of criminal activity either," I said. "I'm beginning to think Nathan's all above board."

"I don't know," she said. "Bad luck seems to follow him. I just wonder if there's a reason..."

"Hey," I said, "I just realized I don't have a current address for him. He's not living somewhere onsite, is he?"

"He's staying at Rancho De Los Vaqueros."

"Really?" Rancho De Los Vaqueros was a dude ranch and resort outside of Wickenburg. A very expensive dude ranch and resort.

But stays at pricey resorts also weren't a crime, as Uncle Bob pointed out when I called him later.

"But where did he get the money?" I said.

"That's a tough one to figure out, at least legally. You sure he actually has the money?"

"What do you mean?"

"The average American household has over ninety thousand dollars in debt," said Mr. Trivia Buff. "Maybe this Nathan guy's got champagne taste and a beer budget."

I jumped up from my desk and paced the few feet across the office. "There's got to be something."

"Why?"

"Because..." I went with Marge's idea. "Bad luck always follows him around."

"I get the feeling you just don't like the guy, Olive."

"I don't. I think he's highly fed and lowly taught."

"Is that Shakespeare talk for 'asshole'?"

"Sort of."

"Just remember, that's not a crime either."

"Ivy!" A tall athletic, brunette was wrangling an Old English-style lamppost through the Berger Performing Arts Center's loading dock door. "Did you come to help?"

I ran to hold the door. "Sorry, Theresa, not really." Theresa was the artistic director for New Vintage Theater, where I'd been painting flats when I got Marge's call about Lassie. "I'm here for another callback for *Annie Get Your Gun*."

"Cool that you got called back again." Theresa set down the lamppost and rubbed her shoulders. She may have been a fit thirty-something, and the lamppost may have been a not-that-heavy prop, but still. "Can I help you with that?" I said. "I've got a few minutes."

"Yeah. Let's just get it on the stage." Theresa grabbed the top of the lamppost and I took the bottom, and we headed through the propped-open door that led to the backstage of the Boothe Theater, the smallest space in the multi-stage Berger Center—the only one that New Vintage Theater could afford.

"Glad I could help." I was. I liked Theresa and her theater company. They presented wonderful shows on a shoestring budget, minimizing the costumes and sets (like this one lamppost for their production of *Jekyll & Hyde*), but maximizing the talent. The theater did cool takes on the classics and new works by local talent (thus the New Vintage name) partly to save money on royalties, and partly because they truly liked the plays. It was the kind of company actors loved to work for—which was good, because most of the time they still couldn't pay. Shoestring budget, you know.

We set the lamppost down in the stage left wing. "When does *Annie Get Your Gun* run?" asked Theresa.

"They start rehearsals in a month."

"Did you hear we got the grant for *Twelfth Night*? We're going to be able to pay people and everything. If you don't get Annie, we'd love to have you audition for Viola."

Viola! She was one of Shakespeare's greatest heroines, clever and resilient. Sure, she had to dress like a boy to get what she needed, but she did it on her own terms. But…"How much are you going to be able to pay?"

"Two-fifty."

"A week?"

Theresa's cheeks colored. "For the run. Plus a take of the house."

If there were any profit, she meant, which there usually wasn't. Especially with Shakespeare. And though it was highly unlikely I'd be cast as Annie, Arizona Center Stage might offer me a smaller role, maybe in the chorus. I'd make at least two hundred and fifty dollars per week for the entire rehearsal period and run of the show—eight weeks as it stood right now. My work at Duda Detectives paid a good portion of my bills, but not all. I needed the money. "Um…" I said.

"Why I don't I check back with you in a few days?" Theresa said. "I know you have to focus on your callback right now."

"Thanks." I exited the backstage area into the hallways that connected the theaters.

"And Ivy," Theresa called from behind me. "Knock 'em dead."

CHAPTER 44

After the last note of "Doin' What Comes Natur'lly!" I held my sassy pose and smiled at Larry Cooper, who was sitting in the middle row of the Berger Performing Arts Center Mainstage Theater. He scribbled some notes, his face impassive, and whispered to the musical director who sat next to him. Then he looked up and smiled at me. I hoped, hoped, hoped he wasn't going ask me anything about the plot. I may have been an actor, but I didn't think I could act like the ridiculous, untrue, borderline offensive storyline had any merit at...well, you get the picture.

But Larry didn't ask me about the script. He just said, "Lift up your skirt. I want to see your legs."

I drove home from the theater and flopped down on my couch. Stupid director. My legs? Really? That was how he would decide whether to cast me? My cell buzzed. I ignored the first few rings. I didn't want to talk to anyone. But curiosity got the best of me, and I glanced at the phone. Nathan. "You're late," he said when I picked up.

"For what?"

"For the emergency meeting I put on your Outlook calendar."

This was the first I'd heard of such a calendar. My suspicion that Nathan was covering his ass was confirmed when I heard a Philly-accented voice in the background say, "Just ask her if she'll do it."

"Since Billie and Mongo are..." Nathan cleared his throat. "No longer with us, we need to replace them."

"I don't see how I can replace Billie. I'm already in the melodrama. And as far as the chuckwagon cookout, the only thing I can cook is beans. Hey, maybe we could have a cowboy all-bean supper? It'd be pretty authentic, I think."

"Worstideeverheard."

"It is not the worst idea you've ever heard and you really should be nice to someone when you're asking them a favor." Take that, Mr. Mumbly.

"Okay, okay. I'm not asking about the melodrama. Frank will replace Billie there."

"Frank?"

"Yeah. He offered to help, and all he has to do is hold up signs, right?" Nathan hadn't actually seen the show yet.

"Right. It could work. Especially if Frank dresses up like an old miner."

"I'll tell him. And we're not going to be doing those chuckwagon cookouts for a while so we don't need to replace Billie as cook—"

"Because of the water problem?"

"I think we got a handle on that, but no cookouts. We're also going to close on Sunday evenings for a while, but until I find someone, I need you to bartend at the saloon Saturday nights."

The only cocktail I knew how to make was rum and Coke. Oh, and vodka and orange juice, whatever that drink was called. "I really don't think—"

"You'd start work at five, after the shows are over, and stay 'til closing at nine. We'll pay you double whatever Arnie's paying you for the melodrama, and the tips are good."

"Okay." I could expand my repertoire. "Oh. What about those tours I'm supposed to be giving? Doesn't sound like I'll have a lot of time and—"

"You really won't have time, since we also need you to replace Mongo. The tours can wait. And before you ask, yeah, double-time for this new job too."

Hmm, that meant Arnie would be paying me for the investigation, plus my salary for the melodrama, and Nathan would double my actor's salary for the bartending and the..."Wait, Mongo?"

"We need a gunfight. Chance said your Annie Oakley was pretty good."

"Chance is back?"

"Not yet, but he's done this before." I seriously doubted Chance had been in quite this situation before. Did Nathan know something, or was he shining on the investors who were listening in? "We'll have some sort of duel between the two of you."

"Oh. Uh..." I wasn't crazy about anyone pointing a gun at me, especially with two unexplained deaths.

"You can check Chance's gun every time," Nathan said.

"Well..."

"And you can write your own script."

My own script featuring Annie Oakley. "I'm in," I said. "You'll have a gunfight this weekend."

CHAPTER 45

"What's Campari?" I sniffed the bottle. "It smells like medicine."

"Tastes like it too," said Uncle Bob. "But some sophisticates like it." He grinned at his girlfriend, who did look awfully sophisticated with her expensive haircut and nice clothes, especially next to Uncle Bob with his two-day beard and Day-Glo orange Hawaiian shirt.

"No making fun of my cocktail choices." Bette poured a measure of the liqueur into a glass of ice, then topped it with fizzy water. "Campari and soda is a perfectly fine drink."

Pink took a drink from the glass Bette offered him. "I like it. And I'm not sophisticated." He belched just to prove his point, though the ink stain on the pocket of his short-sleeved shirt was already a pretty good indicator.

"Campari is an aperitif," I read from a library book I picked up on the way to Bob's house. "Helps with digestion."

Pink belched again. "See?"

"This is the guy you want to me to fix up with my girlfriend?" Bette asked Bob.

We were all gathered around Uncle Bob's kitchen table, which was filled with an array of bottles. Bette had picked up the Campari, but most of the liquor came from Uncle Bob and Pink (Detective Pinkstaff). I contributed tequila, peppermint schnapps, and something called Mama Walker's Bacon Maple Breakfast Liqueur (left over from a cast party). Oh, and a lime.

"What is this?" Uncle Bob picked up the aforementioned fruit. "A kiwi? What kind of drink do you make with a kiwi?"

Okay, so the lime was a little brown.

"No," said Pink. "I think it's some sort of dog toy." He threw it against the floor. It actually bounced a little.

I grabbed it before it rolled behind the refrigerator. "No making fun of my lime either."

"Or she'll slip it into your drinks," Bette said.

"I think throwing it at us would do more damage," said Uncle Bob.

Pink belched again. That Campari was good stuff.

Bette turned to me, and her hair swung in a shimmering blonde sheet. For the umpteenth time, I had to stop myself from asking for the name of her hairdresser. First of all, Bette lived in Denver. Secondly, I suspected her haircut cost more than my weekly salary. "Now, Ivy, is this a full-service bar you'll be working at?"

"I don't know." I hadn't spent much time in the saloon. "There were a lot of bottles in the back."

"What kind of liquor?"

"Brown? Oh, and there's some cheap wine and five different kinds of beer on tap, plus six bottled ones." Okay, I had stopped in once or twice.

"Brown..." Bette mused. "Mostly whiskeys, probably."

"It is a saloon, after all," said my uncle. "People probably want to order authentic Western drinks."

I flipped through the pages of *Drinks for Dummies*. "How in the world am I ever going to learn all this stuff? Can't I just make people rum and coke?"

"Hey," Bette said, "you and Bob just gave me an idea. You can just make the drinks you know how to make. We'll come up with a limited menu of cowboy-type drinks—"

"I'd need a really limited menu," I interrupted.

"And you can steer people toward the ones you know best."

"I don't—"

"You are a persuasive actor, after all."

I shut my mouth. A little flattery went a long way with me.

We decided to focus on beer (easy-peasy, pour it in a glass), tequila, whiskey, and a very few mixed drinks. In the next two hours, I learned the basic classifications of tequila (Blanco, Reposado, Añejo and Extra Añejo); the difference between Canadian whiskey, bourbon, and rye; and how to make an Old Fashioned, a Whiskey Sour, and Texas Tea. I also sampled them.

"Gluhhh," I groaned. "I think I need some Campari."

"I'm not sure that's how it works." Bette poured me some anyhow. "But I guess it can't hurt, especially since you're sleeping here tonight."

"I can't stay here. I have a script to write."

"You're staying here," said Uncle Bob. "There's a cop right here who'd ticket you for even looking at your car keys." I seriously doubted that, since Pink was lying on the couch with his eyes closed. Still, Uncle Bob was right.

"What's the script?" asked Bette.

"I get to be Annie Oakley in a gunfight."

"And you're writing it? I didn't know you were a writer."

"Guy who owns the place probably doesn't want to pay royalties," my uncle said quietly.

Oh. Of course. What the hell, I didn't care. "It's going to be great. I love Annie Oakley. Did you know she secretly put a bunch of women through college? When I told Billie that..." Billie's smiling face came back to me. I swallowed the lump in my throat.

"Billie's the one who just died," Uncle Bob explained to Bette.

"I hope there's a heaven," I said. "I hope she's with Mongo now."

"He's the one who was shot earlier."

"Did you say you're doing a gunfight?" Bette asked me. I nodded. "Are you sure you want to do that? Sounds like it could be dangerous with everything going on."

"I'll be careful. I get to check Chance's gun every night."

"But—" began my uncle.

"I've done this before." Yes, just the one time onstage, but that counted. "Plus I'll be shooting blanks, and they'll use squibs."

"Squibs," Pink said without opening his eyes. "Squibs. Funny name. Like a squid's lips."

"Squibs?" asked Bette.

"They're just little charges—like teeny bits of dynamite—you set off by remote control. Used all the time in the film industry. We'll set them up so a tin can flies off the porch railing when I shoot it, stuff like that. And a squid's lips would be squips," I said to Pink. "So..." I turned back to Bette and Bob. "Squibs and pre-checked blanks. Perfectly safe."

CHAPTER 46

"Why are there dead slugs on the counter?" I wailed. "Who wants to see dead slugs first thing in the morning?" Especially when their stomach feels like a half-full water balloon, all the juices sloshing around in...

I swallowed hard and turned away from the slimy brown things. Pink shuffled past me and peered at the saucer. "DOA," he sniffed. "Murdered by beer."

"I've been murdered by whiskey. I feel like hell. Maybe I'm actually dead. Maybe this is hell. There would be platefuls of dead slugs in hell."

"You two are such weenies." Bette pushed past us and picked up the plate. "I just set these down for a sec while I used the ladies." She poured the dirty beer carefully into the sink and slid the slugs into a garbage can. "We're leaving in a minute, but Bob wanted to get in a little gardening before we left." Uncle Bob often baited slugs with saucers of beer. "He even put the bat house up this morning."

"Bat house?"

"He put up a Robin house too?" said Pink.

"No wonder Bob likes you. Same awful sense of humor." Bette smiled. "And Ivy, I think you gave him the idea for the bat house—talking about bats while slapping mosquitoes or something? Anyway, we're off to Sedona." Bette had an unexpected break in her schedule so she and Uncle Bob were making the most of it. She grabbed her purse from the counter. "We'll be back Monday," she said over her shoulder as she went into the garage. "You two are on your own for breakfast."

Pink and I looked at each other. "You want breakfast?" he asked. His hair (what there was of it) was mashed down on one side from where he'd been sleeping on the couch.

"No."

"Coffee?"

I considered it. The fact that I was thinking about not having the best beverage in the world showed just how bad I was feeling.

"It'll probably taste good." Pink grabbed the Pyrex pot from under the Mr. Coffee and began filling it with water. "Some guys swear that a raw egg with Worcestershire works for a hangover too."

I nearly heaved. "Maybe just coffee."

I eventually got my gag relax under control and sat down with a cup of coffee. I'd thought Pink was in the same shape as I was, but obviously not, since he scrambled himself a mess of eggs. I tried not to look at them (or smell them) as he sat down at the kitchen table across from me. "I can't believe you can eat."

"I didn't have that much to drink. Just a beer and that Campari stuff."

I thought back. No, I hadn't seen him drink anything else, but...

"I tell you what though, I'm never getting double-stuffed meat lovers pizza with extra onions ever again. Or at least I won't eat a whole one."

Ah.

"Did I hear you say something about guns last night?"

"I'm going to be in a gunfight at Gold Bug Gulch. As Annie Oakley."

"You ever shot a gun before?"

"Sure."

Pink gave me that look he probably gives motorists who say they didn't know how fast they were going.

"Just a few times," I admitted. "Onstage. A rifle. Or a shotgun. Not sure which."

Pink sighed. "You really shouldn't handle a gun without proper training."

"We're just using blanks."

"You really shouldn't handle a gun without proper training." He now gave me the look he probably gave speeders as he wrote the ticket. "You know, I'm off for a few days. I could give you lessons. We could go out in the desert, do some target shooting."

I took a sip of my coffee, stalling. Detective Pinkstaff had been on the Phoenix PD forever, so he knew how to shoot. He was one of Uncle Bob's best friends, so I knew he was trustworthy. But Pink had asked me out once. He'd taken it with good grace when I said no, but every so often I caught him looking at me in a more-than-friendly way. Plus there was the fact that I was a little afraid of guns with live ammo in them. And Uncle Bob wasn't much of a gun fan. He often said that people with guns were more likely to get shot by other people with guns.

"We don't have to tell your uncle." Pink read my mind. "And if you're going to be using a gun—even with blanks—you really should know how to do it safely."

"All right." My stomach flip-flopped as I spoke. I hoped it was just the hangover.

CHAPTER 47

"Wow." I held the rifle in one hand and rubbed my shoulder with the other.

"Yeah," Pink said. "Wow." He stared off into the near distance.

I meant "wow," real ammo has way more kick than blanks, but now I followed Pink's gaze to the paper target he'd hung on a dead mesquite tree.

"Pretty good, huh?" I admired the holes clustered within the paper head of the target.

"You've never shot before?"

"Nope. Hey, I missed one." I pointed at a bullet hole outside the paper head.

"By an inch. You never shot any kind of gun before?"

"Just blanks onstage as Annie Oakley. So I did pretty well?"

"I've never seen anything like it. You, lady, are the best natural shot I've ever seen."

"Does it always hurt this much?" I rubbed my shoulder again.

"What?" Pink gazed at the target like it was a mirage. "Yeah, I suppose it does. But you get used to it. Let's go for another round. See if that's just beginner's luck. Okay, check your form: feet shoulder-width apart?"

"Check."

"Back straight? Head erect?"

"Check and check."

"Breathe in. Now align the sights, breathing out as you do."

I did, but I didn't say "check" since I was busy breathing.

"Hold your breath as you pull the trigger and..."

The rifle cracked and bucked in my hands, but I kept my eye on the target.

"Hold up!" Pinkstaff shouted. He didn't really need to since I'd put down the gun and was rubbing my shoulder again. "There's someone out there."

I squinted out past the paper target. Sure enough, a figure was picking its way through the trail-less desert.

"What in the hell?" Pink stared at the figure, which was beginning to look like a man wearing a cowboy hat. "Why would anyone be out here in the middle of nowhere?"

"Hunting?"

"He's not carrying a rifle that I can see."

"Maybe he's lost. We should go see if he's all right."

We headed out through the brush. "Watch out for the cholla," I said to Pink. He seemed like kind of a city guy.

The figure was beginning to look familiar. "It's Chance," I said. "He works at Gold Bug, but nobody's seen him since Billie died. Hey, Chance!" I yelled. "You okay?" I handed Pink my rifle. I didn't want Chance—anyone really—to know I'd been practicing. Not sure why.

I walked toward Chance. "We've been worried about you." Maybe we shouldn't have been. He was freshly shaven and wore clean clothes. He looked like someone who'd been on vacation, not grieving in the desert for three days. "Everybody's been looking for you."

"Yes," he said in that weird clipped voice he sometimes had. "I spoke to the police."

"Where have you been?" I looked in the direction he'd come from. "Oh, you must've been at Frank's house." It was the only thing around here for miles and Chance was on foot.

"No." He bit off the word. "Camping."

It was so patently untrue (besides the clean clothes, he carried absolutely no gear) that I didn't know what to say except, "We have an extra rehearsal tomorrow. We're adding a new gunfight."

Chance nodded and walked past us, tipping his hat at Pink.

"What's going on with him?" Pink watched him as he went down the road.

"I don't know," I said. "But I just realized I skipped something really important."

* * *

I couldn't believe I hadn't done a background check on Chance. Yeah, okay, I had checked out Mongo and Billie and Josh and Nathan, learned a little about the mine and the investors and The Golden Girls, but I hadn't done my due diligence on the guy who started this whole thing by shooting Mongo. I silently berated myself as Pink and I bumped along the dirt road back to Gold Bug Gulch, going about five miles an hour.

"Crap," Pink said as a rock hit the undercarriage of his old Ford Taurus. "Remind me to take my Hummer next time."

"You have a Hummer?"

"Do I look like the kinda guy who'd have a Hummer?" Pink wore a wrinkled short-sleeved button-down shirt, polyester pants, and hard-soled shoes. To go target-shooting in the desert. Not exactly a Hummer-guy kind of look. He shook his head, rolled down his window, and lit up a cigarette—the fourth one I'd seen him smoke that day. "Never have figured out why you're such a good PI when you believe everything everyone says."

"I do not."

Pink looked at me sideways while blowing a stream of Kool-scented smoke out his open window. "Didn't you believe in Jackalopes until you were eighteen?"

"Fifteen," I said. "And those postcards looked so real. Hey, is that the coolest house or what?" We'd come to the crossroad that led to Frank's house. I pointed down the hill, where the house's whitewashed walls stood in cool relief to the brown desert. "It's made of straw, well straw bale. It's going to be on some green home tour coming up soon."

Pink peered through the dusty windshield. "Nice. As long as you don't mind living in the middle of nowhere."

"I think the guy who owns it—Frank—prefers that. Sort of a desert rat. You should see where he used to live. Just a shack. Dirt floors, even."

"So what happened? What's his story?"

Dang.

I forgot to do *two* important things.

CHAPTER 48

I sat on a bench in front of the saloon and booted up my laptop. No sense in fighting the traffic to go into the office for an hour, and okay, it just felt nice to sit in the sun. I couldn't access all of Uncle Bob's fancy databases from here, but I could begin my background checks on Frank and Chance with Google. It's amazing what you can find out about people if you know where to look.

Or not. I turned up a pitiful amount of information that told me nothing except that Frank was called "an environmental activist" by some and "a dangerous agitator" by others, depending on what side of the development fence they were on. Chance's acting career was well-documented, but I couldn't find anything else on him, and no mentions of him were more than a couple years old.

I sat back on the bench to let my mind work on the problems, when, *poof*! A flour sack on the porch exploded. Then a bullet clanged against a bell. And finally, Chance lost his hat to my bullet.

All in my mind, which had decided to work on the gunfight script instead of the investigation. I tapped away on my keyboard. Three good shots should do it. A squib in the flour sack could create the explosion. A little fishing line and a yank from Chance should take care of his hat. The cowbell I was thinking of hung from the roof of the saloon's porch. Hmm...for the time being, we could use fishing line again. Someone would have to tug on it, but we could work that out.

Okay. That was the action. Good. But the script, the actual words...I thought hard. I paced the creaky floorboards of the saloon porch. I even meditated. But I was an actor, not a writer. I was used to saying someone else's words, not creating my own. Wait, someone else's words...

I had it.

I typed away, happy. An hour later, I closed my laptop, put it in my duffel bag, and hopped off the saloon porch. I was headed to the parking lot when Josh's hammer began echoing through the empty street. Ah. Finally, a chance to talk to him alone.

I jogged partway to his forge, so I'd be sure to catch him. "Hi, Josh," I said when I arrived, a little out of breath.

Maybe I said it too quietly, since Josh didn't turn around, just kept hammering. "Hi," I said again.

He looked over his shoulder. When he saw me, he moved awkwardly, placing his body in between the anvil and me. Huh. Why?

"Hey," I said, "I forgot to ask—"

"I'm pretty busy," he said. "So—"

"Just a real quick question for the history tour," I said. "You own this smithy, right?"

"Yeah." The forge glowed behind him in the dark room.

"Are you open for customers? I mean, this blacksmith shop isn't just for demonstration—people can buy your stuff?"

"Sure. I mostly make decorative objects: chandeliers, fire grates, that sort of thing."

"Is this the only business you own?"

"Yeah." A little suspicion in Josh's voice. "Why?"

"Just wondering if you had any other outlets for your work, maybe a shop in Wickenburg or something."

"No. This is it."

I pressed on. "No other business deals in the works?"

He pressed his lips together so tightly they almost disappeared. "No. Somebody been spreading rumors?" He hefted the hammer in his hand, as if testing its weight.

I suddenly wondered about the wisdom of confronting a man with a legendary temper by myself in a remote place with many heavy tools at hand. "No," I said. "Sorry to bother you." I left the smithy, and Josh's hammer took up its rhythm again. But once outside, I crept back toward its entrance, staying hidden behind the front wall. I peeked around the corner. What was on the anvil that Josh didn't want me to see? I peered into the darkness, and saw...nothing. Josh was not creating a new tool or a piece of art. He was pounding with all his strength, on an empty anvil.

CHAPTER 49

The sun was just setting when Matt called. "You still on the west side?" he asked.

"I'm on the road into town, almost to Sunnydale."

"Great. Meet me at Sunny Palms Golf Course. I have something I want to show you."

When I pulled into the parking lot, Matt was waiting with a cooler. "Follow me," he said as I got out of my pickup. "But be quiet."

He led me to a little grassy hill on the edge of the fairway, sat down, and patted the ground next to him. I took a seat and watched him open the cooler, which held cold fried chicken, two apples, and two beers. Matt opened one for me. "Just wait."

I was still feeling a bit raw from my bartending lesson at Bob's, so I sipped the beer politely, then set it down in the grass. I grabbed a piece of chicken, leaned against Matt, and watched the sun set, the sky turning from orange to gold to purple.

"There." Matt pointed not at the sky, but at a place where the golf course bordered the desert. "Do you see?"

I peered into the growing darkness and saw movement. Small figures that nearly blended into the desert brush and the gray dusk light. Only when they hopped onto the grass could I see them properly.

"Bunnies." I hugged Matt around the neck. "I love bunnies."

"I know."

Dozens of cottontails made their way slowly, tentatively, out of the cover of the desert and onto the cool green grass of the golf course, nibbling and hopping and generally being the cutest things on earth.

"I saw them when I came to look for Lassie the other night."

"You came out by yourself?"

"I knew you were busy with the Gold Bug investigation and

everything, so..." Matt shrugged. "I thought I'd see if I could find anything. No Lassie, unfortunately, but..." He waved at the busy party. A few long-eared jackrabbits had joined the crowd. "I thought you'd like this."

"I love it." I kissed him, then put down my chicken leg and kissed him again properly. So properly, in fact, that we both had to stop. "Van Morrison aside, I'm pretty sure we could get arrested for making love in the green grass," I said, panting a little. "But my house is safe."

"I can't stay over tonight," Matt said. "Big day tomorrow, you know."

Did I? What was happening tomorrow? It was Friday. I had a rehearsal for the gunfight, but I was pretty sure that wasn't it.

"I mean, I'm looking forward to it, but..." Matt sighed. He leaned back on his elbows. "You know. Family."

"Yeah." I had no idea what he meant. "You know, you don't talk much about your family." I hoped he would, right then, so I knew what was up tomorrow.

"Well, we're Irish-American." Matt rolled over on his side and looked at me. "My great-great-great grandfather came to America during the Great Bacon Famine."

"You mean the Potato Famine?"

"Well, there wasn't any bacon either."

I really wanted to know about Matt's family, so I smacked him, in a nice way. "Would you be serious?"

"Would you please let us be?"

We both looked surprised that he said it.

"Sorry, Ivy. This sneaking around is getting to me. I feel like we're having an affair or something. Or that you actually aren't really into us, that maybe you're keeping your options open."

"No. Not true. You're the only option I want." I kissed him again for proof. "So, your family..."

"I don't know. You'll meet my mom tomorrow. You can see for yourself."

"Tomorrow?" Dang. My mouth spoke before my brain had a chance to put the brakes on.

"Tomorrow." By the inflection in Matt's voice, I knew he'd caught the question in mine. "Don't tell me you forgot."

"Um..."

Matt stood up and brushed the grass off his jeans. "My mom is coming in tomorrow so she can be there for the party that your brother and the guys at the group home are throwing in honor of my graduation. I hope you can make it."

He left.

Had Matt really told me about the party? How had I forgotten? "Because you're so self-involved," my mother's voice said in my head. She was right this time.

I sat in the dark a few more minutes, hoping that the sight of happy little bunnies would make me feel better.

It didn't.

CHAPTER 50

I texted Matt when I got home: "Looking forward to your party." I should have apologized. But I didn't. And he didn't respond.

After a sleepless night, I got up and drove into the office. Uncle Bob was with Bette in Sedona, so there were no Friday morning donuts and only enough coffee in the can for half a pot. I made some anyway. I could go to Starbucks after I ran a background check on Chance and an asset search on Frank.

But when I finished running them through our databases, I just sat in my chair for a minute. Or ten. Then I called my uncle. I needed some extra brainpower. "I'm on a well-deserved vacation," said Uncle Bob's voicemail. "So I'm off the grid for a few days." Arghh.

A walk to Starbucks and coffee helped my mood (a little) but not my brain. I stared at my computer screen a few more minutes then made another call.

"There's gotta be something," Pink said.

"Hardly more than I got off Google yesterday. Frank's been in a couple of altercations having to do with his environmental activism, but nothing else. And a quick asset search shows that his house is mortgaged, but whose isn't?"

"How 'bout the other guy?"

"Chance? That's really weird. All I could find was a couple of theatre reviews and a mention of him in some indie Western on IMDB—the Internet Movie Database."

"You sure Chance Keeler is his real name, Miss Ivy Meadows?"

"Duh." I slapped myself on the forehead. "Sometimes I can't see the desert for the cactus."

"Not sure that metaphor works," Pink said. "But it's true, anyway."

* * *

"Any way you can get access to Gold Bug's employee records?" I asked Arnie over the phone. This was a long shot. Arnie was not the most computer literate guy in the world, and Chance might be using his stage name (if that's what it was) at Gold Bug too. Actors often made their stage names their legal aliases. For example, legally, I was both Olive Ziegwart *and* Ivy Meadows. I could get paid under either name.

"I'll see what I can do," Arnie said.

Okay, I had all the information I was going to get for now. Time to put it altogether using my favorite tool: a whiteboard. I was a visual thinker. Maybe because I was easily distracted, or maybe because I always had so many thoughts running around in my head, or maybe just because I liked colored markers—whatever it was, seeing ideas written out on a nice clean whiteboard just made things clearer.

I grabbed a bunch of markers and wrote "Gold Bug Gulch case" in nice big letters across the top of the board. Then:

1. Why shoot Mongo?

2. Why kill Billie?

3. Are the two deaths connected—and are the other "accidents" at Gold Bug (sewer, snakes, and tires) part of the same plan?

I chewed the end of a blue marker. Uncle Bob had taught me that most crimes could be put down to power or passion. Power included money, prestige, and the need to one-up someone. Passion covered revenge, sex, and love. Mongo could've been killed for revenge: Josh had that long simmering feud with his family. Chance could've killed Mongo for sex and love. Billie could've killed him out of jealousy—she had suspected another woman. I wrote those down.

There was also that supposed business deal, whether with Josh or someone else. Mongo's partner could've lost money and/or power. I wrote that down too.

Now, Billie's death. Josh and Billie were connected via the Golden Girls, and there was money involved, so power could've come into play. Chance could have killed her too, that love and sex motive again. He was definitely more into her than she was into him. And if he had killed Mongo for Billie's love, only to be rebuffed by her, well...

I wrote both of those suspects and motives down, then chewed on my marker some more. Several problems with my scenarios. The deaths and the accidents felt connected. But the timing was off. Why commit murder first, then go to vandalism? And the motives were problematic. Billie could have killed Mongo and then someone killed her out of revenge for his death, but it seemed unlikely. No one besides Billie and his tavern friends seemed to really miss Mongo. Josh and Chance could be responsible for both deaths, but when you added in the sewer and car sabotages and the reptile release, the deaths seemed less personal and more about Gold Bug Gulch itself. That pointed more to the power motive: someone wanted Gold Bug shut down so they could...what? Did Josh want his family's property back? Would Frank kill people over endangered bats? And what about Nathan? Could someone have made him an offer he couldn't refuse?

CHAPTER 51

I spent the whole morning spinning my investigative wheels. The only thing I had to show for four hours' worth of work was a whiteboard full of scribbles and a couple of chewed-up markers.

And still no response from Matt.

But it was also a school day *and* a workday for him, plus he probably needed to pick up his mom from the airport. Sure, my denial mechanism was in high gear, but there was nothing else I could do.

Yes, there was.

"I'm sorry," I texted him. Then I got in my truck and drove west.

I stopped in Sunnydale and trekked across the golf course to a tree by a water hazard where I'd set up a camera. I grabbed my laptop out of my backpack, downloaded the camera info into it, and sped through a night's worth of thirsty animals: bunnies and coyotes and...hey, a small sturdy figure waded into the manmade pond and lapped at the water. Could it be? Then another similar but much larger animal waded in next to the first one. It was big enough I could see its long snout and tusks. Sheesh. I must've been desperate, mistaking a baby javelina for a pug. I sat back on my heels. There was one more thing I could try.

I didn't relish the thought of being clonked in the head by a golf ball, so I got off the fairway before making my call—aiming for a low stuccoed wall that divided the yards from the golf course. I sat on the wall, punched the numbers into my phone, and tried to muster some enthusiasm. After all, if I was about to give up a big chunk of change, I'd better be damn excited about it. As the phone rang, I calculated. Since Arnie had hired me for the Gold Bug investigation, my part-time job at Duda Detectives was more like full-time, at least for the next week. I'd also get the extra money from the melodrama, bartending, and the gun fight. Then I'd be back to part-time money until I got a show. If I were cast in *Annie Get Your Gun*, I could be assured of a decent paycheck. If not, well, I did love beans.

"This is Southwest Pet Search and Rescue. How can I help you?"

"Hi, Joy, it's Ivy."

Silence.

"Ivy Meadows? We met the other day?"

"Sorry. Bad reception up here."

"Up here?" Maybe she was just on top of Camelback Mountain, here in the Valley. Joy looked like a climber. Please let her be a climber.

"I'm in the White Mountains." A mountain range about five hours away. "We're on a search and rescue job."

"For a dog?"

"No, Sam and I also volunteer for a couple of counties' teams. A hiker got caught in an early snowstorm."

Hikers routinely got in trouble in Arizona, especially tourists. They either didn't bring enough water with them, forgot that it snowed in the higher elevations, or fell off rocks they shouldn't have been climbing in the first place.

"Ivy? Are you there?"

"Yeah. I want to hire you and Sam to look for Lassie."

"We won't be home for at least another two days, depending on when we find this guy. Remind me, when did Lassie disappear?"

"Last Sunday."

"Twelve days ago?"

"Yeah, but one of the wildlife cameras snapped a photo...I guess it would've been Sunday night, maybe early Monday morning."

"Did you get any photos of predators?"

"Coyotes. And...are javelinas predators? I saw a mama and a baby."

"Yeah, and they're more aggressive when their young are around...Listen, for twelve days Lassie has been spending her days and nights outside, without access to regular food or water. And once small dogs get disoriented and slow, they're easy targets. If you're hoping to find her alive..."

I didn't remind Joy that Lassie was a him. Instead I said, "I think I hear what you're telling me."

"I'm so sorry," she said, "but unless you want to find her body, I'd save your money."

I hung up and slumped back on the hard stucco wall, scraping the palms of my hands on its surface until they felt raw. Like the rest of me.

CHAPTER 52

Ten minutes later, I mustered enough energy to make another call. "I want to shoot something."

Silence on the other line. Again.

"Can you hear me?" Maybe Pink was out with the search and rescue team too, though I didn't know why they'd want a detective from the Phoenix PD.

"Yeah. But it's not such a hot idea to shoot things when you're mad. Who you mad at?"

"Myself. The world. Maybe javelinas."

"Tell you what. You pick up some lunch and meet me at the Gulch in an hour. We'll see if you've cooled off by then."

"Deal." I slipped off the stucco wall. "See you then."

Pink was waiting in the Gold Bug parking lot when I got there. "Why are your lips blue?" he said as he climbed into my pickup.

"Huh?" It was eighty degrees out.

"Look in the mirror."

I did. My bottom lip was the lovely royal blue of my favorite marker. "A, uh, pen exploded."

"In your mouth?" Pink grabbed the In-N-Out Burger bag I handed him. I'd really wanted Mexican, but wasn't sure I wanted to be in a small space with a guy who smoked menthols and ate beans. He peered into the bag. "This all for me?"

"Yeah. I already ate."

"You feelin' better?" Pink was already halfway through his burger. A big-bite taker, that guy.

"If you're asking if I've cooled off, the answer is yes. I'm not just cool, I'm cold. Cold as in cold case, cold trail, cold-stupid-detective-who-couldn't-find-her-ass-with-a-flashlight cold."

"Okay." He bounced on the seat as my pickup hit an especially big pothole. "But could you not take that out on your truck?"

"Sorry. It's just that nothing's going well. Not just the Gold Bug case, but I can't find Lassie, I still don't know if I got this theater gig, and I had a fight with...never mind."

"The case I've been working on just blew apart too." He crumpled up his burger wrapper and put in in the bag. "Guy killed his wife, got acquitted, then confessed right afterward. Bragged about it on Facebook. Can't do anything about it. Double jeopardy."

"Are you trying to make me feel better or worse?"

He shrugged and started in on his French fries. "Sometimes a little reality check can go a long way."

"Damn." Pink stared at the tin cans now scattered on the desert floor. "You must be feeling better."

I was, though it wasn't really Pink's reality check. It was the text from Matt: "Sorry. Forgot to charge my phone last night." He must have had a sleepless night too. "See you tonight." And the best part: "XXOO."

"You nailed every can." Pink tossed his stub of a cigarette to the dirt and ground it under his heel. "I oughta recruit you."

"I'd make an awful cop." I handed Pink my rifle and started picking up the cans. "I'm not even sure I'm a very good PI. Uncle Bob says if you look up 'gullible' in the dictionary you'll see my picture."

"There was that time you thought that three-timing actor was—" Pink checked my gun to make sure it was fully discharged.

"Yeah." I cut him off but quick.

Pink opened the door to my pickup and set my rifle behind the seat. "And the time you believed that guy when he bought you—"

"Pretty gullible." I tossed the cans into the pickup bed, then went back and picked up Pink's cigarette butt. A good steward of the land. Frank would be proud.

"And Bob told me how you were buddy-buddy with some criminals when—"

"They were nice." I climbed into my pickup. We had rehearsal pretty soon.

"So yeah, I guess you would make an awful cop. But damn." Pink looked at the bullet-riddled cans in the back of my truck. "You are one hell of a shot."

We got back to the Gold Bug parking lot a few minutes before my afternoon rehearsal. I parked next to Pink's car, then hopped out and went around to him to say goodbye. "Thanks a ton." I gave him a friendly hug. "I'll talk to you—Ow! Damn!" I couldn't move.

"What?" Pink released me.

"My earring. Must have caught it on my shirt." I couldn't see it, but I could feel the tug whenever I tried to lower my arm. "Must be my collar, or around my shoulder somewhere. Can you unhook it for me?"

Pink leaned in. "I think I see it...damn, I really need my glasses." He peered at my ear, so close I could smell the menthol on his breath.

"And who is this?" said a voice close behind me. Chance.

"Got it," Pink said. My ear was released and he backed away.

"This is Detective Pinkstaff of the Phoenix—"

"And I thought you were single," Chance said.

"I am," I said. "I mean, I'm not exactly, but—"

"You act single," Chance said.

"I do?" I did?

"If you have a man, you should act like it. Nice to see you again." He tipped his hat at Pink. "I would keep an eye on her if I were you." He turned and walked toward the Gulch.

What was all that about? I suspected it wasn't really about me, probably had something to do with Billie and Chance and Mongo, but...I acted single? That didn't sound good. What did that say about the way I felt about Matt?

"That was that Chance guy, right?" asked Pink.

I nodded.

"There's something not right about him. Fake."

"He is an actor."

Pink stared after Chance, who walked with a slight cowboy swagger. "I think he's acting right now."

CHAPTER 53

After Pink drove off, I walked the dirt road to Gold Bug's saloon. Chance sat waiting for me on the steps. "Is Nathan in his office?" I asked. He shrugged an "I don't know," but I caught something else on his face. "What?"

"Women," he muttered.

No way I was getting into my love life with him, so I walked up the steps and into the saloon. "Nathan?" I called. "We're about ready for the gunfight rehearsal." Nathan needed to pull the fishing line that rang the bell and push the button on the remote to set off the squib in the flour sack. I heard a noncommittal grunt from the office. "Meet you out front in five," I said.

I walked back down the saloon steps to a still morose Chance. "Can I have the keys to the theater?" He handed them over without a word. I walked next door to the opera house, unlocked the stage door, and went to my dressing room. My rifle hung on its hook. I checked its chamber: empty. I pulled a box of blanks from my duffel bag (bought them myself at a gun store called Tombstone Tactical) and carefully placed them in the chamber of my rifle. I put Annie's hat on my head, locked the stage door as I left, and walked back to Chance. I gave him the keys back, then reached inside my duffel bag and pulled out another box of blanks: pistol-sized this time. "Here."

"I already have some."

"Use these." I pushed the box under his nose.

"Yeah, okay." Chance spun the chamber on his gun and shook the bullets out into his hand. They all looked like blanks—the ends were crimped, but I still felt better having him use the ones I purchased.

Chance began loading. "You going to watch me load them?"

"Wouldn't you?"

I didn't think anyone could be more grudging, until Nathan pushed open the swinging door of the saloon. "Can we get this over with?"

"You mean rehearse the biggest reason people come out to Gold Bug Gulch?"

"It's not the biggest—"

"You think they come for the food?" Chance laughed. It was nice to see him in a better mood. Sort of.

"So, Nathan, you do everything from up there." I pointed to a balcony that ran along the second floor of the saloon. Its floor was the roof of the saloon porch. "You'll find fishing line attached to the railing. Just yank it directly after my first shot and it will ring this." I pointed to an old bell that hung from the porch roof. I handed Nathan a remote. "On my second shot, push the button on this remote—I've already placed the squib in the flour sack."

"NowIhatotakorderfromawom," he said under his breath.

"Why yes, you do have to take orders from a woman, especially when you ask her to direct. Now Chance, on my third shot, you—"

"I know, I pull the line on my hat. I read the script. In fact, I have a question about the song."

"Song?" said Nathan. "In a gunfight?"

"Don't worry, you won't have to pay royalties."

"But..." Chance began.

"All right. Places, everyone."

Nathan climbed the exterior staircase that led to the balcony. I went down the road toward the blacksmith shop, and Chance walked the opposite way, toward Gold Bug's entrance.

"And...lights up," I yelled. No lights out here, of course, but it was the universal theatrical signal for "let's go."

I addressed the invisible townspeople, the audience who would gather in the streets. "So I heard you all here in Gold Bug are down a sheriff. I'm right sorry to hear about his passing." I took off my hat and placed it over my heart. Oops. Strike that blocking. My Annie Oakley pigtails were sewn to my hat. I cleared my throat. "I also heard you might need a little protection 'til your new lawman arrives in town. I've got a little break right now—I'm touring with Buffalo Bill Cody's Wild

West, you know—so I thought I'd stop a while here in the Gulch, just to make sure things stay peaceable." I settled my hat back on my head.

"Well, well, well." Chance strode into town, spurs jangling. "What have we here? A new gal in town. And a pretty one too. With a gun. That's cute, little missy." He pulled out his pistol and twirled it around his finger.

"You could shoot your foot off doin' that," I said. "And it's Miz Annie Oakley to you."

"Well, *Miz* Oakley, awful nice of you to worry 'bout me. But you can stop now. In fact, you don't need to worry 'bout anything, including the Gulch, 'cause I aim to be the law here."

"I don't see a badge."

"Badge? I don't need no stinkin' badge."

I put that line in just for Chance. "Then by whose authority do you act?" I said.

He pointed the gun at me. "Smith and Wesson's."

I raised my rifle too.

"Come on, pretty thing. Put down that gun. Women like you are made for lovin', not for fightin.'"

"I ain't afraid to love a man," I said. "I ain't afraid to shoot him either." Ha. Annie Oakley really said that.

"But here's the problem. I ain't afraid of no gal with a gun. You know why?"

I shook my head.

"Everything I can do," he began.

"Louder," I said in my director voice "And don't talk, sing. You know the tune." I'd sent Chance a YouTube link of the original song.

He sang: "Everything I can do, you do much badder. Everything you do is badder than me."

"No, it's not."

"Yes, it is."

"No, it's not."

"Yes, it is."

"No, it's not." I aimed at the bell hanging from the saloon porch.

"Yes, it—"

Bam! Clang! The saloon bell rang right on cue. It really did look like I shot it.

Chance lowered his gun. "Where in the world did that come from?"

"Nathan pulled the fishing line attached to the bell."

"I know that. The song."

"*Annie Get Your Gun*. It's that song, 'Anything I Can Do.'"

"I *know* that, but 'badder'? Is that a word?"

"It is now. And we're moving on, people," I yelled. I loved being a director.

The rest of the gunfight went smoothly. Even Nathan seemed impressed when the flour sack blew up. At first. "Are we going to need a new flour sack every show?" he grumbled.

"Just every other show. You can turn the sack around and use the other side."

After the gunfight, the rehearsal for the melodrama seemed tame. Frank held up the signs for the audience, practiced leading the boos and hisses and applause, and helped me change my costumes. He also agreed to wear a miner's outfit, said he had something that fit the bill.

When rehearsal was over, I changed back into street clothes and left by the stage door, the last one out of the opera house. Chance was waiting for me, holding the keys. He waited until I cleared the door, then locked the theater behind me.

"Hey, Chance," I said. "You ever hear anything about Mongo and a business deal?" Maybe Billie had mentioned something.

"Mongo? No way." He snorted. "Didn't have the brains for business."

"That's what I thought. Somebody told me he was about as bright as that *Blazing Saddles* character." No one really did, but maybe I'd get more out of Chance if he thought we were both down on Mongo.

I waited. Nope. Nothing more.

Still, I'd created an opening for my next line of questioning. "Mongo was a nickname, right? Not a stage name, I mean, since he wasn't really an actor. Chance Keeler is a way better stage name."

"It's my real name." Chance began walking down the road to the parking lot. I had to do double-time to keep up with him.

"Come on, actor to actor. My real name is Olive Ziegwart." To show him what a casual conversation this was, I added, "It means 'victory nipple' in German."

"No, it doesn't."

"What?" My dad had been telling us that all our lives.

"It means guardian of victory. Well, I guess it could mean victory nipple. 'Sieg' does mean a victor, and German for nipple is 'brustwarz.' Breast-wart."

"Breast-wart? Wow, even better."

"It is?" Chance was a literal kind of guy.

"How do you know all this?" I asked.

A look of panic flashed across Chance's face at my innocuous question. Huh. He hurriedly composed himself, but picked up his pace. I could barely keep up. "Wagner," he said, using the Germanic pronunciation.

"Wagner?"

"I studied opera."

"In Wyoming?"

I swear I saw that panicked look again, just briefly, before Chance scowled. "I am an actor, you know. We studied the classics. And when we studied opera, we learned some German and Italian. Didn't you?"

I had only attended community college (money issues), and I had never studied opera, so I kept quiet. The fact did not escape Chance.

Chance gave a little "I knew it" snort. "So the girl from Arizona should not make fun of the man from Wyoming. Especially since we study shooting there too."

I tried to keep up with Chance as we walked to the parking lot, but soon gave up. By the time I reached the lot, the only sign he'd been there was the cloud of dust his Jeep left behind.

I walked toward my truck, and wow. Mingled with smell of dust was another one. Someone had been smoking a particularly potent type of weed. Couldn't have been Chance or Frank, since they'd been in rehearsal with me. I guess it could've been Nathan, but he didn't seem like the stoner type.

Probably some kids from Wickenberg decided that this parking lot was a good spot to get high. It was always pretty empty when the Gulch was closed. But wow, this, um, fragrance was worse than Pink's cigarettes.

The skunky smell got stronger as I neared my pickup. What did they do, sit in the back of my truck and smoke?

Maybe they had. The smell was definitely concentrated around my pickup. So much so that I slowed down and took a good look. No one in the bed of the truck. I peered into the cab. The sun had set, the light fading to gray, but I would have been able to see anyone inside. No one. I opened the door. I decided to lock it from that time forward, because...Whoa. I was nearly bowled over by the smell—and by something else. It ran toward the open door: a tiny, terrified, incredibly cute, and unbelievably smelly baby skunk.

CHAPTER 54

Romantic relationships were not my forte. Oh, I liked men, and they liked me. I'd had a few boyfriends, even sort of serious ones, but something always seemed to happen. I suspected that something was me.

But even forewarned with this superficial bit of insight into my personality, I still managed to blow any chance I had at happiness with a man. And I was doing it again.

I stood in the corner of the living room, watching the party at Cody's group home swirl around me. It was an unusual mix of people: college students, guys with cognitive disabilities and their family members, and a few neighbors. They were all celebrating Matt's upcoming graduation, and I was hiding in a corner.

Cody ran up to me. "Isn't this great?" Cody loved parties. "I picked out the cake." The cake crumbs on his blue shirt told me he'd sampled it too. "Why are you over here?" He sniffed the air. "And why do you smell funny?"

I'd done what I could to air out the truck. I'd taken a shower, washed my hair, and changed clothes, but..."There was a skunk in my car."

"Oh." Cody considered this information for a minute. I expected him to ask me why, but the mystery of the skunk was not the question he wanted answered. "Okay. But why are you over here?"

"I...have a headache." I lowered my voice. "Why are you having this party now?" I was a little afraid that Cody or Matt had already told me this too and I'd forgotten, self-involved creature that I was. "Matt doesn't graduate for another two weeks."

"Stu will be on vacation with his family." Stu, a good guy with

Down Syndrome, was Cody's best friend at the group home. "They're going to England. He's going to bring me back a rock." Cody had recently begun collecting rocks. A nice inexpensive hobby, but a heavy one. "Hey, would you get me one from Gold Bug Gulch? Maybe one with gold in it?"

"Even better, you can pick one up yourself. You're going to come see my show pretty soon, right?" Matt had told me he would bring him out.

"Right." He frowned past me at the cake table, which had been set upon by bunch of his roommates. "Uh-oh. I better get a piece of cake for Sarah *now*." He ran off, wobbling a bit as he often did when he was excited. Part of his brain injury.

I stayed in my corner.

Two people inside my brain were fighting, circling round and round, and occasionally throwing each other to the mat. One of my little mind wrestlers was a romantic optimist: "Cody's excited about Matt's graduation. This is the perfect time to tell him about you and Matt." The other half of my brain, the security-conscious pessimist said, "No, wait. You've got two more weeks. A lot can happen in two weeks. Take that time. Protect everyone."

Because my mind was deep in its wrestling match, I didn't notice Matt come up beside me until he touched me on the arm. Sarah stood behind him, smiling shyly over his shoulder. Cody followed her with two plates of cake.

Matt put an arm around my waist. He pulled me close to him, then frowned. "Have you been smoking pot?" he whispered into my ear.

"What? No. Oh," I said. "Skunk."

"Much better," he said, and then...

"He kissed you!" Cody looked at me, wide-eyed.

"On the lips," said Sarah.

Matt watched me. I knew what I should say. "He's just excited, a graduation party and all." That wasn't what I should've said. But it's what I said.

"I'm done with school in two weeks," Matt said quietly, giving me another chance. "And I start my new job in a month."

"I bet the guys are going to miss you." I was swimming away from the life ring Matt had tossed, but the security wrestler had pinned my romantic optimist to the mat. Nothing I could do. Matt's arm dropped from my waist.

"I am," said Cody. "But he's going to come see me a lot. Right?"

"You bet." Matt turned to me. "Are you going to miss me?"

What did that mean? Was Matt trying to get me to confess our relationship in front of Cody? Or was he threatening to break up with me?

"There you are." A short older woman bustled toward us. She had Matt's curly hair and his gray eyes but none of his relaxed ease. Instead, she looked as tightly wound as a home permanent.

"Hi, Mom." Matt stepped away from me. "You know Cody."

"Hi." Cody stuck out his hand and she shook it gingerly.

"And his girlfriend, Sarah." Sarah gave a little wave and half hid behind Cody, maybe because she caught the disapproving look that flashed across Matt's mom's face.

"And this is Ivy," Matt said. "Cody's sister."

"It's so nice to meet you." Matt's mom pressed my hand. "Interesting perfume, dear. Don't they call that Mary Jane?" Great, Matt's mom thought I'd smoked a joint before the party. She turned back to Matt. "That was Daphne who called. She said to tell you that she is so sorry she couldn't make it, but with the baby so close..."

Matt's older sister was due in the next few weeks. First grandkid for his folks. Everyone was pretty excited. "That's the reason I'm here now," she said to me. "You know, at this party instead of the actual graduation ceremony. Don't want to miss our new baby boy." Back to Matt: "And you know Katie was just sick that she couldn't make it, but she couldn't leave her folks." To me: "Katie's dad has the Alzheimer's. She moved back home to take care of him and her mom and manage the farm. Of course, she still works too. Her company is letting her telephone-commute—is that what you call it?"

Katie? Matt had just the one sister, Daphne. I glanced at him, but he was focused on his mom. And his jaw was clenched.

"Everyone is so proud she's doing so well. Did she tell you she got a promotion?" she asked Matt.

"Mom." The muscles in Matt's neck stood out like wires.

"In fact, her company is flying her to Paris next month. I'm going to stay with her folks then, because, well, she can't miss Paris. Oh." She still smiled at Matt, but her eyes narrowed, a gray-eyed fox. "You'll have some time off then too. Maybe you could go too, and—"

"*Mom.*"

"Who's Katie?" I said brightly, hoping it would look like I was defusing the tension when I really just wanted to know who this annoyingly fabulous Katie was.

"Oh, didn't you know?" his mom said. "Katie is Matt's fiancée."

The pessimist wrestler in my head said, "match over," but I summoned an enormous amount of willpower and pulled Matt out of the party to a far corner of the backyard. His mom probably thought I needed a hit. "Katie?" I said.

"Ex-fiancée," Matt said. "*Ex.*" He stood close, but faced away from me.

"Don't you think you should have mentioned it?" I said. "Something like, oh, I was supposed to get married once...Wait. When *were* you supposed to get married?" Matt had dated my friend Candy before me. He never said too much about his romantic life prior to that.

Matt didn't say anything. This was uncharacteristic.

"When?" I repeated.

"Well, after Candy and I broke up..."

"*After?*"

"I went home for a week, and..."

"I remember. We were already friends. In fact, I remember you saying something about me being your best friend, which was obviously not true because—"

"Ivy, just shut up for a minute."

Whoa.

"This is what happened. I went home and reconnected with my high school sweetheart."

"Re-connected. Huh. Is that a euphemism for—?"

"*Ivy.*"

I shut my mouth, but I finally understood those cartoons where steam came out people's ears. I thought it literally might.

"We talked a lot, about old times, about our families, about how we used to think we'd get married and…" I heard him swallow, even from two feet away. "She got the wrong idea."

"That sounds like wishful thinking, not an ex-fiancée."

"Yeah, well, things went a little further than they should have before I broke it off."

"How far?"

"Katie said something to my mom, who was so excited she gave her my grandma's engagement ring."

"Your mom gave Katie a ring?"

"She always wanted Katie and me to get together. Now even more, since she thinks it might bring me back home to Grand Island." He made a frustrated noise deep in his throat. "You'd have to know my mom."

"I guess, so, because this sounds like some pretty fancy sidestepping, mister."

"Fancy sidestepping?"

"Don't try to distract me. You know what I mean." I walked away from him. "I can't believe you didn't tell me." That dang mental wrestler said, "Told you to protect yourself," then he whispered something else. "Wait," I said. "Why does your mom think you're still engaged?"

"Well…"

I waited. Not long, but as long as I could. "Why, Matt?"

"Katie still has the ring."

"*What?*"

"I told her to give the ring back, but Mom wouldn't take it and…you'd have to know my mom."

"Fine. Let's go get to know her." I stared walking toward the house. "And you can tell her you're not engaged anymore."

"And tell her about us?"

I stopped walking. I didn't mean to. And it was just for a second.

But it was a second too long.

CHAPTER 55

It was way too early in the morning. I was nursing a "fight with my boyfriend" hangover (and maybe a little one from the beers I drank afterward). I hadn't heard a peep from Arizona Center Stage. I was tromping through the desert outside Sunnydale searching for a dog I loved who had probably been eaten by a coyote or died of dehydration or run over by a car. In short, I was a little depressed.

So when my phone rang, I nearly didn't pick up. It was Arnie, and I didn't want to tell him about my lack of news about Lassie or the feeling I was beginning to have about Gold Bug: that someone was sabotaging his newest venture. But my mother did raise me to be polite, and that means answering my phone when it rings. I picked up.

"And how are you this fine morning?" Arnie chortled. Glad someone was in a good mood. "Guess what? I hacked into Nathan's computer."

"You what?" Arnie was no computer whiz. Maybe he bought a new gadget. I should find out what it was, might come in handy.

"Hacked?" Marge was on the other line. "He means he looked at Nathan's laptop when he left the room to take a leak."

"Same difference," said Arnie.

"Anyway..." I said.

"Anyway, I found the employee records. Chance's real name is Gun. Great name for a cowboy, right?"

"Gun? Someone named their kid Gun?"

"No," said Marge. "They named him Gunther. Somebody put a nickel in Arnie's slot this morning, is all."

Arnie chuckled.

"Wow," I said. "Gunther seems almost as unlikely. Must have been teased like crazy, growing up in Wyoming."

"Wyoming?" said Arnie. "No. I saw something about a visa."

"A visa? For Chance—I mean Gunther?"

"Yeah," said Arnie. "Gunther Schmidt is from Munich. Hey, you want to come over for breakfast?"

After I picked up donuts (which was what Arnie was really angling for), I went to Marge and Arnie's house, where we had a nice breakfast, and I drank about a gallon of Marge's good coffee. I didn't offer any information about Lassie, and they didn't ask.

"So Nathan said you're gonna do the gunfight." Arnie propped his walking cast on an ottoman and put his after-breakfast cigar in his mouth. As usual, he didn't light it. I think it was more of a tasty prop than anything else.

"As Annie Oakley. I thought we'd tie it in to the melodrama. Maybe we'll draw a bigger crowd." The gunfight was free to watch. The melodrama cost ten bucks (five for kids).

"You are really smart!" said the clock on the wall.

"Couldn't have said it better myself," said Arnie.

"Did you hear Gold Bug is clear to serve water now?" asked Marge. "The police are still investigating Billie's death, but Nathan paid some private company to expedite the testing. No cyanide anywhere."

"Bet he's happy." Concessions were the backbone of the operation. Most of the money was made from the burgers and beer in the saloon, the popcorn and lemonade sold at the opera house, and the crank-your-own ice cream Josh sold in a stand outside his forge. Of course, it also meant that someone probably tampered with the water for the cookout, but Nathan seemed much more concerned about the business than the deaths.

"Nathan spent a bundle," Arnie said, "but he's breathing easier now."

"Whose money?" I bit into a jelly donut and red goo slithered down my hand. "Gold Bug can't have very much in the bank yet. Which brings me to another question: Nathan is more of a manager than an owner, right? I mean, he doesn't even own twenty percent."

"What?" Marge looked hard at Arnie. I took the opportunity to lick the jelly from my hand.

Arnie shrugged. "He's got bad credit."

"Like father, like son," she said.

"Hey." Arnie took the cigar out of his mouth so he could look properly wounded.

"Whose money did he spend?" said Marge.

I stood up to make my getaway. "Would you look at the time?"

"Sit down, Ivy," Marge said. "This could be important to your investigation. You are still investigating, right?"

Double whammy. I sat down. Time to start thinking like a detective. "Why is Nathan so invested in this venture? Seems like he doesn't have that much to lose."

"He does get a salary. For managing the place."

"I've seen the accounts. It's not that much money, and I'm sure he could find other work." I remembered Nathan sweating over the plumbing. And again when he met the investors. "He treats Gold Bug as way more than just a job," I said. "There must be another reason."

"For one, he doesn't want to let me down," said Arnie. "You know, he finally finds his old man, offers him this great investment opportunity, and then bankrupts his poor old dad."

"Bankrupts?" I said.

"Just a figure of speech," Arnie said, but Marge took a deep breath.

"You said, 'for one.' What's the other reason?" I asked.

Arnie chewed on his unlit cigar. No, chomped, as if it were a piece of really tough celery.

"Come on, chickie," Marge said, though the endearment sounded forced. "What's up?"

"You know how I hired Ivy to make sure everything was on the up-and-up out there?" Arnie's jaw worked furiously. "It wasn't just because I was worried about the project."

"Yeah?" Marge said.

"Nathan...well, he doesn't really know his investors." Chomp, chomp, chomp.

"That's not unusual. But..." I prompted.

"They're friends of friends back in Philly." Arnie took the soggy cigar out of his mouth. He'd chewed it in half. "And he thinks they're Family."

CHAPTER 56

"What?" Marge's face was red. "You knew this and…"

"The investors are related?" I said. "What's wrong with that?"

"Babe, I didn't know until we were already in." Arnie pleaded with Marge. "And by then, there was Nathan to consider and…"

"Are they the wild cousins or something?" I said. "The bad sheep of the family?"

"I cannot believe you put us in bed with the mob."

Oh.

Shit.

Marge picked up her purse from the kitchen counter and walked past the couch to the garage door without so much as a glance at Arnie. "And I hope you're comfy there, because no one else is going to be sleeping with you."

I knew next to nothing about the mob. Sure, I knew organized crime existed, and from time to time I'd hear about the Mexican mob, La Familia, but it all seemed like something out of an old movie.

This new information threw another wrench into the works. Maybe the investors killed Mongo and Billie in order to send a message to Nathan. But what sort of message? That he needed to make Gold Bug work? Or did Nathan have debts or ties he didn't tell Arnie about?

I called Uncle Bob. "I'm not available right now but if you'll leave a—"

I hung up. Still in Sedona with Bette, I guessed. I didn't want to leave a message about organized crime on his voicemail, and besides, Arnie had said Nathan *thought* the investors were mafia. I started to call Matt, to talk things through, like I always did. Luckily I remembered his ex-fiancée before his phone even rang. I hung up and dialed again. "Hey, Pink," I said, then stopped. What exactly did I want to talk to him about? Impulsively spilling my guts had got me in trouble before. I needed a little time to think through my questions before I asked them. So when he said, "What's up, Ivy?" I didn't tell him I was worried about the mob. I just said, "Do you have time for a little target practice this morning?"

Bam! Bam! Bam!

"Dang," I said. "Missed that last shot." I squinted at the target Pink brought. Two of my shots had hit the paper head, but one was several inches past the left ear.

"You seem tensed up. Keep your legs straight, but relaxed. And don't tighten your fingers—don't want to slap the trigger. Now, try again."

Bam! Bam! Bam!

"Huh." Pink stared at the target. "Exactly like the first time." Even the missed shot was nearly in the same place as the first one. "Try again."

I did. Same results.

"Interesting," Pink said as we drove back to the Gulch in my pickup. "You're off your game today. Any reason why? Maybe it's the same reason you asked me out here today?"

"Let me see, I had a fight with my boyfriend, can't find my friends' dog, and I'm worried that the Mafia is somehow mixed up in Gold Bug Gulch." Okay, I just thought it—didn't say it out loud. Not yet. Instead I said, "Hey, I forgot to tell you. Chance is really Gunther Schmidt from Munich. A German cowboy. Wild, huh?"

"Not as much as you might think. The Wild West is big in Germany. They even got theme towns like the Gulch there."

"You sound like Uncle Bob."

"Who do you think told me?"

The strip of cottonwoods came in sight, a beautiful soothing green. I rolled down my window to catch the cool air from the creek, inhale its scent.

Hey. There was a cowboy hat where it shouldn't be, behind a boulder overlooking the creek. It was attached to Chance, who was hunched down behind the rock. Then, movement on the other side of the rock. I slowed down the car. Was the person Chance was hiding from about to find him?

"Why'd you slow—"

I shushed Pink, who'd been blowing smoke out the passenger window. Too late. Don't know if he heard Pink's voice or the sound of my truck, but Chance turned around. So did the other man. It was Frank.

A look I couldn't define—fear maybe?—flashed across Frank's face in the second before he recognized me. Then his expression relaxed into the easygoing one I knew. "Hey, Ivy."

"What're you boys up to?" I said. "Looking for gold?"

"Bats," Chance said. "We're looking for bats."

"Yeah, I thought I saw some a few nights ago," Frank said. "Might be roosting in those trees down there." He pointed toward the creek, but not in the direction he and Chance had been looking.

"Good luck. See you soon, Chance." Our first of the day's three gunfights was in an hour.

"I'll be back," he said in a very good Schwarzenegger imitation. Ah, now I knew why his voice often sounded forced and clipped. He was trying to hide his German accent.

"Ivy." Pink watched the men in my rearview mirror as we drove away. They hadn't moved.

"Yeah, they were lying." I swerved to avoid a big rock in the road. "Even I know bats don't fly during the day." I went around a bend and pulled the pickup off the shoulder, where it'd be hidden from Frank and Chance. "Wanna go see what they were really looking at?"

"If I'd have known I was going to be tromping through the dirt, I'd have worn different shoes," Pink grumbled as he followed me down a sort-of path to the creek, slipping and sliding in his hard-soled shoes.

"You did know you'd be tromping around in the dirt when you agreed to help me practice shooting," I said. "And watch out for the quicksand."

"In the desert?"

"There's some near that old snag."

"You've got to be shitting me. Quicksand in the desert."

"Fine, take your chances. See if I help you out of the muck as it swallows you whole. Hey, shhh. Listen."

I crouched down behind a fallen tree, where I could just see the boulder where Chance and Frank had been hiding. Where they still hid—I could see movement behind the rock.

"Shhh," I whispered to Pink, who had joined me. "Can't you breathe softer?"

"Gotta stop smoking," he wheezed.

I peered over the log in the same direction Chance and Frank had been looking. Only the creek, sparkling in the sunlight, trees swaying above it in the breeze, birds flitting from branch to branch and singing of their love of water and trees in the desert.

"There." Pink pointed. "Just to the left of that big tree."

I squinted. "The big tree. Thanks. That narrows it down a whole bunch." I heard it then. Josh's voice. I followed the sound to, yep, the left of a big tree. Josh stood on the edge of the tall grass, in the shade with his back to us.

"You see who he's talking to?" whispered Pink.

"No." Whoever they were—it looked like a small group of people, maybe three—stood back in the woods. Their silhouettes blended into the trees and tall brush around them.

I looked over at Frank and Chance. They were so intent on Josh and the group with him that they hadn't noticed Pink and me at all.

"Can you hear what they're saying?" Pink cocked an ear toward the creek and frowned. "Damn, I'm getting old."

"Shh." I listened hard. And above the sound of birdsong and the burbling creek, one word floated up to me. "Gold."

CHAPTER 57

"Bats, huh?" Standing outside the stage door, I put my Annie Oakley hat on my head, tugging it down snug so it wouldn't fall off. "I never knew they flew during the daytime."

"Didn't today." Chance took the blanks I handed him and filled his pistol. "Let me see your bullets too."

I opened the breech of my rifle and slid out the rounds. "See, all blanks. I marked the ends of them with red nail polish so it's easy to tell."

Chance grunted his approval and I placed the rounds back into my rifle. "I didn't know you and Frank were friends."

He shrugged and looked down the street, where about a hundred people had gathered for the upcoming gunfight.

No way he'd answer any questions about him and Frank shadowing Josh, so I chose another, more innocent question: "Is that where you went after Billie's death?"

"Thought you said you weren't single."

"What? No, I mean, yes, I mean, *what?*"

"I saw you with him again. Your man. In your truck."

"Pink is not my—why does it matter?"

"It matters to the man you are with." He snorted. "Women."

I turned on him. "I have had it with you guys saying 'women' all the time. It's offensive and it doesn't mean anything anyway."

"It means you are all the same."

"We are not. This is obviously about Billie, but that's not fair. You already knew about her and Mon—" Dang. He'd distracted me. I needed to wrestle back control of the conversation. "Let's not get off topic here. We're not talking about me or Billie. We're talking about you, Gunther."

Chance didn't move, but something clicked behind his eyes. "You talkin' to me?" he said in his best De Niro.

"Yes, I am, Gunther Schmidt from Munich."

"So you know."

"Why hide it?"

"Who would hire a cowboy named Gunther?"

"You could go by Gun." I thought of Arnie. I wondered if Marge had come home.

"Gun. Gun. Shit, you're right."

"And why make up the whole story about Wyoming?"

"Because no one would hire—"

"A cowboy from Germany. Right. But you're an actor. You can play lots of roles. Is being a cowboy so important to—"

"Yes." Chance cut me off. "It is. And it's time for our shootout."

"Folks, we hear word there might be a gunfight coming up," Nathan's voice said over the loudspeakers mounted on the front of the buildings. "So we'd like you to line up on the sides of the streets, for safety's sake." The crowd obediently got into place, and Chance and I did the same.

Nathan played the beginning of the musical accompaniment for "Anything You Can Do" over the speakers as Chance and I opened the show with the bit of dialogue I'd written. The audience laughed appreciatively at all the right places. Then right on cue, Chance sang, "Everything I can do, you do much badder. Everything you do is badder than me."

"No, it's not."

"Yes, it is."

"No, it's not."

"Yes, it is."

"No, it's not." I aimed at the bell hanging from the saloon porch.

"Yes, it—"

Bam! Clang!

The audience applauded madly.

Chance scowled and sang, "Any bell you can ring I can ring louder, I can ring any bell louder than you."

We bantered back and forth until Chance squeezed off a shot. The bell tinkled (via a pull from the fishing line). "I rang it louder, didn't I, folks?" I shouted. The crowd roared in my favor. Audience participation was always a hit.

I sang the opening line to the song's bridge: "I can shoot my dinner."

"I'm a breadwinner," sang/boasted Chance.

"I can really bake." I aimed at the flour sack.

"You should see *my* cake."

"Without no flour?" *Poof!* The sack exploded. "Don't look so sour," I sang to Chance.

The rest of the song went swimmingly. We finished the gunfight at one fifteen. We had two more scheduled showdowns, one at three and one at five, with melodrama shows at two and four, then I needed to tend bar from five 'til nine. I could change into my melodrama costume in five minutes, so if I were quick about it, I had just enough time to do a little investigating.

CHAPTER 58

I moseyed down the street, nodding at oldsters and chatting with little kids, until I reached the mouth of the blacksmith shop. A small crowd had gathered outside. I joined them, standing on tiptoe to see over their shoulders.

The orange light of the glowing forge reflected off Josh's face like the devil light at a haunted house. His hammer clanged against the anvil, and sparks flew from the piece of iron he held with his tongs. His eyes narrowed behind his safety glasses as he concentrated on the next blow. Then those eyes flicked up and looked straight at me.

Had he seen Pink and me spying on him?

"Not someone you'd want to be mad at you," said a guy in the crowd.

Josh must have heard the comment. He held my eyes for a moment longer, then said, "Actually, it's sort of the opposite." He lifted the piece of iron, now curled upon itself like a snail shell. "Before I found smithing, I was an angry man." Frank's crooked nose flashed in front of me. "Now, this work burns away the rage like an impurity in the metal." He dunked the piece of iron into a vat of water. It sizzled, and steam rose like an instant thundercloud. "Smithing is actually very calming."

He didn't look calm to me—the muscles in his arms tight and ropy, his hands clenched, his jaw jutting forward...

Someone beside me made a little noise, like a chuckle stuck deep in his throat. He had his back turned to me and wore a plaid Western-cut shirt, so new it was still creased from the package. He turned and I recognized him, along with his group of similarly clad friends. Nathan's investors. Right behind them was Frank, whose weathered face was scrunched up in concentration. Was he trying to listen to the investors' conversation? I slipped behind him, so I could listen too.

"Pounding stuff makes me feel better too," said New Shirt. His buddies all laughed.

"Me, I like shooting things," said a guy in a new black cowboy hat.

"I'm a man of simple tastes," said another. "I just like money."

Someone jostled me right into Frank. "Oh, Ivy," he said, "Crap. Am I late for the show?"

I followed his gaze to an old clock mounted on the front of the bank across the street, which was being retrofitted into the Saguaro Savings and Loan Shooting Gallery. "Yeah," I lied. "I thought I'd better find you. Let's go."

We wove through the crowds of tourists in the streets. "So you and Chance are friends?"

"Not really. He seemed interested in the bats though, and I'm always looking for more allies in the fight against—"

"But you're really not friends? So he didn't stay at your house after Billie died?"

Frank sighed and scratched the top of his head. "Okay." He lowered his voice. "I've been helping him out, so he came to me when Billie died. He was heartbroken. A couple days before, they'd been out at some bar. Chance was happy he'd been cleared and was acting all goofy. Billie accused him of faking his grief over killing Mongo. They fought, never got a chance to make up. He couldn't get over it, wanted a place to hole up for a few days. No crime in that."

"You've been helping him out how?"

Frank kicked at the dirt with the toe of one of his new-looking hiking boots. "All Chance ever wanted was to be a cowboy. He grew up with pictures of John Wayne on his walls, watched *True Grit* so many times he knows the lines backwards and forwards, even moved here so he could live the cowboy life."

Did Frank know that Chance had emigrated from Germany? Did it matter?

"This," Frank spread his arms to encompass the dusty town, "is heaven to him. He had just one problem: He's afraid of horses. I've been teaching him to ride. Secretly."

"And to shoot?"

"No. He already knew how. He's not a great shot, but...listen. I know what you're getting at. And yeah, I'm not above a little justified environmental activism, and sometimes I enlist my friends for help. You know, until they started this tourist trap, this land," he waved toward the grove of cottonwoods and the glint of sun off the creek, "was being taken back by nature, the way it was intended to be. Do you know how many riparian areas there are like this in all of Arizona?" He glared at the signs for ice cream and cold beer and "Get Your Wild West On" photos. "They could do this capitalist crap anywhere. So sure, I may have had something to do with the plumbing issue—"

"And the flat tires? Escaped rattlers, maybe?"

"Maybe. And I may have had a little help, but—"

"How about cyanide?"

"*But*—" Frank looked me straight on with those blue blue eyes, "—I would never kill anyone over bats."

CHAPTER 59

By the time Frank and I made it through the crowd to the opera house, we were well and truly late. Strike that: I was late. And I blamed Annie Oakley. I mean, when little girls tugged on my buckskin fringe and wanted their picture taken with Annie, how could I say no?

Frank had no such problem, as he basically looked (and smelled) like a crusty old miner, so he was waiting by my dressing room door when I got there. "Already got your saloon girl wig set backstage," he said, "but I need that costume you're wearing."

I ran into my dressing room, stripped off my Annie Oakley costume, opened the door a crack, and handed the dress and wig/hat to Frank.

"Hey, are we good?" he said. "About my, uh, fervent environmentalism? You understand how I feel about this place, right?"

"I do understand, but—"

"So the place smelled like sewage for a while. Can you honestly say that a tourist attraction is more important than a sacred place, especially one of the last ones left?" If Frank's gaze were any more intense, it would've bored a hole through the door.

"All right. Can't say I approve of your methods, but I do want the gods to keep talking in the cottonwoods. Maybe there's a compromise?"

"Maybe. And thanks." Frank gave me a quick grin and headed toward backstage.

I shut the door. The clock on the wall said seven minutes before two o'clock, which meant two minutes until places. Yikes. I already had on my saloon girl costume, which I wore underneath pretty much everything when I was on duty at Gold Bug, so I grabbed my ingénue dress off the hanger, Velcroed it up the front, pinned my hat and wig on my head, and began to slip into my shoes.

Then I saw it.

"Aaah!" I fell hard on my side, trying to get away from my attacker. Instead it tumbled out of the shoe I'd kicked over and charged toward me. "Wrong way!" I shouted at the skittering scorpion. "Turn around! Turn around!" It didn't. Instead it flicked its tail up so it'd be ready to sting me.

I didn't move. It didn't move. Forget the gunfight, this was a real standoff.

Chance came flying through the door.

"Scorpion!" I pointed at the little monster as it turned to face Chance.

"Hasta la vista, baby." He stomped it flat with his boot, then turned to me. "And places."

"Cuttin' it close." Frank stood next to me in the wings as the lights dimmed, marking the beginning of the show.

"There was a scorpion in my shoe."

"Big one or little one?"

"I don't know. About two inches long, sort of yellow-tan."

Frank nodded. "Bark scorpion. You're lucky—those ones are the worst. Killed one of my friend's dogs. You should always check your shoes out here."

He was right. Arizona was home to a whole host of scorpions, and anyone who'd ever camped in the desert knew to check their shoes before putting them on. Scorpions liked their nice dark comfy interiors. So sure, Frank's relaxed attitude may have been warranted when it came to the scorpion in my shoe—if it hadn't been for the reptiles onstage and the skunk in my car.

Someone was definitely sending me a message.

"You saw *The Godfather*, right?" I slid a drink to Arnie across the saloon bar. "Where they put a horse's head in the bed? Do you think the Mafia would use scorpions and skunks?"

"I don't know," he snuffled, eyes filling up for the umpteenth time. "I don't know anything."

When I came in for bartending duty a little before five, I saw Arnie sitting on a stool by himself. I'd poured him only sarsaparillas, but since he couldn't tell me how long he'd been there, he didn't know how many drinks he'd had before I arrived, and it was nearly his bedtime (eight o'clock), I took out my phone and called Nathan. No answer.

"Guess I'd better go home." Arnie slid off his barstool. "Even though no one is waiting for me." He took his keys out of his pocket.

"No, wait. Let me drive you home. It's been a long hard day for you."

"Aren't you on duty 'til nine?"

"Yeah."

"Too late. I want to go now." He started toward the door, clomping in his walking cast.

"Remember how you said you didn't see so well in the dark?"

Arnie shuffled to a stop.

"Let me try Nathan again." I called again. Still no answer. "Hey," I called to the saloon's waitress, a fiftyish woman who'd waited tables in Wickenburg for most of her life. "Could you get Nathan for me?"

She pursed her lips. I could tell she made that face often—the wrinkles around her mouth didn't lie. "Nope."

"Please?"

"Nope. Not unless you want me to leave this crowd hungry."

Crowd was an overstatement, but she *was* the only waitress.

"Couldn't you swing by the office real quick?"

"I could, but he's not there. Hasn't been around all evening."

Arnie resumed shuffling in the direction of the door. What could I do? I couldn't leave the bar unattended, and it's not like I could call for a ride out here in the middle of nowhere.

Someone pushed open the swinging doors to the saloon. "Where you off to, chickie?" Marge. Thank God.

"Marge! Thank God." Arnie and I were obviously on the same wavelength.

Marge walked toward her husband, a warm smile lighting her face. "About time you came home, don't you think?"

"I'm so sorry," Arnie choked out.

"I know, chickie, I know." Marge held out her arms and Arnie hugged her like he was coming home from war.

"You forgive me?"

"Of course. And I trust you did what you thought was right. That's what love's all about," she said, looking straight at me. "Trust."

I stared at Marge. "How did you know?" I whispered.

"Women's intuition. Plus Matt told me. He wanted to talk to someone who knew you. I was supposed to keep it secret, but..."

"When did he tell you?"

"He called...Thursday, I think it was."

Thursday. Before our fight, then. I slumped forward on the bar and rested my chin on my hands.

Marge reached over and touched me on the cheek. "You want to talk later? I gotta get Arnie home right now, but..."

"Yeah. Maybe later. And I think maybe you two need to talk to Nathan. About your...concerns." The saloon may not have been full, but there were still plenty of ears listening.

"I've been trying all evening," said Marge. "He's not answering his phone."

Huh. The waitress was standing near, eavesdropping. "You know where Nathan is?" I asked.

"Nope." She made the prune face again. "And he disappeared before telling me my schedule next week."

"Disappeared?" Arnie's big ears perked up.

"Nobody's seen him since noon or so," said Prune.

"I did," I said. "He helped out with the gunfight..." But only the first one. One of the dishwashers had filled in the other two times. I hadn't questioned it, just figured Nathan was busy.

"Then you know more than me." The waitress clomped off.

Arnie's bald head wrinkled in worry.

"He's probably in Wickenburg," I said, "celebrating the fact that things went right for a day." I made sure I looked calm on the outside, but inside, a scorpion skittered toward me and raised its tail in warning.

CHAPTER 60

After Arnie and Marge left, I tried Nathan's phone every fifteen minutes. He never picked up. "Have you seen Nathan?" I asked, oh, everyone.

"Probably went home with a hangover," said one of the dishwashers. "He was hittin' the sauce pretty heavy."

"When?"

"All day. In his office."

Ah. That's all it was. I was being silly. The scorpion had set me on edge, but really, it was just a common pest, and Nathan was just a common drinker. Still, I slipped into his office during a lull. Yep, an empty bottle of Jack Daniels and a dirty glass. Only one. Nothing else of interest. I even checked under the desk in case he'd passed out, and in the closet in case someone had stuffed him in it. It'd happened before.

"You know what Nathan drives?" I asked Prune-ella back in the saloon.

"An Escalade," said the eavesdropping dishwasher. "Just got it."

"An Escalade," huffed the waitress. "And us all makin' minimum wage." Maybe her prune face was justified.

Once I was off bartending duty, I jogged out to the parking lot. Almost all of the tourists had gone home, so there were just a few battered employee cars left in the lot—along with a newish red Escalade. If Nathan went home, he didn't drive there.

I couldn't shake off my sense of dread. I called Marge. "No need to tell Arnie this," I said, "but I'm worried about Nathan. I'd like to make sure he made it home okay."

"I'll have somebody check his casita at Rancho De Los Vaqueros. I'll call you back."

When Marge called about fifteen minutes later, I was on my way home. "He's not there," she said, "but the night watchman said he'd keep an eye out for him. You think we should be worried?"

"Nah." After all, I didn't have any real reason for suspicion. "I'm probably being silly. I've had a lot going on these past few days." It was true. My intuition was probably fried from lack of sleep and yeah, maybe lack of Matt. Things would look better in the morning.

Except they didn't. "Ivy?" whispered Marge over the phone. "Nathan never came home last night."

"Gluhhh," I said. My vocabulary was not great first thing in the morning.

"I know it's early, but I thought maybe you could look for him before your shows today."

I rolled over and looked at the clock. Six a.m. My first melodrama show was at eleven. Gunfight after that. "Okay."

After a quick shower and a stop at Filiberto's drive-through for a breakfast burrito, I was on the road. I pulled into the Gold Bug parking lot just before eight—and right after Chance.

"What are you doing here so early?" I asked.

He shrugged. "I like it out here. Why are you here?"

"I need to talk to Nathan." I walked into town with Chance. "I couldn't find him yesterday, and he's not answering his phone, so I thought I'd come out and catch him before the place opened." Nathan's car was still in the lot, so my sort-of lie sounded plausible.

When we reached the saloon, I tried the door. Locked. I knocked on the door.

"Nathan? Nathan!"

"Strange," Chance said. "Maybe he's still hiking."

"Hiking?" Nathan seemed about as likely to hike as to dance *The Nutcracker*.

"I saw him yesterday, after our first gunfight."

"Did he have a backpack on?" I asked.

"No."

"Hiking boots?"

"No."

"So why...?"

"He was heading into the desert. Nothing to do out there but hike."

I sat down on the saloon porch to think, watching Chance walk down the road to wherever he was going. Nathan walked into the desert without camping supplies. Where would he go?

I jogged back to my pickup, got in, and headed down the road out of the Gulch, passing Chance along the way. Guess he was going for a hike too.

When I got to Frank's house, I parked outside next to his Prius.

"Hey," I said, when he opened the door, "am I too early for the tour?"

"Tour?"

"The green home tour. Isn't it today?"

"It's not for a couple of weeks."

"Dang. Sorry. Hope I didn't wake you."

"Nah, I'm an early riser. Want a cup of coffee?" He led me inside the house. Yes. My subterfuge worked.

"Thanks, but I've already had about a gallon," I lied. In fact, I'd only had one cup and would've killed for another, but it didn't fit with my plan. "In fact, can I use the facilities? Everything at Gold Bug is still locked up."

"Sure. Bathroom's on the other side of the house." He pointed through the windows past the enclosed garden to the opposite side of the square house. "You can go either way to get there."

"Thanks." I went left and walked through a dining room and kitchen. Frank followed but stopped in front of a burbling coffeemaker. Nothing else made a sound. No sign of anyone in the rooms.

I turned a corner into the section of the house Frank had pointed out and found the bathroom. I used it, then crept out the door without flushing the toilet and searched the bedroom next to it. The room was spare with whitewashed walls and nowhere to hide except the closet, which held only clothes and boots. I stole back to the bathroom, flushed the toilet, washed my hands, and then walked past the bedroom and into the section of the house directly across from the kitchen/dining room segment. It was a big open room, with a bunch of comfortable chairs, a desk in a corner, and a big picture window facing the garden. Nowhere for Nathan to hide.

"Looks like you're taking the home tour all by yourself," said Frank, who had come around the corner, torturing me with the fragrant cup of coffee in his hand.

"Can you blame me?" I walked up to Frank, then turned my back to him to look at the courtyard again. I'd been checking out the garden as I went, but wanted to take it in from this angle. "This is one amazing house." No Nathan in the courtyard either. "I bet after this home tour, you'll see a lot more houses designed like this."

"That's the point," said Frank. "Showing folks that sustainability can be beautiful."

I managed to leave pretty quickly (though dang, that coffee smelled good), jumped back in my Jeep, and drove out to the main road. Where else could Nathan have gone? Maybe...

I headed back down the dirt road. Hey, was that Chance? I swore I saw a cowboy hat duck behind a mesquite. I looked around me. Nothing but desert. If it was him, he was probably just hiking, or maybe going to Frank's house for his secret riding lessons. I kept going until I hit another junction. Yep, there was Billie's trailer, about a half-mile away. I pulled off the side of the road and walked toward it, staying off the road and as hidden by the scrub as I could. If Nathan was there, I didn't want to scare him away.

I tried the back door. Open, like I figured. Billie had said she always kept the place unlocked in case Mongo came back in the middle of the night. "Besides," she'd said, "what's going to happen to me in the middle of the desert?"

Oh, Billie.

I opened the door as quietly as possible and crept inside. The living room was dark, but there was an open bag of Doritos on the coffee table. Would they have been there since Billie's death? I walked over and put my hand on the back of the old-fashioned box TV. Still warm, so...

"You found me." I felt the cool barrel of a pistol on the back of my neck, Nathan's breath warm near my ear. "Who sent you?"

"Arnie." I was surprised my mouth could form words.

"Yeah, right." He grabbed my left arms from behind, fingers pressing deep into my upper arm.

"Okay, Marge." I maintained my outward sense of calm, while

squeezing my legs together so I wouldn't wet my pants. "But Arnie's worried too. About you. And the mob."

Wrong thing to say. Nathan pressed the gun harder into my neck. "Hodoyunowabutha?"

"I know about it because Arnie wanted me to find you." I skipped the part about Arnie hiring me to investigate his long-lost son. I mean, there was a gun on my neck. "You can call him."

I didn't move, and neither did the gun, but I heard Nathan dial his cell phone. "Papa?" he said. "Are you safe? Ivy's here and—"

I heard Arnie's muffled voice.

"Okay. Yeah, I'm okay, but I think I'll take a couple of days off. No, everything's all right. Promise." He hung up and removed the gun from my neck. "Papa says you're all right."

"Whew." I turned around to see Nathan holding a curling iron. "That was what you held me at gunpoint with?"

"Yeah." Nathan chucked it on the couch. "I hate guns."

CHAPTER 61

"Why should I tell you?" said Nathan. "My father wanted you to find me. You found me. You don't need to know why I'm here."

"Is it the investors? The Good, the Bad, and the Ugly? Are you afraid of them?"

"No," said Nathan, but I caught the slightest nod. A micro-expression, they call it. He was hiding from them. "And you're not telling anyone where I am. *Capiche?*"

Capiche? As if the micro-expression wasn't enough subliminal evidence. After a bit more haggling, I agreed to stop asking questions. Nathan was safe, and I'd done my job. Part of my job. A very small part of my job. Like swatting a fly during a swarm of locusts.

I drove back to Gold Bug in a foul temper. Even as I berated myself for being a bad detective, I understood something bigger was to blame for my mood.

I hadn't heard from Matt since our fight Friday night. I knew, oh I knew, that I was as much to blame as he was (if not more), and I knew Marge was right about trust, but every time I picked up the phone, that little wrestler inside my head said, "Right. You're calling the guy with the fiancée?"

So when I heard the ping and saw that I had a text from Matt, I nearly drove off the road. Instead, I pulled off onto the shoulder. I don't text and drive and there was no way I could wait until I got to the Gulch to see what he said. "Coming with Cody today. See you then."

No hugs or kisses or emojis, but still, he'd made the first move. I suddenly felt ten pounds lighter. I texted back ("Great!"), pulled onto the road, and shushed the overly security-conscious voice in my head with a loud country song I found on the radio. I drove to Gold Bug with the windows rolled down, letting the warm desert wind ruffle my hair, almost happy.

But the day went by with no sign of Matt or Cody. Luckily I had theater to save me. When I was onstage in the melodrama or out in the streets channeling Annie Oakley, I was in the present moment: trying to get away from the evil Neville Blackheart or happily shooting bells and flour sacks and hats off heads. Theater had been my safe place ever since Cody's accident. A place I could relax and be myself, which seems odd considering that I was always playing a role onstage. I guess it was because I felt accepted in the theater, so I could soften the shell that protected me from the harsh outside world. The only other place I felt comfortable enough to let down my guard was in the company of Uncle Bob or Cody, and recently with Matt. Lately though, I'd felt the shell harden again, like a thin layer of ice that protected my heart. And froze it.

That shell grew a little thicker as the hours passed without seeing Matt, but when I bowed during curtain call for the last melodrama of the day, I heard a voice yell, "Yay, Olive-y!" Cody. Yes, there he was, his blond hair catching the light. And next to him sat Matt. A warmth spread through me. Because of Cody? Because of Matt? I didn't care. I was just glad to feel a bit of a thaw.

Cody hugged me as soon as I stepped outside of the stage door. "You played three people! You were so good."

"I second that." Matt hugged me too, and I rested my head against his chest where I could hear his heartbeat. He let me go. "We haven't missed your gunfight, have we?"

"We've got one more. Wow, you wouldn't believe..." I stopped. Oh, this was hard. I wanted to tell Matt about everything that happened the day before—Gunther/Chance, Frank's sabotage, the scorpion, Nathan—but I couldn't with Cody there.

Wait. With Cody there. The little voice whispered inside my head. Was this Matt's way of manipulating me so I would tell Cody that Matt and I were a couple?

I only had a second to contemplate this unpleasant new thought when I heard, "Olive!"

"Dad?" I turned around, and yes, there he stood in scuffed cowboy boots and a pearl-snap-button Western shirt. He looked like he'd been born in those clothes, they suited him so well. My heart ached, just a little.

"Sorry I missed the melodrama. There was an accident between Prescott and Wickenburg. Stopped traffic for a while."

"An accident?" Cody's eyes grew wide.

"Don't worry. No one hurt."

Not only did my dad drive down here to see me in a show (a first), but he recognized Cody's fear. Things were definitely looking up.

"I promise to catch the show another time," Dad said. "Maybe with your mom."

Like that'd happen.

"But there's still another gunfight today, right?" he asked.

"Yeah, right before sundown." I looked at the clock mounted on the bank. "We have about twenty minutes. Want a quick tour of the town first? I need to practice. I'm supposed to start giving tours one of these days."

My emotions were a jumble as I led them down the dusty street. I was worried about Matt and happily confused about my dad's newfound interest in my life. Only Cody felt safe, so I took his arm as we walked. I pointed out the saloon. "Did you know that men used to trade bullets for whiskey?" I said. "That's where the term 'shot of whiskey' came from."

"Cool," Cody said.

We passed the reptile house. "What's the most dangerous animal in the desert?" I asked them.

"Rattlesnake?" my dad said.

I shook my head.

"A Gila monster?" Matt said.

"Nope."

"Vampire bats?" Cody said.

"No vampire bats in Arizona," I said. "Give up?"

They all nodded. "Man," I said. "Men—and women—are more likely to kill you than any other animal."

"Trick question. No fair," Cody said.

"And that's why we have the jail right here." I pointed out the adobe structure.

"Nice transition," Matt said.

"Thank you." I gave a little curtsey. "And that's the hanging tree..." I stopped. A noose hung from the tree. I swore it hadn't been there last week. Decoration, or something more sinister?

"Cool," Cody said again.

"Yes, indeed."

I'd ask Nathan about the noose later. Right now I was going to focus on my family, who had come all this way to see me. I entertained them as we made our way to the end of the Gulch, where a small crowd stood in front of the blacksmith's forge. Josh's hammer banged against the anvil.

"It sounds mad. Like a mad bell," Cody said.

The ring of the hammer did sound angry. Was Josh too? I stood on tiptoe to catch a glimpse of his face when I heard another bell.

"And that sounds like you have a text," Cody said. "Who from?"

I took my cell out of the pocket on my Annie Oakley costume. "Not sure. Oh, I have two." I didn't recognize the numbers, so I checked the texts. "First one is from...Arizona Center Stage." I tried to keep the excitement out of my voice and failed. "They're asking me about my schedule. They want to add another week in Tucson."

"Sounds like you got the part," Matt said quietly.

"They didn't say that," I said. "I'm supposed to call them."

"Who's the other one from?" Cody was always interested in my life. I liked it.

"It's from a friend of Uncle Bob's in Nevada. I need to call him later. Looks like he found some info I needed."

"Is he a PI too? What did he find?" asked Cody.

"Remember that gold mine we saw during the horse ride in the desert?"

"Can we go in it now?"

"Not yet. I was just finding out..." I felt a tap on my shoulder. Uh-oh. I wasn't watching the time. It was probably Chance or Frank or..."Arnie? What are you doing here?" He looked horrible, his shirt wrinkled, his glasses dirty and slightly askew, his pant leg riding up his walking cast.

"I'm pulling you out," he said too loudly. "You need to stop this investigation."

"Arnie," I said, trying to shush him.

"Investigation?" my dad said, as if one person blowing my cover wasn't enough. I looked around to see who might have heard, but I was hemmed in by a group of tall teenage boys.

"On top of everything that's already happened, the sabotage, the deaths—"

"*Arnie.*" I'd been keeping everything on the QT, and now look where we were.

"Now Nathan won't come out of hiding. I talked to him again, but he said no. It's too much. Something's seriously wrong."

"*Arnie,*" I said pointedly, though the damage was already done. "Nathan's just tired from everything going on. Plus he has a hell of a hangover." Could be true. There was that empty bottle of JD.

"Doesn't matter. You're out, Ivy. No more gunfights. I don't want to lose someone else I love."

"But we came all this way to see her in the gunfight," Cody said. "Even my dad came."

"What?" said someone near us. "No gunfight?" Another person picked up the news and the "no gunfight" grumbling escalated.

"It'll be okay." I touched Arnie's arm. "I'll recheck Chance's bullets, just to be sure. Not to worry folks," I shouted to the crowd. "Annie Oakley does not dodge a challenge. The gunfight will go on as scheduled." Then quietly, to Arnie, I said, "I'll just do this one gunfight before calling it quits."

"I'm calling this quits too." I really wished Arnie had learned to talk quieter. Or put his hearing aid in. "If I have anything to do with it, this is Gold Bug Gulch's last day in business."

That news spread through the crowd even faster than the "no gunfight" news. The clanging from inside the forge sounded louder and angrier.

"Really? Are you that worried?" Then I remembered something else. "You said 'lose someone else you loved.' What did you mean?"

"Lassie's dead."

"What? Did something happen?"

"Oh, Ivy, you know as well as we do. He's been gone for two weeks. You haven't seen any sign of him for nearly a week." Arnie's eyes shone wet behind his glasses. "Even if he did find enough food and water, there are the coyotes and..." The tears that had gathered in his eyes spilled over.

"I'm so sorry I let you down. I really wanted to find him. I wish..." I couldn't say any more. Instead I hugged Arnie hard, so he couldn't see I was crying too.

CHAPTER 62

"Folks, we hear word there might be a gunfight coming up," the dishwasher's voice said over the loudspeaker. My cue to be in place for the gunfight. I released Arnie, nodded goodbye to my family and Matt, and ran the half block to the opera house dressing room. I grabbed my rifle off its hook and checked the chamber as I ran to the staging area where Chance and I convened before the gunfight. Everything was just as I left it, bright red nail polish indicating the gun was filled with blanks. I met up with Chance and checked his gun. All good. I made sure that the dishwasher was in place to ring the bell, ran to the middle of the street, and began the show. "So I heard you all here in Gold Bug are down a sheriff," I said to the crowd. "I'm right sorry to hear about his passing."

"Yay, Olive-y!" I couldn't see my brother, but I knew he was there. And my Dad. And Matt. I was glad they were here to see what would be the last gunfight at Gold Bug Gulch.

"I also heard you might need a little protection 'til your new lawman arrives in town..."

The crowd was the biggest in Gold Bug Gulch's short history, and they were really into the gunfight, roaring at the slightest joke and applauding at pretty much anything Annie Oakley did. "Don't look so sour," I sang as I aimed at the flower sack. *Poof!* It exploded and the crowd went wild.

"Anything you can shoot, I can hit cleaner," sang Chance. "I can hit anything better than you."

We argued back and forth in song. The crowd loved the show. I did too. I was going to be sorry to give this up, even with other theater work on the horizon. "No you caaan't," I sang with gusto as I took aim at Chance's hat. I loved Annie. I loved this role. I loved feeling so strong, so sure, so—shit!

As soon as I pulled the trigger for my last shot I knew something was wrong. The gun kicked way too much for a blank. And now I knew what people meant when they said time slowed down for a moment. I saw the hole in Chance's hat, the look of confusion on his face, the splintering of wood as my bullet hit a wall behind him. And then it was over and the crowd cheered and I bowed automatically. Chance did not. He just picked up his hat and hightailed it out of there.

I stood shaking in the middle of the road.

Cody ran up to me and hugged me. "Is badder a real word?" he asked. "And why are you shaking?"

"Nerves." And because I could have killed someone, I thought. How did this happen? Someone must have disguised a real bullet, color-coded it so it would it look like a blank in the chamber. Someone who knew about my nail polish trick and knew where I kept my gun. Which could be almost anyone. I'd bragged about my brilliant idea in front of Chance, Frank, Nathan, and even Josh.

"Everything okay?" Matt's hand on my shoulder was gentle.

"Um..." If I told him, he'd insist I stop the investigation right now. Which was smart. But if I stopped now, I'd have failed Arnie, Billie, and myself too. "Just upset about Lassie." As I said it, that cold reality hit me again, and my eyes filled. I wondered if he'd been set upon by coyotes or hit by a...I shook my head to get rid of that vision. Not what I needed to concentrate on right then.

"Your dad's going to take Cody home for a visit," Matt said. "I thought maybe you'd like to come home with me."

I wanted to, more than anything. But I had to find out who put live rounds in my gun, why Nathan was hiding, and yes, okay, there was Katie the fiancée..."I can't," I said.

Matt walked away.

I called 911.

"What's your emergency?"

I wanted to say that I just let the best thing in my life walk away from me. Instead I said, "Someone put live rounds in my gun." I spoke quietly into my cell phone. The crowd was leaving for the day, but still I stood apart from them, careful not to alarm anyone. "It's supposed to be filled with blanks."

"Is anyone injured?"

"No, thank God."

"Then it's not an emergency. You can call—"

I hung up and called Uncle Bob. "I'm on a well-deserved vacation," said my uncle's voice. "So I'm off the grid for a few days."

"Dammit." I felt madder than I knew was reasonable. "Remember when I was worried about you getting together with Bette, and you said you wouldn't abandon me? Feeling pretty abandoned right now, Mr. I'm-Off-The-Grid. Oh, and someone tried to make me shoot someone." I hung up and calmed myself down before making the next call. It went to voicemail too. "Good thing you taught me to shoot," I said to Pink's voicemail. "Someone did it again, switched blanks for bullets. No one was hurt, thank God, but..." But what? Why would someone have done that? So I'd kill Chance? "Gotta go."

I headed in the direction Chance had taken. Who would want to kill Chance? And why? I guess it meant that Chance was innocent of Mongo's death. Unless...

Unless he wanted to put the blame squarely on someone else's head. But what a stupid dangerous thing to do, knowing I could kill him. Then again, I'd heard of suicide by cop. Chance could be broken up over killing Mongo and losing Billie. And getting shot in a gunfight would be the way a real cowboy would want to die.

Wait. I stopped in my tracks. Chance was either the victim or the perp. Either way, by chasing him I was putting myself in danger. I stopped, reversed, and ran back through the town, sidestepping the few tourists straggling down the street in the fading light. I ran to the stage door, into the opera house, and down the hall to my dressing room. My duffel bag was on the counter underneath the mirror. At the bottom of the bag, I found the box of shells I'd bought for target practice. I began to load my rifle, then stopped. Were there one or two fewer bullets in the box? My red nail polish shone like a stoplight on the counter next to my blush and powder. I picked it up. The top wasn't screwed on tight. Did whoever replace my blanks use my nail polish to disguise my own bullets?

It didn't matter right now. I loaded my rifle with live ammo and was almost out the stage door when my cell rang. I didn't recognize the number.

"Ivy," Frank said. "They've got me."

CHAPTER 63

"Where?" I slung my rifle over my shoulder as I ran out of the opera house. "And who has you?"

"In the mine. I'm in the mine, and God help me, I think there's a body..." The line went dead. I redialed but, dammit, I was beginning to think cell phones were the work of the devil.

I ran to the parking lot, jumped into my skunky pickup, and tried to start her. And tried. Finally I popped the hood and took a look. It was nearly dark outside, but I could still see that my battery was AWOL. Literally AWOL, as in gone.

I suspected it hadn't walked off by itself, but there was no way I'd let some battery-rustling varmint get the best of me. I called Pink again and left a message asking him to meet me at the mine and to bring a battery for my truck. I ran down the dirt road through the now-empty town. Dang, why was I such a slow runner? The mine was about a mile and a half away. Who knew what would have happened to Frank by the time I got there?

I had a brain wave. I jogged to the corral. Yes, the horses were still there, saddled up and everything. I opened the gate to the corral and left it ajar. I headed toward my fuzzy friend. "Hey, Toby, remember me?" The donkey looked at me with big eyes as I approached. "We shared some coffee." He stayed still. I hiked up my skirt and managed to get on his back without the mounting block. Amazing what adrenaline will do for you. "I need you to take me to the mine." Toby regarded me over his shoulder. "And we need to go fast, okay? Fast." I pressed my heels against his sides and he took off at a trot. I steered him out of the corral and down the road toward the mine into the rapidly darkening desert.

I soon realized that Toby might have been faster than me, but not by much. At this donkey's pace, Frank would be a goner before we reached him. We'd have to take a shortcut.

I pulled Toby's reins, steering him off the road and toward the stand of trees that marked the creek. He balked. "C'mon, Toby, I know you can make it down this hill." He reluctantly went forward, picking his way down the rocky slope toward the woods. The dark, dark, incredibly dark woods. No moon tonight, and the trees that promised life and water in the daytime now looked like something out of Grimm's fairytales. Something that would swallow you whole and never give up the body.

"Stop it," I told myself out loud. "This is not a fairytale, these are just woods, and you have technology." I whipped out my cell phone. I'd never downloaded a flashlight app, so I found the brightest photo I had, one of Matt and Cody at Encanto Park. It lightened my screen enough to help a little. We were just at the edge of the riparian area when I realized I was almost out of battery. At the mouth of the really really dark woods. "We can do this, Toby," I said and turned off my phone.

CHAPTER 64

"Aaah!" I'd forgotten about the night snakes, or whatever they were. They rustled in the grass around us, jostling the grass near the ground, then shaking the tips in a weird low-high pattern, as if they were jumping. Wait, jumping snakes?

"Come on, Toby." I didn't want to kick him, so I pressed my feet against him again, hoping he'd recognize that as a "get going" signal. He didn't.

I gave him a little kick. "Toby!" The snakes around us rustled and hopped, but Toby just plodded along. "I should have picked a horse," I said out loud, and Toby picked up the pace. "Yeah, a horse would go so much faster." He trotted a little faster. Looked like a little healthy competition worked with donkeys too.

But we weren't fast enough. "Ivy!" said a German-sounding voice behind us. "Stop!" We didn't stop. "Don't be so pig-headed," Chance panted as he ran after us. His American accent was gone. "You must stop."

No way I was going to stop, but he would catch up with us soon enough. What could I do? We were almost out of the tall grass. The creek gurgled nearby and I could just pick out the outline of the old snag against the near-black sky. Ah.

I nosed Toby towards the water. "Let's see, you killed one man."

"Accidentally!"

"And then your girlfriend died." We were close to the creek now.

"I did not do it."

"And you want me to stop all by myself in a dark deserted place."

Toby and I splashed across the creek, Chance right behind us. We were almost in place.

"What we've got here is a failure to communicate."

"Nice try."

"You must...I...I cannot find the words. Just stop."

I pulled on Toby's reins and we stopped, just to make sure Chance was in the right spot. I could barely make him out in the inky darkness, but I was pretty sure we had hit our mark.

"Thank you," Chance said. "Now...Hey! What in the hell?" He flailed his arms around.

"It's quicksand," I said.

"Quicksand? In Arizona?"

"I know, weird, right? Not sure how deep it is, but I wouldn't struggle if I were you. Now, Toby and I are off."

I nudged Toby and he began trotting at a decent pace.

"Wait!" cried Chance. "Stop! You can't leave me here."

"Frankly, my dear, I don't give a damn." Ha.

My noble steed and I hurried through the woods and climbed the hill out of the riparian area. In a few minutes we were on the desert road that led to the mine. Toby must have recognized where we were, and good thing too, because the desert was black. Not just dark, black. The sky was filled with flickering stars, but their light didn't reach the desert floor.

Ahead of us, the darkness gathered itself into something deeper than black: the mine. Its mouth was blacker yet. A piece dislodged itself and flew toward us. Shakespeare's words leapt to mind:

"Ere the bat hath flown,

His cloistered flight, ere to black Hecate's summons

The shard-borne beetle with his drowsy hums

Hath wrung night's yawning peal, there shall be done

A deed of dreadful note."

"Just bats," I said to Toby, though Macbeth's warning rang in my head. "Harmless bats. Aaaah!" I ducked as dozens of them whooshed out of the darkness and over our heads.

"Ivy?" Frank's voice came from the yaw of the mine. "Help me. Please. He hurt me."

I nudged Toby, but he wouldn't budge. No amount of kicking, wheedling, or telling him he was better than a horse worked. Finally, I dismounted. Now what? I had to get Frank out of the mine, but I might need to protect him from bad guys too. I could take my rifle, but it seemed like a bad idea to discharge a gun inside a mine. No. I'd have to go in unarmed and hope that Frank was alone, or maybe had a big rock. I slung my rifle across Toby's saddle and crept toward the mine.

"Ivy!" a different voice shouted from far behind me. Josh's. He must have noticed Toby missing.

"Ivy," pleaded Frank's voice, a hollow echo from within the mountain. "Don't trust him. Hurry."

I stepped inside the mine. Wow, and I thought it was dark outside. I literally couldn't see my hand in front of my face. I reached out and felt a stone wall, cool under my fingertips. I slid my cellphone out of my pocket. Really wished I'd taken the time to download that flashlight app. I turned it on and pulled up the photo of Matt and Cody. It was one of my favorite photos. Matt had that smile I loved, the one where his eyes got all scrunchy and...

Really, Ivy? You're going to think about that now? I shook my head and held out my phone. The photo's blue-sky background wasn't bright enough to let me see more than four feet. I could walk the four feet in the dark, turn it on, and repeat. Maybe my battery would last until Frank and I were out of here.

"Ivy." Frank's voice sounded weaker. "Where are you?"

"I'm coming," I yelled, clicking off the phone.

The blackness was absolute. My chest contracted. It was hard to breathe: As the darkness pressed in on me, so did the weight of all the dirt and stone above me, the mass of earth that could crush and bury me so I'd never be found.

I shook my head again, trying to shake off my growing fear. I had never been claustrophobic before. Then again, I had never been in a pitch-black abandoned mine before. Huh. My internal dialogue echoed in my head as I inched forward. Fear. Abandoned. Abandonment...

I had it. I knew why I was sabotaging my relationship with Matt. Too bad my revelation came when I was trying to rescue someone from a scary dark mine in the middle of nowhere.

"Hurry. Please hurry." Frank's voice cracked.

"On my way!" I hurried. For three steps. Then I stopped. Had I gone four feet? I reached for my phone. Footsteps crunched behind me. "Ivy?" said Josh.

"Run!" yelled Frank.

I did, stumbling into the darkness, trying to get my phone on for some light. After only a few feet, I ran smack into a wall in front of me. "Ow!"

"Turn right," said Frank. "The tunnel's to the right."

"No! Stop!" Josh's footsteps were close. "Stop!" A burst of noise from behind me. Josh must have stepped up his game. I did too, stretching one arm in front of me so I wouldn't hit another wall, and trying to turn on my phone with my other hand. Yes! The blue screen glowed.

Strong arms grabbed me from behind. My phone flew out of my hands and the light went out. I waited for it to crash against the mine's stone floor, so I could find it by sound. Nothing.

"Don't move," said Josh. "Not a muscle."

I didn't, afraid he might have a knife or gun. Then I heard my phone smash again a rock. A rock far, far, below me.

"That shaft is almost a thousand feet deep," Josh said. "And it's right in front of you. We're going to back up now."

"Frank?" I yelled into the darkness. "Where are you?" No reply. Omigod, did he pass out?

"We're backing up. *Now*." Josh's arms pulled me backward, my feet scrabbling to keep up.

"But Frank—"

"I don't know what Frank's up to, but he just tried to kill you." Josh slowed his pace but kept his arms tight around my waist.

"No."

"You don't think the fall down that shaft would've killed you? Well, maybe the fall wouldn't have. Being left there for a few days would've done the job."

"He must have thought I had a light. I could've gotten around it safely if I had a light."

"And if you'd gone much farther, you would have run into bad air. It knocks you out, then kills you. In fact, let's get a move on. I'm not sure about the air right here either."

"But Frank. He's hurt." And told me not to trust Josh. I leaned back into Josh and pretended to stumble, so I could touch his side, see if he wore his gun belt. He did.

"I don't know what happened to Frank. But don't you think it's strange he tried to lure you to your death?"

"I think it's strange that you came running after me into a dark mine in the middle of the night." I pretended to stumble again, grabbed his gun from his holster, and threw it as far as I could into the darkness behind us.

In a flash, Josh turned to face me, grabbed me, and slung me over his shoulder like a side of beef. I kicked at him. "Stop." Josh tightened his grip on me.

"Frank!" I yelled into the darkness. "I'll get help. Don't give up."

A groan from somewhere in the darkness. "He's still alive!" I kicked harder and landed a good one in the near vicinity of Josh's gonads.

"Stop it now, or I'll bang your head against this rock wall." Josh's voice had changed into something hard and dangerous.

I stopped kicking. We had to be almost of out of the mine, and he couldn't carry me all the way to Gold Bug Creek. As soon as he set me down I could kick him again, make a run for it. I could make into the top of the hill where my cell was in range and...

Shit. My cell would never be in range again.

CHAPTER 65

The sky lightened slightly, from blackest black to black. We were out of the mine.

Josh kept walking, gripping me tightly. He didn't have a gun anymore. He might have a knife, but I could put space between us pretty quickly. My eyes were adjusting to the darkness. Maybe I could make a break for Frank's house, call 911, and...No. Pretty sure Frank didn't have a landline, and he'd called me from his cell, so—

A horse whinnied and Toby brayed an answer. They sounded pretty close.

"Ivy? Are you still there?"

At the sound of Frank's voice, Josh turned toward the mine, me still slung over his shoulder. His horse, Blackie, stood behind Toby, who looked at me with eyes that said something was wrong.

Wait.

Frank reached me at Gold Bug by phone. His cell wouldn't have worked in the mine, wouldn't have been in range anywhere around it, unless he was at the top of a hill. So he couldn't have called...

"Hey there." A scrawny figure emerged from behind a mesquite tree, brandishing a pistol. "Looks like I made it out of that mine just fine." Josh started to turn around. "Don't," Frank warned. "I'd hate to shoot a man in the back, but if I had to..."

"Be pretty obvious you killed him in cold blood," Josh said.

"Not if no one ever finds the body. Bodies, I mean. Which was the plan all along."

"Toby," I whispered to the donkey. He was only about fifteen feet away. "Come to Mama."

He didn't move.

"Too bad you're not as dumb as you look," said Frank.

"Are you talking to me?" I said loudly, then whispered again, "Dammit, Toby, don't act like a horse." The combination of the two magic words worked. Toby sidled nearer. Just ten feet away.

"Yeah, the dumb blonde act almost fooled me. But Chance told me you'd been digging around. Then I overheard you'd been in touch with a PI in Nevada, and well, I knew you'd eventually figure out that I'm behind Acme Arizona."

"You own the mineral rights to the mine?"

"All mine." Frank chuckled. "Get it?"

"Who are you?" Josh asked me.

"I'm a PI."

"Not a very good one, as far as I can tell. Maybe I shouldn't have worried about you after all." Frank shrugged. "Too late now."

I needed to keep him talking, buy some time. "Hey, I figured out who Chance is."

"Who is he?" Josh asked.

"Gunther Schmidt. He's from Munich and is scared of horses. Dammit," I added for a certain donkey's benefit. Toby shuffled a few steps closer.

"You may have figured that out, but you didn't figure out he was my compadre," Frank said.

"I don't think blackmailing Chance makes him a compadre," said Josh.

"Frank blackmailed Chance?" I asked. "Over what?"

"Chance's visa is expired."

"Actually, it's not." Frank sniggered. "Nathan extended it. Dumbshit cowboy never even checked; just took my word for it. When he figured out who switched his blanks for bullets, all I had to do to keep him quiet was threaten to turn him over to immigration. Also reminded him he had no proof and a pretty good motive to kill Mongo, whereas little ol' me..."

"Chance just told me today after the gunfight," said Josh. "Real bullets again, Frank?"

"Worked before."

"So you killed Billie too," I said. "Must have found one of those old drums of cyanide in the desert." I could almost touch Toby.

"Cyanide." Frank clucked his tongue. "That's nasty stuff. Place should've been shut down after that 'accident.'"

I was so disgusted I could taste it. "You are cold-blooded."

"Like a snake. 'S how I survived in the desert for so long. Now this snake says it's time to stop your yakkin' and head toward the mine."

Josh didn't move.

"Don't worry, I'm not going send you down a shaft. Just into one of the areas filled with carbon dioxide. It's not a bad way to go, from what I hear. Just a few breaths and you're asleep. Forever."

"Hey, why did you say I was a bad PI?" I hoped my question would distract Frank so he wouldn't hear me whisper into Josh's ear: "Let me down on the count of three."

"Because you didn't realize that I couldn't have called from a cellphone. Or notice the way my voice crackled when I talked." Frank held up something in the hand that didn't hold the gun. "Bought top-of-the-line walkie-talkies, but still sounds pretty bad to me." He held the transceiver to his mouth and said, "Ivy? I'm hurt." His words drifted out of the mine.

"One," I whispered to Josh.

"And you suspected Josh." Frank laughed. "Old trustworthy Josh, savior of mice."

"Mice?" I said to Frank, then whispered, "Two."

"And you made him throw away his gun. Stupid girl."

"Three!" Josh dropped me. I rolled toward Toby, grabbed my rifle from his saddle, and stood up in one fluid move. Being a dancer paid off in the most unexpected ways. So did being an actor. Though I was literally shaking in my boots, I channeled Annie Oakley's confidence. "I'm not stupid. I'm armed." I pointed my rifle at Frank.

"Full of blanks."

"No, it's not. I changed them out in case you needed help."

"Right."

I shot the rifle into the air. "Sound like a blank to you?"

"Maybe. Anyway, I ain't scared of a little girl with a gun."

"Who you calling a little girl?" I fired another warning shot into the air and took the time to check my stance, my grip, my everything.

"'Cause even if those are real bullets, you wouldn't kill me. You don't have it in you."

"You're right." Breathe in. "I wouldn't kill you." Breathe out. "I'd just shoot the rifle out of your hands."

"Ha ha..."

And pull.

Crack! Frank's rifle flew out of his hands. "My thumb!" he yelled.

"Damn!"

"Damn," Josh said admiringly.

"Damn," I said, keeping my rifle trained on Frank. "I *am* Annie Oakley."

CHAPTER 66

"Can I use your bandanna?" Josh asked.

I took the red kerchief from around my neck and handed it to him. He expertly bandaged Frank's thumb with my costume piece. He'd already tied up the lousy, no-good, murderous bushwhacker with a length of rope from his saddlebag.

"Got me so trussed up I'll fall off the damn horse," muttered Frank.

"No, you won't," Josh said. "'Cause you're not riding." He fastened the rope to his saddle. "You're walking. Don't worry, I made the rope long enough for you to walk behind without Blackie kicking you, but…"

As if on cue, Blackie raised his tail and dumped a load.

Frank jumped out of the way. "Shit."

"That's what you get for killin' folks." Josh mounted his horse, and I hoisted myself onto Toby.

"I still don't get it," I said as we headed back toward Gold Bug. "Two people dead over bats?"

"I told you I'd never kill anyone over bats. And I don't lie."

I wanted to point out that he did kill and probably also lied somewhere along the line, but I still hadn't put all the pieces together, so instead I said, "So…?" I wanted to give him enough rope to hang himself, so to speak.

"Gold, woman. There was gold in that mine. Found two nuggets bigger than my thumb. 'S where I got the money for my house and car."

Josh made a noise in his throat but still faced forward, walking Blackie at a pace slow enough for Frank to keep up.

"And you bought the mineral rights," I said. "So you could get more gold."

"'S not a crime."

"And he'd need the land around it so he could re-open the mine," said Josh.

"Reopen the mine? But wouldn't that disturb the bats?"

"No endangered bats in there," said Josh. "Just common old bats."

Frank chuckled. "Yep."

"But still, doesn't mining cause all sorts of environmental degradation?" I turned to look at Frank. He'd seemed so sincere. "I thought you were an environmentali—"

"I am." Frank raised his voice. "This land is ruined. For God's sake, woman, there are drums of cyanide buried all over this place. Even gets into the water." The smirk in his voice made my hands curl into fists. "But my box canyon, now that's pristine. For now. With the money I get from the mine, I could save it for future generations."

"You killed people to shut down a tourist town so you could open a mine and buy another piece of property?"

"*Sacred* property."

"I think the desert sun has addled your brain."

"It's not the sun," said Josh. "It's the gold. Gold makes people crazy. Too bad there isn't any in that mine."

"'Course there is," snorted Frank, trundling along in the dirt road behind us. "I sold those nuggets I found. They were real. Fetched a pretty penny."

"They were real," said Josh. "And they were everything you were going to get out of that mine. My grandpa salted it years ago when he had a couple investors on the hook. Problem is, he did it after a bout of drinking. Couldn't remember where he put those nuggets. The investors never found them and neither did he."

Frank stopped walking. "No gold? You're shittin' me."

"Nope. No gold. Just common old bats."

Frank sat down in the middle of the dusty road. "No gold?" he whispered to himself. "No gold?"

Josh turned around. "C'mon, Frank, get up. I don't want to drag your scrawny ass over all these rocks."

"I want to talk more about gold," I said to Josh. Though he had saved my hide, I still wasn't sure of him. He could be complicit with other goings-on. "Who are the Golden Girls?" It was a risk, asking him straight out like that, but I still had my rifle and he'd seen me shoot. "Do they have anything to do with the mine?"

"The Golden Girls? Billie's outfit? Nothin' to do with mining. It's a scholarship program for young women in rural Arizona."

Oh, Billie. Golden-hearted Billie.

"For a guy who doesn't have any money, you sure donate a lot for girls' scholarships."

Josh shrugged. "I gave some of the money from the land sale to The Golden Girls."

"Paying off your dad's debt?"

"At the beginning. Then I saw what Billie was doing for those girls. Decided to invest in the future, so to speak."

"Josh Tate, one of the good guys," snarked Frank.

"If it's legit, why so cagey about it?"

"The organization is all above board," Josh said. "But some of the funds..."

"Come from the game, right?"

"Don't think the proceeds are exactly legal."

"You ever join in on the game? With the Philly investors, maybe?"

"What? No."

"You all seem pretty chummy. I saw you with them a couple of times at the forge and then again down by the creek."

"Yeah, I'd been talking to them about...down by the creek?" Though I couldn't see Josh's face in the dark, he tilted his head toward me. "Oh." He straightened up in his saddle. "Those weren't investors. Well, maybe they will be."

"Good luck with that." Frank still sat in the middle of the road.

"Just you wait and see. I think it might work out in the end."

"What?" I said. "Who were they? What might work out?"

"I'll show you." Josh nodded to our right, where the creek sloshed at the bottom of the hill. He dismounted, then held out a hand for me. I took it and swung off Toby. "What about Frank?" I said in a low voice.

"Blackie won't move unless I give him the go-ahead, and Frank can't pull a thousand pounds of horse. Still," Josh got out another rope from his saddlebag, "might as well make it interesting." Josh tied the rope into a lasso, swung it over his head, and then looped it over a cholla. He clucked at his horse. "Back up, Blackie." The horse began walking backwards. "Better stand up unless you want to get sat on," Josh said to Frank.

Frank scrambled to his feet. Josh grabbed Frank by the rope that encircled him, and pulled him toward the lassoed cactus.

"Oh no." Frank dug in his heels. "You're not planting me in any cholla patch."

"I'm not, long as you don't move." Josh fastened the rope around Frank, so he was tied to Blackie on one end and the cholla on the other, with only about six inches in between Frank and the devilish cactus. Josh stepped back to admire his work. "You'd better stay still. You move just a couple inches, you'll get skewered."

Josh led the way down the hill. "That was brilliant," I said, partly because it was true, and partly because I was walking into the dark woods with a man who had a pretty diabolical imagination and I wanted to be on his good side.

I lagged behind Josh as we climbed down the rocky slope, pretending I couldn't see well (my eyes had actually adjusted to the darkness), when I really wanted to make sure I had enough room to shoot a rifle if need be.

We reached the brushy edge of the riparian area. "Shh," Josh said. "Follow me, but quietly."

We were silent as scouts as we wound through the cottonwoods to one of the spots with the long grass. Suddenly it shivered, as something moved just inches in front of me. Wait, was this a trap? Could you kill someone on purpose with snakes?

Josh didn't move, but squatted in the meadow in front me. The grass moved and lightning-quick he reached down into the grass and grabbed something. He walked toward me, his hands cupped around something small. Not a snake. "This here is the real value of this place." Josh opened his hands to reveal...a mouse? "The New Mexico Meadow Jumping Mouse." The little brown mouse lay on his back, Josh's thumb on his white belly. "Just look at those babies."

"Omigod," I said. "His back legs are enormous. Like a kangaroo's."

"The better for jumping, my dear. These guys can jump as high as three feet."

The mouse regarded me with curious little eyes. "He also may be the cutest thing I've even seen."

"And these mice are the endangered ones, not the bats. Not very many them left anywhere and none ever found in this part of Arizona before." He stroked the mouse's belly with his thumb. "This little guy is the real treasure of Gold Bug."

He knelt down and let the mouse go. The grass jumped in several places, as if the other mice were doing a little dance in honor of the return of Josh, the Savior of Mice.

"Is this why you don't want people at your house? You're protecting the mice?"

"Yep." Josh stood up and watched the moving meadow, a smile on his thin lips. "Those investors you thought you saw down here? They're folks from the Wilderness Coalition."

"But I'm sure I heard someone say gold when you all were down here."

"We might have been talking about these little guys—the real 'gold' that's here." Josh smiled as he watched the jumping grass. "Or maybe the gold bugs—they're not endangered but they're not common either, and they're awfully pretty."

I did not think bugs could be pretty but decided not to state my opinion right then.

"But we were probably talking about Gold Bug Gulch. I'm hoping they'll partner with us."

"With the Gulch? The tourist attraction?"

"It'd be Gold Bug Gulch Western Theme Town and Wildlife Refuge. We'd keep the town as a theme park but set aside this riparian area. That's why you saw me meeting with the investors too. They're all onboard. Smart. The Wilderness Coalition will put some money toward maintenance and preservation, and we'll probably double the tourist traffic."

"You might want to be careful, Josh. Those investors, the ones from Philly? I think they're the reason Nathan disappeared."

"I know." Josh turned to me.

My heart dropped out of my body and tumbled into the creek. Josh was too close to shoot. I glanced over my shoulder. Could I make a run for it?

Josh shook his head. "Nathan ran off because he's misdirected. For some reason, he thinks the investors are...connected. They're not. They're just Italian guys from Philly who like the old cowboy-style Arizona. In fact," he smiled broadly, "you might call them Spaghetti Westerners."

CHAPTER 67

"Hello! Is somebody there?" The voice came from near the creek.

"Is that Chance?" Josh asked.

"Yeah, I thought he was after me, so I led him into the quicksand."

"Nice," Josh said. "Nobody ever believes there's quicksand in Arizona."

It took ten minutes for Josh and me to extricate a grumbling Chance. "Sorry about that," I said. "I didn't realize you were trying to save me. I thought you were a bad guy."

"I should wear a white hat." Chance washed the quicksand mud off his boots. "So people know which side I'm on."

"Mongo was onboard too," Josh said as the three of us crested the hill. "He said he just needed to work out one last detail."

Ohhh. That was the investment Billie had mentioned. But...

"Aha," said Frank. "No wonder Mongo was trying to bail on me."

"Wait, what?" I said to Frank. "Were you the business deal he wanted out of?"

"You think I could've afforded those mineral rights all by myself, even with those nuggets? Too bad Mongo didn't have the balls he was born with." Frank chuckled. "Me, on the other hand, I got the balls *and* the brains."

"And that's why you're trussed up and tied to a cactus," said Josh.

"And that's why I'll get away committing the perfect crime. You have no proof I did anything."

"You held us at gunpoint," I said. "And we both witnessed your confession."

"Oh, that'll go over well. A blacksmith with a long-standing grudge against me and Mongo, and a girl detective who couldn't find her ass in the dark. Besides, I'm pretty sure I never actually said anything about killing."

Didn't he? What did we have? I willed my brain to put the pieces together.

"You got nothin'," Frank said. "No witnesses, no evidence."

"I will testify," Chance said. We'd told him he was safe, visa-wise.

"About the blackmail. And the bullets."

Bullets. A tiny cog in my brain started turning.

"And what a great witness you'll make. A guy who works under an alias, who wanted Mongo dead, and then found that Billie didn't want him after all," Frank said. "You got a way better motive for killing those two than I do. After all, would a guy with a lifelong reputation for peaceful activism kill someone over bats?"

"Bats?" Chance said. "I thought it was gold."

"No gold in that mine. Right, Josh?" Frank cocked his head. "You know, I think I have a better case than you all do...kidnapping, maybe aggravated assault. Yep, you might as well untie me now."

My brain-cog was still whirring. "Why did you swap bullets for my blanks? Did you want me to kill Chance?"

"*Whoever* swapped those bullets..." Frank chuckled and I nearly slugged him. "Could've have a double motive: keep a loudmouth fake cowboy quiet and put a nail in the coffin of this damn tourist town."

"Too bad you didn't resist that last impulse." I had it now. "Because we do have evidence: your prints, from where you handled my box of ammunition."

That wiped the smirk off Frank's face. "Uh..." He sucked on his teeth.

"Also, you got me." A menthol cigarette-voice came from the darkness. "And I make a pretty good witness." Pink stepped out from behind a saguaro. "Came when I got your call," he said to me. "But dammit." He looked at his feet. "Didn't have time to change my shoes."

Pink helped the now-regulation-handcuffed Frank into the backseat of his cop car, which he'd parked around a bend in the road. "I'm gonna drop this guy off at the County Sheriff's—there's a substation on Bell Road. You want a ride into town? I didn't bring a battery for your truck. Seemed more important to get out here quick."

"Yeah, thanks. Maybe you could drop me off in Sunnydale?" I could ask Marge to borrow her car to get a battery tomorrow. She'd probably even drive me out to Gold Bug later in time for Mongo and Billie's funeral.

"Do you need us?" Chance looked down at his mud-covered self. "I would rather..."

"You guys can go," Pink said.

Josh swung himself onto Blackie. Chance just stood there.

"C'mere, Toby," I said. He trotted up to me. I stroked his soft ear. "Best donkey in the world." I led him over to Chance. I was the only one close enough to see Chance take a small step backward, his eyes wide

"You'll like Toby," I said quietly. "He's not like a horse. More like a golden retriever you can ride." I handed Chance the reins. As he cautiously mounted, I whispered in Toby's ear, "You be especially good and you'll get your very own Frappuccino."

I swear that donkey nodded.

CHAPTER 68

"So, gold, mice, quicksand, and a Sergio Leone movie?" Marge and I walked down her hall past a door that practically shook with Arnie's snoring.

"Spaghetti Westerners," I said as she opened the door to her guest room. I was so tired I couldn't make my mouth say any more. I flopped on the bed.

"I got it," she said. "Really. Arnie'll be so relieved. We'll see you in the morning."

That was the last thing I remembered before waking up to coffee in bed, courtesy of Marge. "Arnie wanted to bring it, to thank you. But I wasn't sure you'd be decent."

I was. I was lying on top of the covers, still fully dressed as Annie Oakley. "Hey, do you think you have some clothes I could borrow?"

Marge came back a few minutes later with one of her tracksuits. "I brought you a black one. For the funeral."

At least I wouldn't be wearing buckskin. I got dressed and padded out to the kitchen where Marge was slicing bagels, just in time to hear the doorbell ring. "I got it!" Arnie shouted from somewhere in the house. Another ring, the sound of the door opening, then, "Oh my God!"

Marge and I raced to the front door. Nathan stood there, Arnie in front of him, on his knees, crying. And in his arms was a little black pug.

Later, over bagels and coffee, Nathan told us he'd put up a thousand-dollar reward. "Went around to all those posters you hung and slapped an orange sticker over them with the reward and my phone number."

Lassie sat on Arnie's lap, licking cream cheese off a bagel. "Guy called this morning," Nathan continued. "Have the feeling he mighta had Lassie for a couple of days, but hey, money talks."

"You are so awesome!" said the affirmation clock. I actually agreed.

Marge jumped up and hugged Nathan for about the tenth time. He'd started hugging her back around embrace number three.

"So much money," she said. "Let us pay you back."

"Consider it a gift for setting my mind at ease." We'd told him the whole story, except for investigating him, of course. "Besides, I'm flush right now."

Lassie looked at Nathan with love and a little cream cheese on his nose. The look on Marge and Arnie's faces (and my own, I suspected) was a sort of gratitude-skepticism salad.

"Yeah, Papa." He slung an arm around Arnie's shoulder, his mouth full of bagel. "Your son is one damn fine poker player."

Nathan drove me to get a battery. He even paid for it. Then he drove me out to Gold Bug and helped me hook up the battery. Who knew his brusque manner disguised a real softie? Guess he had more of Arnie in him than I'd suspected.

Even so, I didn't want to push my luck by asking to borrow his phone, so I followed him to the saloon. "Need to use the land line," I said to the people who were prepping for Billie and Mongo's wake. "My phone is at the bottom of a mine shaft."

No one looked surprised. Must not be that uncommon out Wickenburg way.

I called Arizona Center Stage and New Vintage Theater, both of whom actually picked up. I spoke to them both, then made another call. "I'm so sorry," I said to Uncle Bob's voicemail. "I know you didn't abandon me. You love me and I love you and I hope you have a great vacation with Bette. You deserve it."

Then I made the most important call of all. "Lassie's home," I said. "It's a long story, but he came home, and I want to too. And...well, you feel like home." I told Matt's voicemail where I'd be and how to find me, then hung up.

"Ivy!" Nathan came out of his office, a sheaf of papers in his hand. "Nearly forgot." He handed the stack to me. "Found these at Billie's place. Thought you might like to see 'em, you being a literary type."

"Thanks." I waved the papers at him as he shut his office door. Then I read the top paper. And the second one. And the third. And solved the mystery of where Mongo had disappeared to all those times.

CHAPTER 69

"I drink too much on Saturday nights," the minister said to the crowd gathered for the funeral.

"And eat like a pig at a trough.

I'm often spoilin' fer a fight.

And am liable to mouth off."

"That was Mongo, all right," said a voice behind me.

"So Mongo was a cowboy poet?" asked Pink. He sat to one side of me on the hard wooden pew, while Chance fidgeted on the other.

"Yeah. That's where he went all those time when he disappeared—cowboy poetry gatherings. Nathan found a bunch of Mongo's poems at Billie's place. I loved this one, and wanted to share it with everyone at the funeral."

The minister continued: "She walks in beauty, like the night

Of cloudless climes and starry skies.

That Old Lord Byron got it right

Like he had seen her deep blue eyes."

A sigh passed through the crowd.

"I don't know what she sees in me.

I'm just an old cowhand.

But when she takes me in her arms,

I become a better man."

"Did Billie know?" whispered Chance. I gave him big brownie points for coming to the funeral. Lots of people didn't know the whole truth of the situation yet, and he'd received more than a few barbed looks.

"I think so. She said something about figuring out Mongo right before she died."

"I...I'm glad."

Josh leaned forward from where he sat in the pew behind us. "Looks like you two made up."

"What?" I said.

"From when you left Chance in the quicksand. Not the nicest thing to do to your boyfriend."

"Boyfriend?" Chance said.

"I thought you two were close," Josh said.

"That's her boyfriend." Chance pointed at Pink.

"Neither of them are my boyfriend," I said. Pink drooped a little. "I'm in love with a guy named Matt."

Mongo and Billie were buried next to each other in the hard dirt of the pioneer cemetery. There was a short graveside ceremony, and after handfuls of earth had been tossed onto the caskets, we all walked toward the saloon for the wake.

Someone tapped me on the shoulder. Finally. My heart lifted. "Matt." I turned and lifted my face to kiss him.

But it was a teenage girl. A clutch of them stood behind me on the dusty road. I bit my lip, dropped my chin, and tried to look like my heart hadn't broken.

"You're the one Billie talked about," said the girl, who was slight with fine brown hair. "We're really grateful to you for telling her about Annie Oakley."

"About Annie?"

"Yeah," said another young woman with deep brown eyes. "We're the Golden Girls. We loved Billie, but we hated that name."

"We knew Billie meant that we were worth a lot, like gold, but it made everyone think of that TV show with all the old ladies."

"Once you told her about Annie Oakley paying for those young women's education, she changed the name."

"We're the Oakley Sisters now," another one said.

I smiled then. Annie would be proud.

CHAPTER 70

After the wake, I crawled into my pickup cab, feeling as low as the skunk who'd stunk it up. Matt didn't come. I told him that I wanted him and where to find me and he didn't come.

I started up the truck and backed up out of my parking spot, looking over my shoulder as I—ack!

"You're supposed to look *before* you back up." Matt came around to my open window, looking better than anything ever. "Unless you asked me out here so you could dispose of my body in the desert."

"No. I asked you out here so I could tell you—what?" Matt's face was scrunched up in disgust. "You look like you just ate poop or something."

"It's your car," he gasped. "How do you stand it?"

"Huh. I guess I got used to it." I opened the door and slid out of the cab, making sure I landed close to Matt.

"Whoa." He took a step back. "You smell like skunk too."

This was not going as planned. "I could take off my clothes."

Matt grinned. Things were looking up.

"Want to take a ride?" I asked. "In the nice fresh air?"

"A ride?" He glanced at my truck.

"A horse ride." I'd asked Josh's permission this time.

"Yeah. Sure. Oh, wait." Matt went back to his car and emerged with two drinks in sweating cardboard cups. "You wanted these?"

"Thanks." I took the Frappuccinos, but held out one to Matt. "Want to share one?"

"Okay." Matt took one of the cups back. We walked down the road into Gold Bug, trading sips of the icy drink. "Sorry I didn't make the funeral. The new employee they hired for the home didn't show up. I tried to call you. Did you have your cell turned off?"

"Not exactly." I gave Matt the short version of last night's escapades.

"That explains the casual funeral attire." We stopped at the entrance to the corral. "Though you may start a trend. You are rocking that tracksuit."

"Why, thank you, sir." I swung open the corral gate. The best donkey in the world trotted over to me. "Something I need to do before we go." I held out the Frappuccino. "All yours, Toby." He slurped it, spraying me in the process.

"Wow, skunk smell plus coffee-scented mule spit," Matt said. "You really know how to impress a guy."

"*Donkey* spit." I held the cup steady for Toby. "Take whatever horse you want."

Toby made short work of his treat and I hiked myself onto his back. Matt settled himself on a bay. We rode out of the corral, side by side.

We bumped along the dusty road in silence for a few minutes.

"Katie really wasn't my fiancée," Matt said finally. "I never even asked her to marry me. It was all a mix-up."

"I figured as much."

"I got the ring back. Well, my mom got it back. I asked Katie to give it back, and then I told my mom about us. Cody too."

"You told him?"

"He said he already knew. That we looked at each other all mushy." Matt cleared his throat. "I hope you're not mad."

"I'm..." I searched my heart. All I found was a big glowing ball of happiness. "I'm...not. Not telling Cody—not telling anyone—that was my way of protecting myself. Last night when I was in the mine, it hit me. I had just called Uncle Bob and accused him of abandoning me. And then I was in this scary old abandoned mine and I thought about abandonment and...remember how I told you about that Russian orphan I met? Val?"

"Russian orphan? You mean the guy on that cruise ship you worked on?"

"Yeah. And I swear this all ties together. One of the things someone told me about Val was that he wasn't any good at relationships because he had the whole orphan thing going on. Fear of abandonment. You know, dump them before they dump you?"

Matt looked at me, gray eyes steady behind his glasses. "You were going to dump me?"

"Not on purpose." That might have thrown most guys, but Matt's face was still open, waiting to hear what I was going to say. "I know I'm not an orphan, but...after Cody's accident, I might as well have had no parents. You know how my mom and dad behaved. They basically abandoned me. I pushed you away so you wouldn't do it to me first. And I didn't want to tell anyone about us, because that would make it worse when you left me, which of course you would."

"And now?"

"And now I know that even if you do leave me eventually, being with you now is worth the risk." There, I said it.

But of course I couldn't leave well enough alone. "In fact, I just turned down a part in *Annie Get Your Gun* so I could have more time with you." Arizona Center Stage didn't want me for Annie, but they did offer me a role in the chorus.

"You turned down a role?"

"I did."

"But..." A smile tugged at the corner of Matt's mouth. Dang, he knew me too well.

"But you're right. I turned down *Annie*, but I did agree to do Viola in *Twelfth Night*." Theresa had offered me the role straight out when I called her.

"And this has nothing to do with your respect for Annie Oakley?"

"Maybe just a titch, *but Twelfth Night* runs for only half the time and there's no tour to Tucson. So I get to spend more time with you."

Matt shook his head, but he was definitely smiling now.

"Thanks for being so patient," I said. "It's one of the things I love best about you."

Oh no.

I said "love." And I said it before Matt ever said anything, which was exactly what I was trying to avoid. A wave of heat engulfed my face. "Oh. Uh, what I meant was..."

"It's okay, Ivy." Matt leaned over and took my hand. "I love you too."

And we rode off into the sunset.

Reader's Discussion Guide

As you may have suspected, there's a little bit of me in Ivy, and maybe a little more than usual in *Ivy Get Your Gun*. The idea for the plot came from a newspaper clipping (thanks, Mom!) about a real-life shooting during a staged gunfight in Tombstone, Arizona. It was an accident, and no one died, but it got my wheels turning. I'd acted in a melodrama at Pioneer Living History Museum, and so decided to use that as Ivy's undercover gig. But I also wanted to include a show that would be familiar to readers: *Annie Get Your Gun* fit perfectly.

That's where this book and real life merged more than I'd planned: Like Ivy, I had a difficult time getting hold of the script and the video, so I began by researching Annie Oakley. I'd always been a fan, but I had no idea what a truly amazing woman she was. Then I received the script in the mail (and yes, I had to get it on eBay from New Zealand) and was able to get the movie from the library. I was stunned. All I had remembered was the wonderful music and cowboy-type shenanigans. I certainly didn't know they changed the real-life ending of Annie's shooting match with Frank Butler. It ticked me off royally, and so I decided to have Ivy tell the real story of Annie Oakley. I hope it inspires you to "aim for the high mark."

"Aim for the high mark and you will hit it. No, not the first time, not the second time and maybe not the third. But keep on aiming and keep on shooting for only practice will make you perfect. Finally you'll hit the bull's-eye of success." – Annie Oakley

Topics & Questions for Discussion

If you could erect a statue of a hero more people should know about, who would it be?

Have you ever been stopped (by someone else or yourself) from doing something because of your gender?

How do you think women's roles have changed in the last 100 years? In the last 50, 25, or 10?

Who are some good role models for young girls?

Ivy finds she's a natural with a rifle. Have you ever found yourself surprisingly good at something right away?

Frank believes the end justifies the means. Do you think this can ever be true? In what circumstances?

Why do you think America's Old West has such a hold on our imagination?

Did you know there was quicksand in the desert? Any other fun facts you learned?

There are several famous cowboy names parodied throughout the book. Can you find them?

Enhance Your Book Club or Class Discussion

Watch *Annie Get Your Gun* (great music), and PBS's *The American Experience: Annie Oakley* (true history).

Listen to cowboy music! Try songs by Riders in the Sky, Slim Whitman, or Gene Autry.

Read *Annie Oakley* by Shirl Kasper.

Google "Sonoran desert animals" to see many of the critters mentioned in this book.

Check out cowboy poetry. YouTube has a bunch of options, as does the Facebook page for the Center for Western and Cowboy Poetry and CowboyPoetry.com.

Extra credit: Erect a bat house! Bats consume their weight in insects every night, plus they help spread seeds and pollinate plants—and unfortunately, many of them are endangered. You can learn more at batconservation.org.

Visit www.cindybrownwriter.com to learn more about me, and to sign up for my Slightly Silly Newsletter, an irreverent look at mystery and drama (with a smidgen of book news).

Cindy Brown

Cindy Brown has been a theater geek (musician, actor, director, producer, and playwright) since her first professional gig at age 14. Now a full-time writer, she's the author of the Agatha Award-nominated Ivy Meadows series, madcap mysteries set in the off, off, OFF Broadway world of theater. Cindy and her husband live in Portland, Oregon, though she made her home in Phoenix, Arizona, for more than 25 years and knows all the good places to hide dead bodies in both cities.

She'd love to connect with readers at cindybrownwriter.com.

The Ivy Meadows Mystery Series
By Cindy Brown

MACDEATH (#1)
THE SOUND OF MURDER (#2)
OLIVER TWISTED (#3)
IVY GET YOUR GUN (#4)

Available at booksellers nationwide and online

Visit www.henerypress.com for details

Henery Press Mystery Books

And finally, before you go...
Here are a few other mysteries
you might enjoy:

NUN TOO SOON

Alice Loweecey

A Giulia Driscoll Mystery (#1)

Giulia Falcone-Driscoll has just taken on her first impossible client: The Silk Tie Killer. He's hired Driscoll Investigations to prove his innocence and they have only thirteen days to accomplish it. Talk about being tried in the media. Everyone in town is sure Roger Fitch strangled his girlfriend with one of his silk neckties. And then there's the local TMZ wannabes stalking Giulia and her client for sleazy sound bites.

On top of all that, her assistant's first baby is due any second, her scary smart admin still doesn't relate well to humans, and her police detective husband insists her client is guilty. About this marriage thing—it's unknown territory, but it sure beats ten years of living with 150 nuns.

Giulia's ownership of Driscoll Investigations hasn't changed her passion for justice from her convent years. But the more dirt she digs up, the more she's worried her efforts will help a murderer escape. As the client accuses DI of dragging its heels on purpose, Giulia thinks The Silk Tie Killer might be choosing one of his ties for her own neck.

Available at booksellers nationwide and online

Visit www.henerypress.com for details

DOUBLE WHAMMY

Gretchen Archer

A Davis Way Crime Caper (#1)

Davis Way thinks she's hit the jackpot when she lands a job as the fifth wheel on an elite security team at the fabulous Bellissimo Resort and Casino in Biloxi, Mississippi. But once there, she runs straight into her ex-ex-husband, a rigged slot machine, her evil twin, and a trail of dead bodies. Davis learns the truth and it does not set her free—in fact, it lands her in the pokey.

Buried under a mistaken identity, unable to seek help from her family, her hot streak runs cold until her landlord Bradley Cole steps in. Make that her landlord, lawyer, and love interest. With his help, Davis must win this high stakes game before her luck runs out.

Available at booksellers nationwide and online

Visit www.henerypress.com for details

GHOSTWRITER ANONYMOUS
Noreen Wald

A Jake O'Hara Mystery (#1)

With her books sporting other people's names, ghostwriter Jake O'Hara works behind the scenes. But she never expected a séance at a New York apartment to be part of her job. Jake had signed on as a ghostwriter, secretly writing for a grande dame of mystery fiction whose talent died before she did. The author's East Side residence was impressive. But her entourage—from a Mrs. Danvers-like housekeeper to a lurking hypnotherapist—was creepy.

Still, it was all in a day's work, until a killer started going after ghostwriters, and Jake suspected she was chillingly close to the culprit. Attending a séance and asking the dead for spiritual help was one option. Some brilliant sleuthing was another-before Jake's next deadline turns out to be her own funeral.

Available at booksellers nationwide and online

Visit www.henerypress.com for details